THE
HOMEPLACE

THE
HOMEPLACE

KEVIN WOLF

To John:

Thanks so much
for coming

Minotaur Books

A Thomas Dunne Book
New York

A THOMAS DUNNE BOOK FOR MINOTAUR BOOKS.
An imprint of St. Martin's Publishing Group.

www.thomasdunnebooks.com
www.minotaurbooks.com

Library of Congress Cataloging-in-Publication Data

Names: Wolf, Kevin, 1951– author.
Title: The homeplace : a mystery / Kevin Wolf.
Description: New York : Minotaur Books, 2016.
Identifiers: LCCN 2016016262| ISBN 9781250103161 (hardcover) |
    ISBN 9781250103178 (e-book)
Subjects: LCSH: Homecoming—Fiction. | Basketball players—Fiction. |
    Murder—Investigation—Fiction. | Plains—Colorado—Fiction. | BISAC:
    FICTION / Mystery & Detective / General. | GSAFD: Mystery fiction. |
    Suspense fiction.
Classification: LCC PS3623.O546 H66 2016 | DDC 813/.6—dc23
LC record available at https://lccn.loc.gov/2016016262

Our books may be purchased in bulk for promotional, educational, or business use. Please contact your local bookseller or the Macmillan Corporate and Premium Sales Department at 1-800-221-7945, extension 5442, or by e-mail at MacmillanSpecialMarkets@macmillan.com.

First Edition: September 2016

10 9 8 7 6 5 4 3 2 1

Dad,
I wrote a book.

THE
HOMEPLACE

If you listen you'll hear the wind.

It seems to always blow across Comanche County. A wind from the north rattles the eaves and brings icy cold down from Canada. From the south it pumps out heavy, humid air that stacks against the mountains and leaves its rain a hundred miles from the county's fields.

If you listen you'll hear it.

Some days the wind howls. Some days it whispers. Many think they hear it laugh at those fool enough to live out here. Some say the wind cries for those who do.

CHAPTER ONE

When Chase Ford was a boy, he couldn't understand why he never heard the sounds of dawn. Why couldn't he hear night tear away along the horizon and day take its place? Why didn't the sky sizzle when the warmth of the sun touched what was left of the cool darkness?

His father, Big Paul, would have called him foolish for having such thoughts. Some part of Chase knew he was only a visitor on this wide-open, windswept splash of prairie. Chase was the first of four generations of Ford men to leave Comanche County. For Chase, leaving saved the best and hid the worst.

But Chase Ford had come home.

As the first spikes of orange painted the gray morning, Chase spotted a deer at the edge of the field. It was upwind. No chance it would scent him. Through the binoculars, Chase could tell it was a big deer. The broken tine on the buck's wide antlers and its graying muzzle meant it was an old bachelor, most likely run off from the herd by the younger bucks to live out what years it had left on its own.

If Chase could be patient, the deer might drift into the stubble field where he would have a shot. His father's rifle would reach that far. He'd seen Big Paul take game a quarter mile or more away too many times to count. But it had been almost sixteen years since he'd held his father's gun. And that many years since Chase had been home.

Chase swung the glasses back, but the animal was gone. He searched the sagebrush at the edge of the field, but the old buck knew all the places to hide on the homeplace better than Chase. For now there was a thermos of coffee waiting in his truck, and for the first time in sixteen years, he had nothing else to do except wait for his next chance at the deer, and listen for those sounds of dawn.

Once, simple fun came from pushing his old truck for every mile per hour he could get. Back then, Chase had let rooster tails of dust chase him home from school, home from practice, and home from errands Big Paul had sent him to run in town. At every chance, he stayed off the asphalt and drove the back roads. It was an easy choice in a county that had forty miles of dirt for every mile of blacktop. In a place that moved so slowly, pushing that old battered truck had made the whole world turn faster.

Now he pushed a new truck to remember what it was like to be home.

A silver blaze of reflected sun stabbed the sky. Chase tapped the brakes. From the top of a roll in the road, Chase spotted a vehicle in the bar ditch ahead. He slowed the Dodge to forty, and from the next hillock he could see a light bar on the car's roof and markings on the tailgate. It wasn't a farmer out checking stock. This was a county sheriff's four-by-four, and a man in a Stetson leaned against the fender.

Chase let off the gas.

The man in the cowboy hat straightened, and Chase recognized the same lean figure that had often been on the seat beside him, racing across these dirt roads all those years ago. Chase pressed the brake pedal and eased to the side of the road.

He powered down the passenger window and leaned across the seat. "That you, Marty?"

A smile spread over the deputy's face. "Well, it's Chase Ford. What they been sayin's true. The prodigal has come home."

Chase jerked up on his door handle and met the deputy at the front of his truck. Hands were shook, shoulders slapped.

"Deb said she saw you at the game night last, but before she could get over to say hello you'd ducked out a side door." Marty rubbed his hand over the grill on Chase's new Dodge. "Boys at the café say you're down to hunt."

Chase nodded. "I towed a trailer down to the homeplace. I can only stay for a few days. It's been a long time since I tasted venison."

"How long has it been?" Marty shifted a match stick from one corner of his mouth to the other. "Back to Brandon, I mean? Folks here thought you'd be down for Big Paul's . . ."

Funeral. Chase filled in the blank spot Marty left hanging on the prairie wind. "Couldn't make it." He looked away and nodded at the four-by-four in the ditch. "Trouble?"

"Yeah, transmission gave out. I called in, and Arlene is sendin' a tow truck. Should be here anytime." Marty leaned his hip on the Dodge. "You know, this county's dead broke, but each fall they still find money enough for Old Man Gray to climb the water tower and repaint those big letters. *Single A State Champs 1992.* That basketball game and Chase Ford are about the best things ever to come out of Brandon." He held out a tin of Skoal.

Chase shook his head.

Marty shrugged and tucked the tobacco can into the back pocket of his Wranglers. "You remember that game up at Eads our senior year? Coaches from six, seven colleges sittin' in the stands. There just to see you play. We thumped 'em by thirty points. We was so far ahead, you told Coach not to put you in at all in the fourth quarter."

Chase remembered. The game was fun then. It changed soon after. "You and I combined for forty-three points that night."

"Yeah. I had four of 'em." Marty smiled the smile that Chase would always remember. "Chase Ford's come back to Brandon. How about that?"

Birdie Hawkins blew out a deep breath and turned away from the banty rooster of a man who paced back and forth down the length of the driver's side of her truck. She slammed the door shut on the state-owned pickup truck she drove every day. Birdie needed that layer of window glass between her and the lunatic outside. She pressed the speed dial number on the state-owned cell phone and waited for it to connect.

Birdie combed her stubby fingers through the thick, brush-short hair on the top of her head. She never thought of herself as a girly-girl. And most people in the county didn't, either. But the little dickhead outside kept calling her *sir*. Maybe it was time she started wearing earrings or eye makeup like Marty's wife begged.

The dispatcher answered the phone on the third ring.

"Arlene, this is Birdie. I need some help out here. Do you know where Marty's at?"

The little man stormed to the front of Birdie's truck. He shook his fist at her and pointed to the field beyond the fence. Birdie didn't want to look at it again, but it was better than watching the turd-bucket rant.

Four brown lumps decorated the sweep of sage brush and prairie. She shook her head. Yesterday they had been living, breathing buffalo worth upward of four thousand dollars each. Today they were fly bait with bullet holes in their wooly hides. Dead buffalo fell under the Sheriff's Department's jurisdiction. If these were pronghorns or deer it would be up to her, as county game warden, to figure what had happened. She had tried to explain that to the little madman doing the war dance, but he didn't want to hear any of it.

Arlene told Birdie about Marty's car trouble and that she'd sent a wrecker out to tow him into town.

"I'll call him," Birdie said, "and, Arlene, do me favor. Run this license plate." She rattled off the string of numbers and letters. "It's a red Ford half ton. With a Brandon Buffalos sticker on the back bumper." Birdie was afraid she knew who the truck belonged to. If she knew, Arlene would, too.

Through the phone Birdie heard a gasp.

"Oh, dear," Arlene said.

Marty plucked his cell phone from an inside pocket of his Carhartt. "Chase, you're never gonna believe who this is."

"Who?"

"Birdie."

"Our Birdie?"

"You bet."

The phone hummed again.

"What's she up to these days?" Chase asked.

"Got on with the Department of Wildlife 'bout ten years ago. They moved her to this district three years back. If you came around more you'd know that." Marty lifted the phone to his ear. "Birdie, guess who's standin' beside me right now—it's Chase. Yeah, Chase Ford—is, too." He tucked the phone under his chin. "Chase, Birdie says, 'Hey.'"

"Hey, Birdie."

"What, Birdie?—That so?—I'll ask him."

Marty tucked the phone down again. "Chase, Birdie's got trouble, and we need you to drive me over to the old McKeever place to give her a hand with somethin'. You do that?"

"Sure. It'd be good to see Birdie again."

The deputy put the phone back to his lips. "We're on our way. This'll be like the old days. You, me, and Chase." He slipped the phone into his jacket pocket.

Chase climbed behind the wheel, and Marty slid into the passenger seat. "What kind of trouble does Birdie have?"

"Somebody killed four buffalo."

Chase jammed his foot onto the gas pedal and glanced at Marty beside him. The deputy wedged one hand against the dashboard and clung to the seatbelt with the other. Outside the prairie snapped by the windows at sixty miles an hour.

"So you saw that Riley kid play Friday night?" Marty said over the roar of the tires on the dirt road.

Chase nodded.

"The coffee drinkers at the café are comparin' him to you. They say Brandon might make a run at the title again this year. Whatcha think?"

It was good that the conversation was about basketball and not about money, or his failed marriage, or the pills. "Just saw him that once," Chase answered. "He can shoot a little bit, but he doesn't play one lick of defense."

"That's what they said about you."

Maybe the folks in Brandon would only remember the boy who played basketball and drove his pickup too fast. "This have anythin' to do with Birdie?" Chase asked.

"It could. Birdie says the boy's pickup is at the edge of the pasture with the dead buffalo. Just a Brandon Buffalo sticker on the back bumper."

Chase took the hard turn at County Road 17 and pushed the truck up to sixty-five. "Marty, Jimmy Riley drive a red half-ton Ford?"

"You know somethin'?"

"Not really. It's just that . . ." Chase bit down on his lip. "After the ball game last night, I drove over to Cheyenne Wells to get some groceries and ice for my trailer. I got back to the homeplace about midnight. My headlights flashed on a red Ford parked down there by those elm trees Grandpa Ford planted. I got a glimpse of a girl's foot hooked over the top of the seat and a bare behind bouncin' up and down. I hit the high beams, and two faces popped up. I think the boy was Jimmy Riley."

"Probably was. That boy doesn't do all his shootin' on the basketball court." Marty tipped his head. "There's Birdie's truck now."

Chase pulled his Dodge in behind the DOW pickup. He and Marty climbed out. The closest dead buffalo had dropped just inside the fence. Three more dotted the corner of the pasture. Birdie stood by the farthest animal, about seventy yards out. She started toward the road when she saw them.

Fresh hay was scattered on the ground near the fence. Jimmy Riley's red pickup was parked near a padlocked aluminum gate. Its tailgate was down, and a half bale of hay sat in the box.

Marty whistled through his teeth. "This don't look good. Somebody put out that hay."

Birdie stuck one of her stubby legs between the strands of barbed wire on the fence and wriggled her wide fanny through. She climbed out of the ditch and onto the shoulder of the road between Marty and Chase.

"It's a lot worse than it looks," she said. "Jimmy Riley is lyin' dead out there behind a soapjack. Boy's stark naked and has a bullet hole in his head."

Chase set his coffee cup on the hood of Birdie's truck. A brand-new GMC pickup with a gold Comanche County Sheriff's Department star on the door wheeled up next to his Dodge. Powdery dust rose up from around the tires and drifted across the prairie.

Sheriff Lincoln Kendall stepped out. He had on the same tan uniform shirt and Wranglers that all the deputies who worked for him wore, but his shirt was shiny new and straight-edge creases had been ironed into his jeans. He tilted down the brim of his black Resistol to shade his eyes against the morning sun.

"He a lawman or politician today?" Chase asked.

Marty slopped the coffee from his Styrofoam cup onto the ground. "With him, one's never too far from the other." The deputy crushed the cup and tossed it into the back of the DOW's truck. "C'mon, Birdie, you're gonna need to explain whatcha know." Marty tapped the side of his face, at the corner of his right eye. "And Chase, you might not want to say hello to the good sheriff 'til he's ready to talk to you."

If Birdie had a choice right then, she'd have told Chase and Marty goodbye, climbed in her pickup, and been fifty miles from Sheriff

Lincoln Kendall. It wasn't that she disliked the man. It wasn't that at all. No, Birdie hated Lincoln Kendall. And she'd hated him since her first day of high school.

"Officer Hawkins?"

She wasn't even sure he'd ever known her first name. He called her "farm girl" in high school and "Officer Hawkins" now.

"Sheriff." Birdie hung her best farm-girl smile on her face and nodded.

"Tell me what you know."

"Deer season opened up this mornin'. I was out before sunup. I was gonna drive the roads, listen for shots, and check licenses. Generally we don't have too much trouble out here. Most folks obey the rules." Birdie knew she was rambling. "I was down along Sandy Creek. Just checked two boys who'd filled their doe tags, when that little fart—" She pointed at the man sitting in the cab of his pickup, staring everywhere except the field with the dead buffalo. And the dead body.

"Officer." Kendall raised his voice.

"Er, that good citizen"—she couldn't help herself—"came barrelin' down the road. Saw my truck. Jumped out and started screamin' that somebody shot his bison." Birdie took a breath. "That's what he called them. Bison."

"Do you know him?"

"Andy Puckett." She'd been the first person with a badge the little dipshit could find. That was the only reason she was here. "He and his wife bought the old McKeever place. Renamed it Pleasant Prairie Winds. Come down from the city on weekends and pretend they're cowboys. Got more money than good sense."

Kendall's eyes flashed at her. "Just tell me what you know."

"I followed him up here and"—she pointed at the pasture dotted with dead buffalo—"he was right. Somebody shot 'em. I called in to let Arlene know. Dead buffalo belong to the Sheriff's Department, not Department of Wildlife."

"The body?"

"While I was waitin' for Marty, we walked out in the pasture to get a closer look at the buffalo. That's when we found . . . uh, it." She glanced at Puckett again and then up at Kendall.

"Did you check for vitals?"

"Crap, no. The whole back half of his head's gone." Birdie's stomach seized; she shut her eyes and saw the bloody smear again. "It ain't pretty. That little fart puked his guts out."

"Officer, mind yourself."

"Didn't mean nothin' by that. Thought you should know in case somebody might find the puddle and think it's evidence. It was him that puked, not me."

"Anythin' else?"

Birdie thought for a minute. "The hay, sir. Looks to me like whoever did this put the hay out and shot the buffalo when they came in to eat. I think he shot the farthest one first and worked his way in."

"Why you say that?"

"If he would have shot the one closet to the fence first, the others would have seen it fall and spooked. By shootin' the farthest, the ones in front of it wouldn't know what was goin' on. They'd just be thinkin' about what they're gonna get to eat. A fella could take his time and pick 'em off one by one." She smiled at the way she'd put things together. "And I think he did just that. A couple staggered around a bit before they fell, but there's only one bullet hole in each of 'em." Her stomach went sick. "Even the boy."

Kendall looked out on the prairie. The muscles in his jaws bunched and then relaxed. "Any ideas?"

Birdie scraped a smooth spot in the dirt with the toe of her boot. "You know, there is somethin' you could check out." She looked up at Kendall, and he was watching her face as if he really wanted her help. "You know Ray-Ray Jackson?"

The sheriff nodded. "I got a call this mornin' about him. He missed a court date, and there's a failure to appear warrant out for him. Somethin' about an overweight truck and an expired license from the next county."

"Sounds like him. I ticketed him about five years back for huntin' without a license and he missed that court appearance, too. One of your boys ended up draggin' him in. 'Member?"

Kendall rubbed his chin. "Seems I remember somethin'. What's that got to do with anythin'?"

"'Bout four months ago, Puckett's buffalo broke through a

fence and got onto Ray-Ray's land. If there's one thing Ray-Ray don't like, it's people trespassin' on his ground. He threatened to shoot 'em if it ever happened again. It ain't much. But somebody ought to talk to him."

Kendall adjusted his hat down so the brim hid his eyes. "I'll send one of my deputies out to his place and see if we can bring him in."

"I could go." Birdie wanted to get as far away from Kendall as she could get.

"Stick tight. The boys from the state are sendin' down a crime scene team, and the coroner is on his way. They might have some questions."

Birdie looked down, scuffed her toe in the dust, and bit back a string of cuss words. She wished she could get away. "Sheriff, better send two men out to Ray-Ray's. He can be a mean one."

Kendall nodded and then tipped his head toward Birdie's truck. "Any reason for Chase Ford to be here?"

"When Marty had car trouble, Chase gave him a ride over here. That's all."

"Tell Ford to leave."

Birdie forced herself to walk back to her truck when every part of her wanted to run away from Kendall. She grabbed her thermos from the fender and filled a worn, plastic Town Pump mug. If she had been home she would have sloshed two fingers of Crown Royal in with the coffee. She looked up at Chase. "That man don't get any more likeable with age."

"Careful, Birdie."

"Careful, my ass. Only thing I like about him is when I remember the blood on his face from when you decked him out behind Saylor's Café."

"That was a long time ago." Chase rubbed the knuckles on his right hand. Birdie guessed he was hiding a smile.

"Anyways, he wants you to get on out of here. The rest of us are gonna wait for the coroner and the state police. Now, go on and get yourself a good cup of coffee." She gulped at her mug. "And, Chase, Mercy's back at Saylor's. You know that?"

CHAPTER TWO

Mercy glared at the man in front of the stove. "I'll not have language like that in this restaurant. My mother wouldn't tolerate it, and neither will I."

He hung his head. "It won't happen again, *señora*."

"It's fortunate that none of our guests heard."

He tapped the spatula on the stovetop, bobbed his head once more, and flipped three pancakes from the stove to a plate.

On the day Mercy Saylor left Brandon, she had vowed to herself that she'd never tie another apron around her waist, never again serve ham and eggs to truckers who eyed her behind, and never again fill coffee cups around a table full of farmers talking about the weather. The day she left for college she was sure she would not work in her mother's café another day. Six months ago, she'd broken that vow, and almost every other promise she'd made to herself.

Dolly Benavidez hadn't shown up for her Saturday morning shift. Mercy had planned on catching up on some paperwork, but she tied on an apron and tried to remember if she had missed any shifts at her parents' restaurant when she was seventeen. Probably. Other things can take priority when you're seventeen. Like the basketball player Dolly was always with. Mercy knew all about that. She'd had her own ballplayer when she was seventeen.

"How do you want those eggs?" Mercy asked the trucker at the counter.

"Sunny side up with ham."

She knew he was looking at her backside.

She grabbed a pot off the Bunn machine and crossed to the table by the front windows. "More coffee here?" Not one face had been shaved that morning. Fish-belly-white foreheads peeked out from under dirty John Deere caps, and every man at the table looked old.

"Whatcha think, Mercy?"

She'd gone to high school with that one. Bobby Jackson had been a sophomore when she was a senior.

"The weather, I mean." He held out his cup. "Today's one of those days when you scrape frost off the windshield in the mornin', and by noon you'll be peeled down to a T-shirt. This time of year it means a front's chasin' the warm down from Wyoming, and we're due for a change. I'll wager we have snow by Monday."

Heads around the table nodded.

Mercy smiled. But her insides turned as bitter as the coffee she poured.

"Mercy, here comes Pop Weber." Bobby tapped on the window.

A battered farm truck came around the curve on the highway that led into Brandon. The driver straddled the dotted line that separated the two eastbound lanes.

Mercy checked the clock over the cash register. Ten minutes after eight. Pop Weber was on time.

Bobby tapped again. "Your mother watched out for him. It's up to you now."

Mercy stepped to the front window. She wiped her hands on her apron and bit her lower lip. Maybe today Pop would remember.

The truck made a hard right turn. Metal fence posts bounced in the back of the truck. It jerked to a stop in front of a boarded-up building that had once been the Brandon Inn. The only other restaurant in town had closed five years before.

A bent old man climbed out.

Mercy opened the front door to the chill outside.

Pop hobbled up the cement steps to the padlocked door of the empty building. He tried the door.

Mercy heard him curse. "Pop," she called, "come on over and have breakfast with us."

Pop tugged on the locked door once more. He put one hand to his forehead and leaned into the glass. A laugh cackled out of the old man, and, like a foggy day melts in midmorning sun, he straightened a bit. He caught hold of the railing and limped down the steps.

Mercy was at the edge of the highway. "Coffee's on over here, Pop."

"When did this place close down?" He asked her that almost every morning.

"Five years ago, Pop."

He tottered to the edge of the highway.

"Look both ways, now."

A semi blasted its horn. Mercy trembled. But Pop stayed where he stood. The big truck sped by. Mercy took another look and crossed. She slipped an arm around the old farmer's shoulders and kissed his cheek. Pop had shaved that morning.

"Some days I just forget things, Mercy. Some days, I forget."

Half of the pancakes in front of Pop Weber were gone, and he was on his third cup of coffee. Two more truckers had ordered ham and eggs, and the men in the John Deere caps were taking turns in the restroom before they left for their chores.

Bobby Jackson put a dollar bill and two quarters next to the cash register. "Whatcha think, Mercy?"

Mercy had heard that question every morning since she'd come back to Brandon and ignored it since that first day.

Bobby's teeth were yellow, but he smiled his best. When he was sure she was looking he slipped another dollar in the tip jar on the counter.

He didn't know the tips were divided up between the waitresses. Mercy didn't get a share.

Three gray-haired women slipped in the door. They waved to Mercy and took seats at their Saturday morning table. It was the same table they sat at on Tuesdays. And Thursdays.

Mercy tried, but smiles were harder to come by now.

Bobby held the door open for two men in camo overalls and orange caps. "Get anythin'?" he asked.

"Filled." One of the hunters smiled a toothy grin. "Gonna have breakfast and head back to the Springs. Too easy this year."

Mercy saw a set of antlers in the back of the hunters' pickup, but the man climbing out of the new Dodge in the parking lot made her smile.

"Chase Ford," Bobby Jackson bellowed out as the door swung closed behind him. He met Chase in the parking lot, and the two pumped hands.

Mercy was untying her apron when Chase came through the door. Her feet moved before her mind told them. She was at the door in front of him with apron strings trailing from her fingers. She wrapped both her arms around his waist, and she pressed her face onto his chest. The top of her head touched just below his shoulders, like she remembered. She squeezed until she felt muscle and sinew. He was still strong, like he'd been all those years ago.

In the next instant he held her at arm's length and smiled down at her.

Tears bubbled up from that place inside her and filled her eyes. Then Mercy did what she'd planned to do if she ever saw Chase Ford again.

"Ass"—the sound of her hand smacking his face filled the diner, and every head turned to look—"hole."

Very few things about his job made Deputy Paco Martinez uneasy. He'd told Marty that. Paco showed his nervousness by jabbering. Marty thought of Deb and their three kids. And prayed that no one would ever come knocking on their door with this kind of news.

How do you tell someone that their wife or husband, son or daughter, is dead?

You just told them. Paco had taught him that two weeks after he was hired on the Sheriff's Department. Be ready for them to break down, cry, faint, or lash out. But just tell them. That was all you could do.

It was bad enough when that loved one had been killed on the highway or in some farm accident. But Jimmy Riley had been shot in the head.

Paco steered the department's car off the highway that divided Brandon into two equal halves and pointed the car toward the grain silos near the railroad tracks. The Pioneer House sat on the town side of Front Street. Once the railroad had put crews up for the night in the old hotel. Now workers in the oil patch rented rooms by the week. New company trucks sat on the street with an equal number of worn-out pickups. Friday night's beer bottles littered the yard.

"You been here before?" Paco tipped his bald head toward the building.

"Too many times," Marty answered. "Noise complaints, drunk and disorderlies. Once two old boys were goin' at each other in the street at two o'clock in the mornin'. That turned into a real rodeo."

Paco tapped a finger on the steering wheel. "Four years ago, I got called here on a shots fired. The vic had a hole in his beer gut but wouldn't say who did it. Paramedics hauled him to the hospital in Hugo. I think he lived."

They parked in the gravel lot at the silos and crossed Front Street to the boarding house. Paco's first year on the job had been Marty's senior year of high school. If Marty had to pick any of the deputies in the department to pair up with, it would be the old man. He looked like a fireplug with a potbelly, but Paco was a darned good cop.

The deputies climbed the empty stairs to an apartment on the second floor that Jimmy shared with his father.

"Smells like the burritos they sell at Town Pump," Paco said.

Marty thought the building smelled more like cat piss.

The only light socket in the narrow hall had a broken bulb. Whatever carpet wasn't stained dark with oil crunched with crusty red dirt, and gravel bounced from their footfalls.

Paco tapped on the door marked with a number eight. "Mr. Riley, Officers Martinez and Storm with the Sheriff's Department. Can we have a few words, sir?"

"What the hell's this about?" A hoarse voice rasped from inside the room.

"Please come to the door, sir." Paco glanced at Marty. "It's about your son."

The voice was louder. "I haven't seen him since Tuesday. If he's in trouble again, I don't know anythin' about it."

"Sir, we need to talk to you."

Springs creaked on the other side of the door. "Okay. Give me a minute."

Paco slipped his hand to his duty pistol and unsnapped the holster. He looked at Marty. The old deputy's counsel replayed in the younger man's head. *The best thing you can do is go home to your wife and kids when your shift is over. Don't assume anything.* Marty's hand hovered over his gun.

The door swung in. Jimmy's daddy filled the space. Tufts of dark, coarse hair fringed the collar of his stained T-shirt, and work-hardened muscles bulged from the sleeves. His eyes were red rimmed, and he squinted even in the shadowy light of the hallway. "What about my boy?"

"Your son's name is Jimmy?" Paco's arm relaxed.

"Yeah."

"Can we come in?"

Over the man's shoulder, Marty could see a box of Frosted Flakes and a Coors longneck on a table in front of a flickering TV.

The man shook his head. "We'll talk right here."

Paco took in a deep breath. "I'm sorry to have to tell you this. Your son's been killed."

The father's hand slid down the edge of the door and grabbed the doorknob. He squeezed until his knuckles turned white. He looked at Paco and then turned to Marty. "Who shot him?"

Marty's lungs seized. And his heart paused. Who shot him? People cried when they heard the news. They asked "How?" Some screamed out and wanted to know "Why?" Not "Who shot him?" *How did he know?*

Riley swung the door open, waved with his fingers for them to follow, and turned into his rented room. He dropped his bulk onto a threadbare couch and looked up at the lawmen. "What do I do now?" He shook his head. "How much does a funeral cost? I don't think I can afford it."

Paco ignored the questions. "Do you need to contact the boy's mother?"

Riley fumbled for a pack of Marlboros on a side table. He tapped the pack on the arm of the couch, pulled one out with his lips, and lit it. "She's dead. Just me and him. Now just me." Smoke flowed from his nostrils.

"When was the last time you saw your son?"

"Tuesday. I left on a run to Syracuse."

Kansas. Marty filled in the state. The town was a hundred miles from Brandon. Two or three of the big oil drillers had yards there.

Jimmy's father continued. "Truck blew a head gasket on the way. They towed me in and I sat and played with myself until they got the parts to fix it. Dropped my load Friday mornin' and came back here. Jimmy wasn't around."

"Any idea where he'd be?" Paco was good at this. He'd keep the man talking. Marty had to listen.

"School. Ball practice. That's the only place he ever is, when he's not sniffin' after that little Mexican girl. I told him to get a job to make some money. He don't listen to me."

"Do you know the girl's name?"

"Somethin' stupid." He exhaled a puff of smoke. "Dolly, I think. Only some Mexican would name a kid somethin' like that."

Marty's guts puckered. Paco was one of the best men he knew, and Marty couldn't let himself look at his friend.

Paco moved on to another question. "Sir, Jimmy had a basketball game last night. Did you go?"

The man shook his head. "Don't have time for such foolishness."

"Where were you last night?"

"Hey, what's this about?"

"We just need to know, sir."

"Sat downstairs with a couple of fellas that live here. We shared a six-pack and shot the shit. You can ask 'em."

He thought drinking beer with his buddies was more important than his son's game? Marty couldn't feel sorry for the man. He wanted to, but he couldn't.

Riley ground out his cigarette on the table, dropped the butt down the open mouth of an empty beer bottle, and lit another. "What do you need me to do now?"

"We can take you to see your son's body." Paco cleared his throat.

"No. I can drive myself."

"Are you sure?"

"Yeah." A lungful of smoke filled the air around his face. "Jimmy"—it was the first time he had said his son's name—"drove a Ford pickup. Any idea where it is?"

Paco almost recited the next words. "Sir, your son's body is on the way to the morgue at Comanche Crossing. You can view the body there. It will be up to the district attorney as to when it will be released." It made Jimmy sound like a thing, not a person. "You can talk to them about your son's truck."

Riley was on his sixth cigarette and still on the couch when the deputies left him. He had never asked anything more about how his son had died. Had it been guessing when he asked who shot Jimmy? Marty shook his head.

The deputies didn't say a word until they were in the car. Paco took a folded paper from his shirt pocket and scribbled down notes for himself.

Marty copied the older man and wrote down things he wanted to remember, but the silence battered his ears. "I saw Chase Ford this mornin'." He needed words to fill the terrible quiet and silence the things that brewed in his mind. "He's stayin' out at the ranch. Gonna try to get a deer."

Paco nodded. "I said hello to him at the game last night."

"Big Paul didn't come to Chase's games, either."

Paco shook his head. The old deputy had ten acres on a creek bottom between Brandon and Comanche Crossing. He and his wife had two little girls. They raised Shetland ponies for extra money, went to church every Sunday, and he coached soccer and softball. Paco never missed his girls' games.

Paco started the car. "The woman Victor Benavidez married has a daughter named Dolly."

"I know." Marty didn't want to hear what he knew would come next.

"Before she married Victor, Isabel kept house for Big Paul and Chase." Paco stared straight ahead. "She came to work for them after Chase's mother was in that accident."

"I remember all the stories people were sayin' back then."

"That Big Paul was plowin' two fields?"

"Yeah. And that the baby girl was Chase's half-sister."

Paco shifted the car into gear. "Most Saturdays, Dolly Benavidez works the breakfast shift over at Saylor's. Let's go see what she can tell us about Jimmy Riley."

Marty wasn't sure he wanted to hear what she might say.

CHAPTER THREE

Birdie stepped over the yellow crime scene tape. She waved for the truck driver to stop and used the keys that Andy Puckett had given her to open the pasture gate. She swung the gate open and tied it off with a piece of baling wire she found in her pickup. No need to shut it. Everything in the field was dead. Including Jimmy Riley.

Sheriff Kendall and the state police had taken her statement and told her she could leave. An ambulance waited to drive Jimmy's body to the morgue in Comanche Crossing. The techs from the state said it would take them the rest of the day to gather what they needed.

Andy Puckett never settled down; he went on a rant again. Finally, Sheriff Kendall let him send for a truck and front-end loader to haul his buffalo to the processing plant so he could save what meat he could.

All the while Birdie couldn't get one thought out of her head. She knew she was right about the shooter. He'd dropped the buffalo one at a time as they came in for the alfalfa hay he'd spread out along the fence. She reached down and picked up a handful. From the feel, it was fresh cut. Couldn't have been in the bale for more than a week. The bale in the back of the boy's truck was a regular sixty pound, square bale. Nothing special about it.

She tried to recall which farmer was cutting and baling, which field had been worked recently, and who sold to whom.

All this farm country could look the same.

Then she remembered.

Birdie hustled to her truck. She resisted her urge to salute the sheriff with her middle finger and jumped in.

She'd talked to Bobby Jackson early one morning last week. He was fueling his machinery near an alfalfa field about six miles from here. Told her he was going to start baling that day.

It was the ground he leased from the Ford family.

Chase rested his elbows on the checkered vinyl tablecloth and touched the side of his face.

"I can get some ice for that." She hid her mouth behind the fingers of one hand.

"It'll be okay," Chase said.

"I'm sorry."

"No, you're not."

"You're right." When Mercy took her hand away from her face, she was smiling. "Your face is as red as it was when you came to pick me up for our first date. Do you even remember that?"

He thought he remembered her face and eyes. But right that minute, everything about her seemed brand new. Her eyes were greener, her hair softer.

Now a few strands of gray showed in the dark hair near her ears. The skin along her jaw seemed softer. Delicate lines marked the corners of her eyes. Her green eyes. Mercy Saylor was a handsome woman. That's what Big Paul had said about her. It might have been the only thing that Chase and his father ever agreed on.

"Our first date. You don't remember, do you?" Lines knitted across her forehead as she waited for him to answer.

"Sure, I took you out to that old barn on McKeever's place to shoot pigeons with my twenty-two. You were a good shot."

"That wasn't a date."

"It wasn't?"

"Birdie came with us, you fool."

Chase grinned and reached for her arm. She pulled away. "Still, you were a good shot."

"And I still am." She flashed with a bit of the anger Chase always enjoyed. "I killed the last thing I shot at."

Anger flashed again on her face, and Chase looked away. He searched for the next thing to say. He nodded toward the corner of the dining room. "That TV's new."

"Dad put it here so folks could get together and watch you play." Mercy put her elbows on the table, knit her fingers together, and rested her chin there. "I was home for Christmas one year. You were playin' in some big game. There must have been fifty people in this little room. Bangin' on the tables every time you scored. Everyone in Brandon was proud of you."

"Were you, Mercy?"

"All that was a long time ago." She looked away. "See there"—she pointed at the wall—"pictures of Chase Ford, the cowboy ballplayer from the high plains of Colorado. Can even dribble a basketball from the back of a horse."

"Quit."

"That's her, isn't it?" Mercy pointed at a poster of Chase in his Lakers uniform.

Instead of his basketball shoes, they had him wear cowboy boots that day. A long mane of his blond hair hung from the back of the cowboy hat on his head. Someone had strapped a pair of pistols around his waist, and his arms were crossed over his bare chest. Two girls in gold and purple bikinis had been posed in the pile of straw at his feet. Chase had thought all of it was just plain silly until his agent told him there was a check for twenty thousand dollars coming his way.

And that was the day he met Billee. She was the bikini girl on the left.

"That's when she was modelin' to pay for her singin' lessons," Chase said. "She hit it big six months later."

"It didn't hurt any that she was bein' seen with the cowboy ballplayer." Mercy looked back at him. "I read all about it in *People* magazine. *Country Music Sensation Billee Kidd marries NBA Star Chase Ford.*" Mercy looked away. "What happened, anyway?"

"It didn't work out. That's all."

"Mine didn't work, either."

Quiet slipped into the room and took the empty chair at their table. Pans and pots clanged in the kitchen. Dishes loaded with eggs and bacon slid over the front counter, and the cash register drawer opened and shut. They both stared out the window, content in that minute to say nothing.

Midmorning sun bathed the prairie in light so clear that Chase could count the few yellow leaves still on the cottonwoods along Sandy Creek half a mile away. Furrows green with winter wheat striped brown fields. A lone tumbleweed disturbed by a speeding semi did slow somersaults across the parking lot.

"I forgot how peaceful this could be," Chase told Mercy.

"I know" was all she said.

Chase drew a circle on the inside of his cheek with the tip of his tongue.

"And, Mercy. Our first date." He waited until she looked at him. "We drove to the Springs. We told your mother that we were goin' to see *The Lion King* but went to *Pulp Fiction* instead. Stopped at Pizza Hut afterward. Got back to your house at two in the mornin'. Sat in my truck for another hour and talked about both our plans to get out of Brandon."

Mercy looked away from him. "Sixteen years later, we're both back."

"I'll be leavin' on Monday, Mercy."

She reached out and touched his arm, and he pulled away. He couldn't hurt her again.

CHAPTER FOUR

Marty crushed a stray tumbleweed under the front tire of the Sheriff's Department's patrol car and eased into a parking spot at the front door of Saylor's Café.

The police radio, hung beneath the dashboard, chirped. Paco grabbed the microphone. "Martinez, here. Marty's with me."

"This is Kendall. You talk to the boy's father?"

"Yes, sir. He's a strange one. We offered to drive him to the morgue. He refused. Said he'd drive himself." Martinez twisted up the volume.

"What's your gut feel? He do it?"

"Tough to read. I say no. But we need to watch him. He already had two or three beers in him this mornin'. I think that's an everyday thing. Boy lived with him, but as far as I can tell the old man let him raise himself."

"There a mother?" The sheriff's voice crackled through the radio.

"Said she was dead."

"We ran a background on him and the boy. Just what we thought we'd find. The father has his commercial driver's license.

Some traffic tickets. Not much else. Arlene is tryin' to contact someone at the school so we can get a look at the boy's records."

Marty's fingers tightened on the steering wheel. No one would say the boy's name. Jimmy Riley was dead.

Paco continued, "The father said his son had a girlfriend. He wasn't real clear on her name. If it's who I'm thinkin', it might be Dolly Benavidez. She works at Saylor's. That's where we are now. We'll see what she can tell us."

"Let me know what she has to say."

"They find anythin' at Ray-Ray's, Sheriff?"

"No sign of him at all. They're on their way over to his brother's now."

"Sheriff?" Marty tapped Paco's wrist and took the microphone from his hand. "Has anybody talked to Coach Porter? If anyone can tell us about Jimmy, it would be his coach."

"Good thought, Deputy. You know Porter. As soon as you finish at Saylor's, go see what you can find out."

Mercy looked up as the café's front door opened.

"Is that Paco Martinez?" Chase asked. "He still workin' for the sheriff?"

"If you came around more, you'd know." She twisted her mouth in a sour grin. "I don't know how many times people have said that to me since I've been back." She waved for the two deputies to join them and looked back at Chase. "I'll go get some coffee cups, and you boys can talk."

"Mercy, I'm afraid they're here on business." Chase's throat tightened.

Mercy tilted her head. "What?"

"They found a body this mornin'."

Her eyes opened wide. "How do you know?"

Before he could answer, Marty stepped up to the table. "Mercy." He touched the brim of his Stetson. "Chase, you know Deputy Martinez."

Chase reached out to shake Paco's hand.

Marty licked his lips. "Mercy, is Dolly workin' this mornin'?"

Mercy felt the blood drain from her face. "She was supposed to, but she didn't show up. Didn't even call. That's not like her."

Marty glanced at Paco.

"What's this about?" Mercy looked from Marty to Paco and then back to Marty.

Paco raised a hand and answered. "We just need to ask her a few questions. That's all."

"What's going on?" Mercy's voice trembled. "Tell me, Marty. You tell me now."

Birdie recognized the old pickup. She pulled off the road at Bobby Jackson's alfalfa field and rolled her window down. Some mornings Pop Weber would stop to talk when he saw her. Some mornings he'd just drive by.

The old man hunched over the steering wheel and never looked her way as his truck rattled by.

Birdie let out a breath. A naked, dead boy cluttered up her mind, and she didn't need to talk to anyone this morning.

Square bales, some still tinged with a bit of green, stretched across the field in neat lines. Birdie stepped up to the closest bale and plucked out a handful of hay. She held it to her nose and sniffed. Fresh cut, like the hay with the buffalo. Three rows down from where she'd left the truck, the bale at the end of one line was missing. Mashed weeds still damp with last night's frost showed where a truck had backed up to the fence from the dirt road.

Birdie walked closer and hunkered down on her heels where the missing bale had been. She snatched a stalk of straw from the ground, mashed it between her front teeth, and studied the ground at the edge of the field. What she saw in the powdery dust, near a strand of sagging barbed wire, stopped her breath.

She fished her cell phone from her jacket and took a picture of the spot in the dirt. She checked to be sure the image came out clear, then punched in the sheriff's number and hit Send. When *sent* showed on the screen she dialed his number.

The sheriff answered. "What are you up to, Hawkins?"

"I just sent a picture. You get it?"

"Just a second."

She imagined Kendall tipping back his hat and staring down at his phone.

"Where are you?" he asked.

"Six miles south. That section of ground the Fords lease to Bobby Jackson. He cut and baled last week. Every row is nice and even 'cept one."

"What are you gettin' at?"

"A bale's missin' from the end of one row. And that footprint in the picture is right next to it. You best send some of the state boys over here."

"I'll see to it that they're on the way, pronto."

"Yeah, pronto." She hoped she wasn't right.

Birdie looked down at a barefoot print in the powdered dirt between the fence line and the rows of cut alfalfa. Toes pointed to the road. She knew enough from tracking deer and coyotes to know the track was fresh. Probably made last night.

The shaft of straw fell from her mouth, and Birdie couldn't think of one reason why a naked boy would lug a bale of alfalfa from the field. But it was the track beside the barefoot print that troubled Birdie most. It was a smooth-soled boot print with a Tony Lama logo on the heel. Just smaller than her own.

Mercy looked up from her cell phone. "It went straight to voice mail," she told Chase and the two deputies.

Marty fidgeted with his coffee cup. "What about her father?"

Mercy stared at her phone. "I gave Victor the day off. He usually closes for me on Saturday nights, but with the pancake supper over at the church, we're plannin' on closin' early." Her stomach boiled with too much coffee and too much worry. "He said he was going to drive to Lamar to see his brother." She shook her head before Marty could ask. "Victor doesn't have a cell phone. Says he doesn't believe in them."

"Then try his house."

"He won't be there."

"Try anyway."

Mercy found his number and hit Send. She tapped her thumb-nail on the Formica tabletop in rhythm with the ringing phone. "Victor?" She covered the phone with her hand and whispered to the men around the table, "He answered." Then she pulled her fingers back and spoke. "Victor, listen. It's Mercy. Dolly didn't come in this mornin'. Is she there?"

Victor's voice rattled through the phone line. "She spent the night at her friend Valarie's and said they were going to the ball game in Limon today. She said something about shoppin' for school supplies. She didn't tell you?"

Mercy's eyes narrowed. "Oh, I guess I just forgot." She looked at Marty and shook her head.

"I could come in if you need help," Victor offered.

"No, we're not that busy. See you tomorrow."

Mercy rested the phone on the table and bit down on her lip. "Dolly told Victor she was spendin' the night with Valarie Maestas. She told him they were going to drive to Limon to see the freshman game and do some shoppin'. Victor said she told me she wasn't comin' in, and I said it was okay." Mercy shook her head and lifted the phone to dial another number.

"Who are you callin' now?" Marty asked.

"I know Valarie's mother." The lines at the corners of Mercy's eyes pulled tighter. "And I remember how easy it was to lie to my parents." When she looked at Marty, he nodded his head.

Birdie dropped her rear end on the tailgate of her truck and lifted a bottle of Walmart water to her lips. She unzipped her jacket and undid the top two buttons on her uniform shirt. The day was warming, and by noon it might be close to seventy. Any other time she would have taken off her shirt and stripped out of the long underwear she'd put on that morning. But not with two officers from state crime scene investigations and Sheriff Kendall just ten yards away. Why give them a show?

Yeah, like they'd even look.

They had finished making plaster casts of the footprints Birdie had found. They photographed everything they could, from every angle they could, and were working on the impressions of the tire treads near the missing bale.

Sheriff Kendall walked to her truck with a cell phone pressed to his ear. He slipped the phone into a shirt pocket and rested his foot on the bumper of her truck. "I don't know what all this means right now, but I'm glad you found it. Good eyes, Officer Hawkins."

Birdie pointed to the cooler in the back of her truck. "Water?"

Kendall popped the cooler's lid and scooped a bottle from the ice. He twisted off the lid and took a drink. He looked out across the field and didn't say anything.

You're very welcome, shit for brains. Birdie was hot and ornery. This was her busiest time of the year. She should be checking hunters' licenses, making sure no one was hunting on ground they didn't have permission to be on, and keeping count of animals harvested.

No.

Jimmy Riley had had the back of his head blown off. The blood and gore replayed in her mind. Somebody had to pay, and that was all that mattered now.

She took the last swallow of water from the bottle. "Anythin' on Ray-Ray yet?"

Kendall shook his head. "He wasn't at his brother's. Bobby said he hadn't seen him. But Ray-Ray keeps to himself."

"Sheriff, I've had a run-in or two with Ray-Ray, and there's one thing I'd bet on."

"What's that?"

"Ray-Ray likes to hunt."

Kendall nodded. "And today's openin' day."

"I might just know where to look." Maybe it was best to call a ceasefire in her battle with Kendall and find out if Ray had something to do with Jimmy's death. A ceasefire wouldn't mean she hated the man any less.

Mercy came back to the table and took the chair closest to Chase. She let her arm brush his. "Valarie's mother said three girls slept at her house last night. And Valarie told her they were goin' to drive to Limon to see a ball game and get a pizza."

Paco asked what the others were thinking. "Was Dolly one of them?"

"She thinks so." Mercy wanted it to be true. "They came in late, and Mrs. Maestas was already in bed."

"Try Dolly's cell again."

Mercy dialed the number. "Straight to voice mail."

Paco lifted his coffee cup, took a sip, and paused as if he was letting everything sink in. "Let's all settle down. We can only go with what we know. Dolly could be in Limon. You know how bad cell coverage can be out there." He took another drink. "Let's assume she's with these other girls. We can talk to her when she gets back."

"And if she's not in Limon?" Marty asked.

Paco was calm. "We'll have to wait and see."

"One thing for sure," Marty thought out loud. "She's not with Jimmy Riley."

Tears filled Mercy's eyes. But not for Dolly.

CHAPTER FIVE

Opening day at ten thirty A.M. should have been Birdie's busiest time. Hunters would be moving from where they had been in the early morning. Those who had game would be hauling the animals to camp and maybe heading into Brandon for breakfast at Saylor's. Those who hadn't filled would be on the roads seeking a new place for an afternoon hunt. Normally, Birdie would check licenses and keep count of dead deer.

This morning, Birdie sped by trucks filled with men in blaze-orange hats and vests and never gave them as much as a nod. She knew Ray-Ray Jackson never missed opening morning, and he wouldn't be one of the hunters on the roads.

The rolling prairie always made Birdie think of some storybook giant's table after a holiday meal. Folds and creases made by the great tablecloth covered the November fields in tones of gold and brown. Here and there ponds and stock tanks filled with dark water stood out like dribbles of gravy.

On the far west side of the county, the giant's younger brother had hidden the salt and pepper shakers beneath the cloth. Jumbles of cottonwoods and tamarack collected in the crinkles between the two high points, and deer thrived in the creek bottoms below.

The two sections of ground belonged to the state, and hunting was open to any who dared the muck and tangles. That place on the map was called by a Spanish name. But Birdie always thought of a wrinkled old man's backside when she recalled what the locals called it. Ray-Ray would be hunting in the Butt Notch, Birdie was sure. It was less than a mile from the old farmhouse he called home. And the same distance from the dead buffalo.

And where she had found Jimmy Riley.

Birdie turned off the county gravel onto a trail road. Weeds scraped the undercarriage as she bumped the truck along the two packed strips of dirt that followed the north fence line. A mile in, the trail zigzagged away from the fence and up the higher of the two hills.

She stopped the truck before she reached the top, where the winds had taken down a dead cottonweed tree sometime last winter. Dried limbs stretched out over the trail road and spilled down the hillside. She killed the engine, sat for a moment, and listened. It was quiet. No gunshots, sounds of car engines, or distant tractors. Only the symphony the wind made over the prairie.

Peaceful.

But the image of Jimmy's body wedged into her mind and stole away the thought as soon as it formed.

Birdie took her binoculars from the glove box, opened the door, and climbed the last fifty yards to the top of the hill. Birdie didn't get a body like hers from walking. Fifty uphill yards was torture. But binoculars beat shoe leather. From the top of the bluff she could get a good look at everything in the Butt Notch.

A gunshot boomed from the jumble of the trees in the valley below. She scrambled the last few steps, dropped to her knees, and raised the field glasses to her eyes.

Ray-Ray Jackson wiped the blood from his skinning knife on a clump of dried grass. An inch of thick fat along back of the fork horn buck pleased him. Ray-Ray could have taken the older, bigger buck from the herd, but he had chosen the younger animal. From its small antlers, he would fashion the handle for a new knife, and the deer's tender meat would feed him through most of the winter.

He decided to hang the buck from the low-slung branch of a cottonwood in the shady creek bottom. He wrapped the carcass in cheesecloth—to keep away the flies—and left it to cool.

No hurry to head home. The lawmen had showed up at his house that morning. The yard dog let him know they were coming. Ray-Ray had slipped out the back, lay on his belly, and watched from a sage-covered hill not two hundred long steps from his house. The two fools in their shiny sunglasses and new cowboy hats had hollered his name and peeked in the windows but never so much as looked for tracks. They wouldn't have found his even if they had. Ray-Ray took the time to be careful that way.

Ray-Ray was sure that some judge from the next county had sent the lawmen. He knew he hadn't shown up for court when he was supposed to, but that had been nearly a month ago, and he was hoping it had all been forgotten by now. Or maybe this had something to do with his run-in with the pretend cowboy who'd let his buffalo break down Ray-Ray's fence. That one deserved all that he had coming. Ray-Ray leaned back against the trunk of the tree and watched the breeze rustle the edges of the cloth he'd wrapped around his buck.

Damn lawmen. Damn sheriff. Damn politicians.

Why couldn't they just leave him alone? He kept to himself. Never bothered anybody who didn't bother him first. Paid his property taxes in cash money over to the courthouse in Comanche Springs each April.

Ray-Ray thought for a minute and then ground what was left of his front teeth together. It had to be. That little butterball of a woman game warden was after him.

It was her, he was sure. Her that sent those lawmen out to check on him. Didn't have the grit to come herself.

Birdie Hawkins, what a bitch.

Still, there was something about her that Ray-Ray liked. She was different than other women. Liked the outdoors. Worked hard. Cared about the deer and other wild things, like him. He thought of her thick body.

Yeah, a woman like her might be nice. Shade to cool you in the summer and warm you when January nights got cold.

A rifle shot cracked the stillness around him.

Ray-Ray turned his face toward the faraway sound.

That would be the city boys he saw earlier on the other side of the Notch. They'd hunt along the edges. Wouldn't want to get into the thick stuff. Boys like that carried new scope-sighted deer rifles, not old Winchesters like his. They wanted to shoot at things out there a ways.

Ray-Ray rubbed the worn metal and smooth wood on his forty-five-seventy.

He liked to get close. Sneak through willows and tamaracks. Get in close enough to see the flies buzz around a deer's nose. That's when the forty-five-seventy did its job. Threw a bullet as big as a man's thumb. Knock a deer flat.

The shot from those city boys' rifle might send the deer back his way. Best if he sat tight. He eyed the buck hung in the tree. But two deer would get him through the winter and leave him another cow to sell at auction house.

Those deer ate his grass. Nibbled at the bales in his alfalfa fields. Drank from his stock tanks. It was only right. And it wouldn't hurt anybody. He'd take another deer. Nobody would know. Not even Birdie Hawkins.

Grass rustled along the creek bank. Not a stone's throw away, two plump does slipped from the shadows. Ray-Ray lifted his rifle.

Wait. Wait.

He put the sights on the lead deer's shoulder. The forty-five-seventy would do its job. A gun like his could knock a buffalo down in its tracks.

Through her binoculars, Birdie chuckled at a hunter in green camouflage pants and jacket. Men like that paid out a lot of money to buy clothes so the deer couldn't see them. But the state said big-game hunters had to wear blaze-orange hats and have so many square inches of orange covering their chests. So, the expensive camo Elmer Fudd had bought at the sporting goods store was lawfully covered with a bright orange vest that matched the ball cap on his head. Silly. But men liked their toys.

And Elmer, or whatever his name was, had dropped the hammer on a nice four-point buck just inside the fence line. Birdie might have spooked the deer his way when she drove her truck in. The hunter didn't seem nervous. He wasn't looking around to see who was watching. He leaned his rifle against the fence, took out his knife, and went about dressing the deer. Good signs. Meant he was legal.

Birdie had about decided that spotting Ray-Ray in the Notch wasn't going to be as easy as she had guessed. Her best chance would be catching him between here and his home. She stood up and dusted off the seat of her britches. She'd walk back to the truck, go check the hunter, maybe give him a ride to his vehicle, and then circle around to the other side of the Notch and see if she could find any sign of Ray-Ray.

Another shot sounded in the bottoms.

Not a crack like the first. No, this was more of a boom. Came from a cannon like Ray-Ray carried.

Birdie slipped her Glock from the holster on her hip. She pulled back the slide just enough to be sure there was a live cartridge in the chamber. Then Birdie started down the hill. If she found Ray-Ray, she wasn't sure what she should do. The sheriff just wanted to talk to him, that was all. Ray-Ray wouldn't like that.

And if she did find him, Ray-Ray might shoot her. Or ask her to come to dinner. He was crazy that way.

Oh well, it would give her something to think about on her way down the hill toward the boom of the big rifle. One thing was for sure. Birdie hated walking.

CHAPTER SIX

Chase, Mercy, Marty, and Paco stood in a shady spot on the steps outside the café. Mercy rubbed her hands over her bare forearms. They'd said goodbye to each other, but no one was ready to leave. A burst of wind from a passing semi brushed Chase's face and rattled the front windows of the café. Without saying a word, Marty dove behind the wheel of the Sheriff Department's car. Paco Martinez jumped for the passenger seat and slammed the door shut. Tires spun and gravel flew as Marty backed away from the restaurant onto the highway and hit the gas. Red and blue lights flashed, and the deputies chased the speeding truck out of Brandon.

"Happens almost every day," Mercy told Chase. "Truckers don't slow down for this one-horse town." She fanned the dust from Marty's car away from her face and looked up at Chase. "Come back in for another cup of coffee?"

"Naw, I've got an appointment at the bank to go over some things about the ranch. Maybe I'll stop by again later on." He tried to think of a reason he wouldn't want to see her again, but couldn't.

Mercy pushed the hair away from her eyes. "There's a pancake supper over at First Methodist tonight. They make it a big deal.

Feed the visitin' hunters. Money goes to the town. We're closin' early. How about you take me? Whole town will be there."

"I don't know, Mercy." Chase wasn't sure what the folks in Brandon thought of him now. He knew now he'd made a mistake going to the ball game on Friday. Finding Mercy back in town complicated a part of his life he wanted to stay simple.

"Come on, people will want to see you. By then everyone in the county will know about the Riley kid." Her green eyes pleaded. "It might take their minds off of some of the bad if you're there."

Chase shook his head. "Ah, okay." Chase gave in too easy. He always did with Mercy.

"Pick me up at my folks' house at six. Like you used to."

The bank manager pointed to a chair, and Chase settled in across the desk from the woman. Chase knew his father never would have done this kind of business with a woman.

The banker pointed to a stack of file folders on her desk and said, "It's nice to do this in person instead of just email. Where would you like to start? Regular ranch accounts, rentals, or your"— she paused—"more altruistic endeavors." She smiled at him.

"Anythin' I should know about the ranch that I don't?"

"I'm sure you're up to date."

"How much is in the rental account?"

She opened a folder, put on her reading glasses, and then turned the papers so Chase could see the numbers. "Bobby Jackson hasn't missed a payment."

Chase took a check from his shirt pocket and laid it on the desk. "I want you to deposit this into that account."

The banker's eyes widened.

"As soon as that clears," Chase said, "I want you to change the account to a trust for the education of Dolly Benavidez. I want her to be able to draw on that to pay for college."

"Does she know about this?"

Chase shook his head. "I'll take care of that. You just draw up whatever papers we need, and I'll sign them before I leave on

Monday." He looked over the banker's shoulder at the few stores still open on Main Street. Plainsman Liquors was the only one with cars in front. Chase bit back an old urge. "Anythin' else?"

"Pop Weber and two other old timers are going to have trouble paying property taxes this year."

"I'll pay again. Like before, no one is to know."

Stalks of knee-high brown grass tangled around the broken, silver-gray tree branches in the dry creek bed. Fresh tracks from two deer led Birdie down the wash. In the shade made by the trees, Birdie found what she expected.

Birdie poked at a slick, sticky gut pile with the toe of her boot. Whoever had dropped the paunch from the deer had taken his time and knew what he was doing. Only a few silver dollar–sized drops of blood dotted the sand. The stomach hadn't been punctured, and there were no knife nicks on the coils of intestines. The liver and heart had been taken from the pile of entrails. Birdie found the place an arm's length away where a knife had been wiped clean on a clump of dried grass.

She studied the deer tracks again. The heart-shaped tracks meant that these two were does. Most likely a mother with a yearling fawn. The two deer had slipped into the creek bottom single file. The hunter had taken the second deer. Good choice. The younger animal would be tender and better eating. She scanned the trees and shadows, guessing where the hunter had hidden.

Birdie poked around at the brush at the edge of the far creek bank. A sunbeam filtered through the bare autumn tree branches and flashed almost golden from a speck of dirt behind a fallen cottonwood. She sucked in a breath and told herself she should have worn her other pants. The pair that made it easier to bend over.

With more effort than it should have taken, she stooped down. Her belt buckle pinched the soft rolls along her belly, but she speared the empty rifle cartridge with her Bic pen like an actor on a TV detective show. It had been fired by a big gun. Birdie didn't need to look at the stamp on the cartridge to know it was a forty-five-seventy.

Like Ray-Ray carried.

Not six more steps away she found another sun-glazed gut pile. No liver or heart there either.

Damn it, Ray-Ray.

She used her phone to take pictures of what she had found and tucked the cartridge in her shirt pocket. The phone had no reception behind the big hills in the Butt Notch. She put it in the pocket with the cartridge and stared up at the hill she'd hiked down.

Crap. She should have worn the other pants.

One trucker sat at the counter in Saylor's Café. The kitchen was clean from breakfast and the clock over the cash register said one o'clock.

Mercy untied her apron. "Diana, I got some errands to run," she told the waitress reading the new *People* magazine at the table by the front window, "I probably won't be back. Close up at four and put the sign on the door tellin' 'em they can eat at the Flapjack Feed over at First Methodist."

Mercy took her coat from its hook by the back door and stepped out into the parking lot. She tossed the coat and her purse on the backseat of her mother's old Lincoln. There was a dark smudge on the bumper. Mercy wiped away the spot with a Kleenex.

She climbed into the car. The warmth from the afternoon sun wrapped around her, and the steering wheel was almost too hot to touch. It reminded her of the bubble bath she had planned before Chase came to pick her up.

Sunlight touched the silvery threads of a spiderweb that stretched from the dried branches of a wild rose to the letters carved in Chase's mother's headstone. He stopped before he brushed them away.

His mother wouldn't have touched them. Not from fear. The small things of nature were what she loved most. She marveled at the swallows' nests along the eaves of the house and how the birds came back year after year. She could name each wildflower that grew in the pastures around the house and knew to the day when each would bloom in the spring.

When a spider spun its web outside her kitchen window, she refused to let his father knock it away. She marveled at it each day that whole summer. Especially on the prairie mornings when drops of dew clung to the silky fibers.

He stood by her grave a long time and thought of the good times and was glad that she hadn't seen the man he'd become. But it hurt him that she'd never seen him play for the university, never seen him on TV, and never met the woman he loved.

He left her there with the wild rose he'd planted the morning he left Brandon, and never looked at the place beside her where his father lay.

Chase paused at one other grave before he left the hill and said a prayer for Dolly's mother, and asked her to forgive him for the terrible things his father had done.

CHAPTER SEVEN

Chase pounded harder on the front door of the small house that Coach Porter called home. No one had come when Chase rang the doorbell or rapped on the doorframe.

From inside the house, ESPN's *SportsCenter* played on a widescreen TV, and lights were on in one bedroom and the kitchen.

But lights seemed always to be on at Coach's house, and his constant companion was TV sports.

Coach had grown up in some farm town in Missouri. Got a scholarship to play basketball for a small college in Nebraska. Was set to be a starter his junior year when, coming home from Thanksgiving break, he'd been in a car wreck on an icy highway. A teammate had been killed, and Coach's face had been cut up real bad. He lost his left eye and his chance to start. He played a minute here or there in games whose outcome had already been decided, but spent most of his time on the end of the bench.

But Coach made the team again his senior year, took the same seat on the bench, and graduated with honors. Fresh out of college and just a few years older than the players who would be on his teams, Coach took the job with Brandon Schools. Chase and Marty were seniors that year. For the first time Chase had to work at a game that had been so easy for him. Coach wrote letters and made phone calls, and when Brandon went to the state tournament, college coaches knew all about Chase Ford. Instead of the junior college in Lamar, Chase left Brandon with a full ride to the University of Colorado.

Seventeen years later, Coach Porter taught history, coached track and basketball, and had made a player out of Jimmy Riley. He was the only man in Brandon whom Chase had talked to in all those years.

Chase stepped back from the door, crossed the porch, and looked down the side of the house. Coach's pickup was in the driveway. Chase took out his cell and dialed Coach's number.

Straight to voice mail.

Like Dolly's.

Down the street, Chase could see the school bus wasn't back from the freshman game. Old Paco said the cell reception was bad in Limon. Chase guessed that Coach had gone along. Maybe he even drove the bus. Coach would do that. Basketball and kids were important to him. All these years later, Chase realized the kids were the most important thing to Coach Porter.

Especially a kid whose father never showed up for a single game.

Chase should have told Coach he was coming for the weekend. Now, Chase wanted to be there when Coach found out Jimmy Riley was dead.

But Mercy said the whole town would be at the pancake supper. He'd see Coach then.

Chase left Brandon for the ranch. It was four hours until he needed to be back at Mercy's house. He'd take his father's rifle and slip out on the sage flats to watch for the big buck he'd seen that morning.

By the time Birdie had reached the top of the Butt Notch's south hill she had used up every cuss word she knew three times and was partway through the list for the fourth. Weighted down by her pistol, her too-tight pants chafed her hips. Sweat soaked the armpits of her shirt and plastered her hair to the sides of her head.

She scooped a bottle of water from the cooler in the back of her pickup, pressed it to her forehead, and used each of the cuss words still available on her list. Cell reception showed four bars and three messages. Two from Sheriff Dickweed and one from Marty's wife.

The first message from the sheriff said, "Call me." The second said, "Call me now."

Birdie let the jerk wait and checked the message from Deb. "You're comin' to the Flapjack Feed, aren't you? The boys want to see their Aunt Birdie. See you tonight."

Seeing the little boys would be fun. Birdie had spent the whole day at the place where Jimmy Riley had been found, or hunting for Ray-Ray Jackson and not doing what the state paid her to do.

Besides, she could nose around at the pancake supper, talk with hunters who came in to eat, and get a feel for what was going on.

She sipped the water and used her binoculars to scan the creek bottom one more time. Still no sign of Ray-Ray. She pressed the callback button on her phone and waited for Sheriff Shithead to pick up.

First ring. "Where have you been, Hawkins?" Sheriff Kendall snapped.

What? No *Good afternoon, officer?* Birdie gritted her teeth so tight she'd need to call the dentist for an appointment on Monday. She fought the urge to tell the turd-breath that she had been risking life and limb to track a dangerous criminal and simply said, "I didn't catch up with Ray-Ray. Found where he shot a deer. Least I'm ninety-nine percent sure it was him that shot it. But never saw him."

"Listen, Hawkins, we got somethin'."

"I hope it's good," she muttered.

"What's that, Hawkins?"

"Nothin'. Go on."

"When the processor in Cheyenne Wells started to butcher the first of Puckett's buffalo, he found a rifle slug. He checked the other buffalo and found slugs in two more." Birdie could hear the stubble on Kendall's chin scrape over his phone. "The state is gonna do a full ballistics study and tell us what they can, but for now we can guess the buffalo were shot with a thirty caliber. The bullets were pretty tore up, but they're guessin' they were a hundred and fifty grains."

Not much. Birdie knew that half the farmers in the county had a thirty-thirty in their pickup, or barn, or behind the kitchen door. Those that didn't have a thirty-thirty might keep an aught-six handy. A lot of hunters carried thirty-caliber guns, and a 150-grain bullet could come from any one of them. She sucked in a breath. "What about the bullet that killed Jimmy?"

"Didn't find it. Through and through shot. But from what the coroner can say so far, the entrance wound could have been from a thirty." The sheriff paused. "Hawkins, what kind of gun does Ray-Ray hunt with?"

She touched the cartridge case in her shirt pocket. "Forty-five-seventy. I picked up an empty by a gut pile down in the Notch. Sure it's from Ray-Ray's gun."

A long silence hung on the end of the sheriff's line. Then, "I still want to talk to him. Go by his farm again."

Rage flared inside Birdie. "It's not my"—the phone went dead—"job. . . ."

Shit fire. She hated that man.

Through the scope on his father's three-hundred Magnum, Chase spotted the tips of the big buck's antlers. The deer had bedded down behind a clump of yucca plants on a knoll just above the winter wheat field where Chase had first seen him that morning. No doubt the old buck had found a sunny spot to chew its cud. The wind was to its back. It could see danger coming from a mile away in three directions, and the breeze would bring the scent of trouble from the other.

Chase leaned the old Weatherby against a fence post and raised his binoculars. He fiddled with the adjustment wheel until the deer came into focus. Through the spear points of the soapweed, the old buck stared right back at him.

No chance to get any closer today. The deer knew right where Chase was.

Hints of a breeze stole away the day's warmth. The sun would be down in less than an hour. Cinnamon-dusted clouds stacked up on the western horizon, and spikes as bloodred as the smears around Jimmy Riley flared away from the setting sun.

Chase needed to get back to his trailer in the ranch yard and wash up. Mercy was expecting him at six.

All through school, every girl Mercy knew had told her she lived in the nicest house in Brandon. Her house sat at the edge of town, north of the highway, the railroad, and the feedlots. The prevailing wind in Brandon always came from the north. It made sense that folks who had a choice would want to live upwind of the noise, smells, and commotion that happened on the south side of town.

Mercy's father was vice president of the bank, and Mama owned the café. Mercy knew she had more than most of her friends and she was grateful, but the house she lived in was really no different from the other houses in the county. The only time the front door was opened was when Mama decorated it for Christmas. When folks came to visit they entered at the back of the house, through the mud room off the kitchen. Mama kept a dozen chickens in the backyard, and her father ran cattle on two sections of ground north of town.

Mama had tried to keep the house clean, but there was always a gritty layer of prairie dust on the vinyl floor in the kitchen and during the summers flies had buzzed in the corners of the windows just like the farmhouses her friends lived in.

Just after four, Mercy opened the back door and ran up the stairs to her parents' room. She started water running into the claw-footed tub in their bathroom, and when the steam fogged the windows she poured in twice as much bubble bath as she should have. Mercy gathered towels and a robe from the back of the door, stripped off the clothes that smelled of Saylor's Cafe, and settled in the hot water to soak away the day.

Chase Ford wouldn't come at six. Chase would knock on the back door at five forty-five. He was always early, and Mercy intended to make him wait.

She scrubbed the stains and grime from her fingernails with a stiff brush and washed her hair. She rubbed handfuls of conditioner into her dark hair, leaned back to enjoy the warmth around her, and stared out of the open bathroom door.

Mercy hadn't touched a thing in her parents' bedroom since Mama had moved to the rest home in Comanche Springs and Daddy had died. His deer rifle still leaned in the corner behind the door, and Mama's full-length oval mirror sat at the end of their bed.

Whenever Mercy looked at herself in that mirror she could still see the reflection of Mama's face behind her. Mama was there when Mercy tried on her costume for the school play, when she dressed up for homecoming, and all those other special times. Mama told her she looked like a lady.

But Mercy wasn't a lady. She was just a girl from a small farm town on Colorado's windswept prairies. She wanted to be something else, something more, but she never quite fit in. Not at the small eastern college she chose. Certainly not with Carl's family in the Philadelphia suburbs.

Now she was back in Brandon. Waiting for the high school basketball star to take her to a pancake supper in the church basement. Maybe this was where she belonged.

No.

The clock downstairs chimed five times. Mercy climbed from the tub, dried herself, and put on the robe. She walked to Mama's mirror and did a most unladylike thing for a woman on her way to church.

Mercy let the robe drop from her shoulders and appraised her naked body. The twenty pounds Carl had teased her so cruelly about had melted away in the stress from their divorce. The months on her feet at the café had taken another ten and firmed her legs. Gravity had been kind, and makeup could hide the wrinkles around her eyes.

She left the robe on the floor, pushed the box of cartridges for her father's rifle to the side of the dresser, picked up her cell phone, and dialed a number.

"Sheriff," she said into the phone. "You know who this is?" She let her voice purr. "I'll see you at the pancake supper tonight, won't I?"

Sheriff Lincoln Kendall tucked his personal cell phone into the shirt pocket behind his badge. He walked back to his deputies and the crime scene agents from the state.

"How much longer do you need?" he asked the lead agent.

"We're wrappin' things up now."

Kendall turned up the collar of his jacket. "I'll leave two of my men to help out. I got business I need to attend to." He wiped his mouth with the back of his hand. "I'll look for your report in the mornin'." He didn't thank them.

The sheriff climbed into his truck and dialed home on the department's cell. "Becky, listen. This thing turned into a nightmare. I'm not sure when I'll get home tonight. Tell the girls I love 'em. And don't wait up."

He started the truck, pulled up onto the gravel road, and punched a button on the police radio. "Arlene, I'll be in Brandon if you need me."

CHAPTER EIGHT

Marty set two cans of Mountain Dew, a bag of Cheetos, and a Snickers bar on the scratched countertop in the Town Pump store. Cecil pushed up his glasses and wriggled the skin on his nose as if to command that they stay in place for longer than a minute. He smiled at the woman in front of Marty, shook open a plastic sack, and dropped the pack of Marlboro Lights she had asked for into the bag. The woman tapped the edge of her credit card on the counter. Cecil screwed up his face, lifted a box of Tampax between his thumb and little finger, and dropped it into the bag with her cigarettes. He swiped the woman's credit card and nodded to her as she left the store.

"Marty, is all this for you?" he asked as the deputy added two Slim Jims to his snacks.

"No. The Mountain Dew is for Paco."

Cecil pushed at his glasses again. The bright yellow Town Pump cap on his head was the only thing he was wearing that didn't need washing. "I heard about Jimmy Riley." He stared at Marty though his thick glasses. "Is it true what they're sayin'? Somebody cut off his pecker?"

"Where'd you hear that?"

"One of those fellas that drives for an oil company said he heard it from those Mexican boys that are buildin' that fence ten miles north of town. Said they cut off the buffalos', too." Cecil jabbed at his glasses again and whispered, "Sound's like devil worshippers to me. I saw a show on the TV about them."

"You're makin' all this up, aren't you? Just like the story you told about Pop Weber not bein' able to remember things because he got lifted up by a tornado and dropped on his head. You think because you tell all these stories people will think you're important." Marty grabbed a Slim Jim, peeled down the plastic, and bit the end off. "'Sides, all those buffalo were heifers and heifers don't have peckers"—he took another bite—"and Jimmy had his. I should arrest you for lyin'."

Cecil shrugged. "Maybe it wasn't that driver that told me. But somebody did."

"How many people you tell this story to?"

"A few." Cecil looked down at the floor.

"Shut up, Cecil, just shut up."

Marty took his bag of food outside. He hadn't gotten a good look at Jimmy's body in the field. There was a lot of blood.

What if what Cecil said was true?

When he looked down at the ragged end of the Slim Jim in his hand, his butt puckered. He tossed the rest of the sausage into the trash barrel. Birdie had found the body. He could ask her.

Hey, Birdie. Did Jimmy have his . . . ?

Paco came around the corner of the building, opened the front door, and hung the restroom key back on its hook. The old deputy stepped off the curb and rested his hip on the patrol car. Marty handed him a can of pop and fished the Cheetos out of his bag.

"Cecil tellin' stories again?" the old deputy asked.

"Yeah. And a whopper this time."

"Anythin' to it?"

"I don't think so."

"Cecil can't help it. I think that's just who he is." Paco popped the top of his pop can and sniffed the air. "Smell that?"

Marty put his nose to the breeze and smiled. "I think I smell flapjacks and maple syrup. They must be startin' to cook over at

First Methodist. Deb's gonna bring the kids, and we're all gonna eat together. What time is it?"

Chase's Dodge pickup rolled down the highway in front of the island of light at the Town Pump. Both deputies waved.

"It's twenty to six," Paco said.

"Them Methodists start servin' at six thirty. I better call Deb." Marty wiped the Cheetos dust from his mouth. "I like pancakes."

In just the light of the flames from a can of Sterno, Ray-Ray lifted two pieces of sizzling bacon with the tip of his skinning knife from a blackened skillet. He laid the bacon on a paper towel he had placed on a rock and set the skillet back over the fire. One by one he dropped strips of fresh deer's heart into the hot grease and added green jalapeño peppers to the mix. He covered the skillet with a tin plate and listened to his dinner sputter and pop.

Ray-Ray lifted his head just high enough to see over the rim of the gulley where he hid. The chubby game warden's truck still sat on the road near the gate to his property. She hadn't just barreled in like the two sheriff's deputies had done that morning. Birdie Hawkins was a smart woman. She had left her truck at the bottom of that little hill, climbed the fence, and was sitting out on the pasture watching his house.

If he believed the state had a right to make him buy a hunting license to kill deer that fed on his land all year long, he might have asked her to share this deer-heart supper. He could have cooked it up in the house instead out on the prairie. Spill some wild honey over scratch biscuits to go along with it. Nothing wrong with that.

Still, it rankled him something awful that the law and government were after him. Why couldn't they just leave him alone?

But he could wait her out. He knew where she was. She was looking for him.

After he ate, Ray-Ray dug into his shirt pocket under his coat for his Zig-Zags and a baggie of homegrown weed. He twisted up a smoke and lit it in the flames from the Sterno. Sterno didn't put out smoke that could be spotted and threw off a good bit of warmth.

He held the first drag of herb deep in his lungs for a long while. Over his head, more stars than a man could count peppered the new night. Ray-Ray liked to watch the stars and hated the way the lights in Brandon hid so many. He bet city people had no idea how many stars there really were. All those electric lights didn't match up with what the Lord had made.

He took another puff, and dreamy warmth filled his head. He heard Birdie's truck start up. He could go to the house now, but Ray-Ray decided to stay on the prairie and try to count the stars.

Marty stepped up onto the curb as Sheriff Kendall pulled into the parking lot at Town Pump. The sheriff rolled down his window, and Marty stepped in close.

"Any word on the Benavidez girl or Coach?" Kendall asked.

"We put in a call to the high school in Limon. The janitor answered. He didn't know much, 'cept the game went in double overtime so they were late gettin' out of there. When they came out of the school, the bus had a flat tire and they had to wait to have it fixed. Bus should be showin' up anytime now." Marty took another sniff of the air. He was sure he smelled maple syrup. His stomach growled.

"Anythin' else, Marty?"

"Brandon won, sir."

"What's that?"

"The basketball game, sir. Brandon won. That Taylor kid hit two free throws with three seconds left."

Paco came out of Town Pump with two cups of coffee. He gave Marty a grin and then handed one of the cups to the sheriff. The sheriff tipped his head. That was about the only way Marty had ever seen the man say thank you.

They stood next to the sheriff's truck on the warm November evening. The sheriff's eyes were tired, and Marty knew he was thinking about all that had happened that day. He had trouble believing it himself. Boys didn't get killed in Comanche County. They died in car wrecks and tractor turnovers, not by a bullet in the head.

Across the highway, near the train tracks, in that old part of town, a sound like summer thunder split the night.

Paco slopped coffee from his cup onto the ground. The sheriff turned his face toward the noise. "That sounded like a gunshot."

Lights blinked on the radios in both the sheriff's truck and the deputies' patrol car. Arlene's voice cracked through the static. "Just got a nine-one-one. Shots fired. Plainsman Liquors in Brandon. Nearest unit, please respond."

The sheriff had the microphone in his hand and the truck in reverse. "This is Kendall. On my way. Martinez and Storm are with me."

Paco followed the sheriff. Marty was in the passenger seat unlocking the patrol car's shotgun from its bracket. The sheriff stomped on the gas. Red and blue flashing lights pulsed over the four-lane road. An oncoming semitruck hit its brakes, and Kendall swung a hard left in front of it. The back end of his truck swayed with the turn. The breath stopped in Marty's chest, and Paco skidded the patrol car inches from the semi to keep up with the sheriff.

Two short blocks down, the owner of the liquor store stood on the sidewalk. Behind him, light spilled from the shattered front window of his store. He pointed across the street.

A man in a white T-shirt sat on the curb. He upended a bottle of liquor into his mouth. A deer rifle lay in the gutter at the man's feet.

Kendall slammed his truck to a stop and stepped out with his pistol leveled at the man. Marty rolled out of his side of the car, jacked a load of buckshot into the shotgun, and flopped over the hood. Paco had his Glock out, moving off to the side.

The drunken man set the bottle on the sidewalk. Marty recognized Jimmy Riley's father.

God, don't let him do anythin' stupid.

"Kick that rifle out into the street," Kendall barked.

Riley shook his head.

The liquor store's electric sign buzzed behind him; the father sobbed; and even with the click of the sheriff cocking his forty-five, Marty's heart pounded louder than everything else.

"I'm gonna tell you one more time, kick that rifle out in the street," the sheriff shouted again.

Marty clamped his face to the stock of the shotgun and poised his finger over the safety. Do what he says. Please, God, just do what he says.

In a blur, Paco dashed from the shadows. He caught Riley around the neck, and as the two tumbled to the ground, the old deputy's foot kicked the rifle toward Kendall.

Marty's instincts jerked the muzzle of the shotgun toward the sky and away from his partner. Kendall jammed his pistol into its holster and snatched handcuffs from his belt.

"My boy's dead." Pain filled each sob in the father's voice. "Dead and bleedin' all over the ground like a cut calf."

The lies Cecil had told the town filled Marty's mind, and he was sick.

Mercy thought she heard a gunshot.

Some hunter taking a chance at deer this close to town?

Birdie would be fit to be tied. Marty, too.

Chase had banged on the door ten minutes ago. She'd make him wait another ten.

Mercy checked her hair in the mirror. Turned her head side to side to be sure her makeup covered those tiny lines near her eyes. A pancake supper in a church basement was as close to high society as Brandon ever got. Mercy wanted to be sure she looked nice. There'd be hunters in camo and orange, farmers in Carhartt overalls, and most of the women would be wearing jeans and sweatshirts.

Mercy would wear jeans, too. The tight Cruel Girl pair the truckers liked to see her in. She'd even caught Jimmy Riley checking out her backside when he stopped by the café to give Dolly a ride home.

Poor boy.

Tomorrow she'd ask the waitresses at the café to give a share of their tips to the boy's father.

She checked her hair one more time and smoothed the front of the tight cashmere sweater she'd chosen.

It was a shame to hide all that under a jacket.

She opened a prescription pill bottle on the dresser and washed down two with Diet Coke. She shut her eyes as they slid down her throat and knew she'd feel the pills kick in before they got to the church.

Chase banged on the door again.

Five after six.

It was like before. When all her friends envied the banker's daughter in the nicest house in town. It felt like high school again. Two of the best boys in the county out for her attention. Mercy wanted everyone to know it.

"I found this in his apartment. Thought he could use it." Marty looked at Jimmy's father in the back of the patrol car and handed Paco a dirty sweatshirt. "It's gettin' cold." He turned to Sheriff Kendall. "We'll just keep him overnight and let him sober up. Right?"

"The liquor store owner is pissed. He wants somebody to pay for his window. I think Riley's gonna hafta stand up in front of a judge and answer for this," the sheriff said.

"What happened, anyway?"

"Owner says he came in asked for a quart of Bombay gin on credit. He told him no way. Riley came back with his rifle and grabbed a bottle off the shelf. When the owner hollered at him, Riley shot out the window. Then he just walked across the street, sat down, and started drinkin'. That's when we got here." Kendall nodded to Paco. "Go ahead, take him on over to Comanche Springs."

Paco climbed in the car and pulled away. In the backseat, Riley's chin rested on his chest. Tears still streaked his face.

"I feel sorry for him," Marty told the sheriff.

"Yeah, I know what you mean. Only thing we can do is catch whoever killed the boy."

"Sheriff, there's somethin' you should know. These were sittin' on the table in his apartment. I took a picture before I picked 'em up." Marty held out a box of cartridges he'd tucked into a plastic bag. "Thirty-aught-six. Federal one-fifty grain. You don't think—"

"Hell, Marty, I don't want to even think about it." The sheriff pressed his eyes shut.

Marty thought the man's shoulders slumped with the weight of the awful day. "Climb in my truck. I'll give you a lift to the church," Kendall said.

"If it's all the same, sir, I'll walk."

The sheriff never looked at him. "You do that."

CHAPTER NINE

In the cool evening air, Chase could almost feel the surge of wind on his face from the speeding trucks on the highway six blocks away. Over the noise, a crack like a distant explosion rolled over Brandon.

Rifle shot? Some hunter making a last try?

The light still shined in Mercy's bedroom. She liked to keep him waiting. Chase stepped away from the back door and fumbled in his pocket to check his cell phone. Two messages. Neither from Billee. Both from his agent.

Even as Chase retrieved the messages, he knew what they'd say. *Need an answer.* Or, *Have you made up your mind?* Or, *What do I tell San Diego?*

Chase didn't need to decide. Not now. He had thought it would be easy, but being home—seeing Marty, Birdie, and Mercy again—made it harder.

Tell them what I told you to tell them. I'll make my decision by Monday.

Chase checked the messages again to make sure he hadn't missed one. But there was nothing from Billee.

From inside the house, stairs creaked. The light in the kitchen flicked on. Then Mercy Saylor opened the mud room door.

A gasp caught in his throat.

A canvas barn coat hung from her shoulders, one arm in its sleeve, the other arm searching to find its place. Her tan sweater stretched tight across her chest with the struggle.

Chase reached in and lifted her jacket to help her find the sleeve.

"You're a gentleman, Mr. Ford," she said, and her green eyes sparkled in the light. She turned and stepped closer to him. "The door was unlocked. You could have come in."

"I tried that one night, and your daddy ran me off."

"I remember." She knotted her fingers in his shirtfront.

Chase pulled back when Mercy tugged to move him closer. He looked up at the night above him. "I forgot how clear the skies could be and just how many stars there really are. It's a nice night, Mercy, let's walk."

She pulled tighter on his shirt. "No, drive me to church in that new pickup of yours."

Birdie eased her truck to the side of the street a block and a half away because the church parking lot was already full.

Damn it. More walking.

She turned sideways, squeezed between two trucks, and checked license plates as she walked to the church. An even number of local and out-of-county vehicles filled the lot. One from Illinois. Birdie would keep her ears up to figure out who the out-of-state hunters were.

She knew she should concern herself with how many hunters had filled their tags and listen for any word of trouble. But she wondered how many thirty-caliber rifles were tucked in cases in the back of those trucks and SUVs, and how many more had been left back at camps. Thirty caliber was the most popular rifle, she guessed. 150-grain bullet wasn't at all special either. Until the tests came back from the state lab, any one of a hundred rifles could have killed the buffalo. And Jimmy Riley.

And why was Sheriff Turd-Breath so keen on talking to Ray-Ray?

Ray-Ray wasn't the most balanced fella in the county. But he had no reason to shoot the boy. And she'd thought hard about that. If Birdie had to bet, that Tony Lama boot print she'd found by the missing alfalfa bale meant something.

A group of hunters opened the front door to the church. Laughter spilled out. A tinge of the aroma of warm pancake syrup floated on the cool evening. Birdie could swear she heard sausage sizzling.

Whipped butter, hot syrup, and Grandma Titus's flapjacks might make a bad day better.

"Hey, Birdie." Over the noise from the church someone called her name. "Over here."

She spotted Marty at the corner of the church building. One little boy hung in his arms; another, in a cowboy hat like his dad's, stood at his side, and Marty held hands with his very pregnant wife. "Birdie, come on. Join us."

Probably wants someone to help with the rug rats. Damn him.

She crossed the lot a half step faster than before, held out her arms, and took the little boy from Marty.

"Don't be teachin' these little buckaroos any of your bad words, Birdie," Marty told her with a smile.

"Like they haven't heard it from you already." She stopped a choice curse and nodded to Marty's wife. "How you doin', Deb? Feelin' okay?"

Marty bent over and pressed his ear to where his wife's sweatshirt stretched tight over her bulging belly. "Deb says this here cowpoke is kickin' up a storm tonight."

Deb patted her husband's head. "Marty, the doctor said this one's a girl."

"What's he know?" Marty tucked his other son under his arm, as if he were carrying a football. "Let's get somethin' to eat."

"Wait for us." It was Chase and Mercy.

Mercy's arm wrapped around Chase's. When they stepped up to the others, Mercy tilted her face until the top of her head rested just below Chase's shoulder.

Birdie thought she saw Chase pull away just a bit.

"Deb," Marty said as he wrestled to keep his oldest boy under his arm, "I told you about these folks. I believe it's the first time me, Birdie, Chase, and Mercy have been together since high school. Tonight will be like old times. Let's go in and eat and tell stories about each other 'til they throw us out."

Marty took Deb's hand. Mercy pulled closer to Chase, and they all walked to the church's front door.

Just like old times. Mercy was up front with Chase and Marty, and Birdie was two steps behind. Marty's little boy rested his head on Birdie's shoulder and fought to keep his eyes open.

The light from the open door brushed over the dirt path from the parking lot. Birdie's breath stopped. She wanted to bend down and look closer, but with a child in her arms she couldn't. In the dust, just where her friends had walked, was a boot print about the same size as the one she'd found in the alfalfa field. The Tony Lama logo showed clearly in the mark from the heel.

Birdie heard the click of boot heels on the church stairs.

"I like your boots, Deb," Mercy said. "Are they new?"

Oh, shit.

Townsfolk and hunters sat at rows of folding tables placed end-to-end in the church basement. The clamor of kitchen noises and conversation echoed off the worn tile floor and painted cement walls. The smell of pancakes dripped like warm syrup from the air.

Chase could feel every head in the place turn when he walked into the room.

"That's him," was whispered in hushed tones at every table.

Chase's shoulders slouched and his head hung in the practiced manner he'd grown used to when he didn't want to be recognized in airports or restaurants or all the other places where he wanted to be just like all the others. At six feet seven, he always got noticed. Some recognized the tall man with blond hair and remembered his championship series with the Lakers. Even more remembered his picture on the magazine covers with Billee.

He wondered which one the folks in Brandon thought of.

The ladies in the church kitchen whispered to one another as they piled flapjacks and sausage on his paper plate. Farmers nodded as he followed Mercy to the end of the long line of tables. Some tipped their heads and told the younger men at tables, "Six-Gun Ford was as good as they come, until . . ."

Chase hated that word. And more than the word, he hated the way so many said it.

He and Mercy took metal folding chairs across the table from Marty and his wife. Birdie and Marty's boys settled in next to Deb. Marty sloshed warm syrup on his pile of pancakes until it dribbled from the edge of his plate and made sticky rivers on the paper table cloth.

"Doesn't get much better than this." He shoveled a forkful into his mouth. "You're sure bein' quiet, Birdie."

Birdie smeared butter and doused syrup on the boys' pancakes. "Wore out. I had a long day."

"Yeah, we all did," Marty said between mouthfuls.

Chase asked, "Any news yet about . . ."

Marty washed down the pancakes with a swallow of coffee. "Last I heard we're waiting for the forensics from the state. That might take a couple of days. Still haven't talked with Coach. He's supposed to be on the bus comin' back from Limon. Don't know just what he could add." He took another gulp of coffee. "There's the sheriff now. He might know somethin'."

Chase turned. Kendall Lincoln—big hat, bigger gun, badge and all—walked down the church steps. He touched the brim of his hat when he saw Mercy. His jaw muscles tightened when he spotted Chase beside her. He hooked his thumbs in his gun belt and leaned a shoulder against the wall.

Half a dozen teenage boys in Brandon Buffalos sweatsuits filed down the stairs past the sheriff and into the line for pancakes.

"Bus must be back." Marty stopped the next forkful of pancakes before it reached his mouth.

Cheerleaders and another group of girls joined the boys. Marty matched names with the faces he recognized.

"I don't see Dolly with them," Mercy said.

"I don't, either." He set his plastic fork beside his plate and mopped his mouth with a napkin.

Above the noise in the basement a cell phone rang. The sheriff straightened, pulled his phone from his belt, and put it to his ear. The man's lips pulled tight.

"Deputy Storm," he called, "come with me."

Marty caught up to the sheriff in the parking lot. He struggled into his jacket and licked sticky syrup from his fingers. "What's goin' on?" He jumped in the passenger seat of Kendall's truck.

"I guess Coach wasn't with the team in Limon." Kendall turned the ignition and slipped the truck in gear. "When the bus got back, one of the boys went over to Coach's house to tell him they won. No answer when he knocked. Got in somehow. Found Coach on floor." The sheriff flipped on the flashing lights. "Says there's blood everywhere. Ambulance should be there any minute."

It took less than five minutes to get to Coach Porter's little house. As they climbed out of Kendall's truck, the sheriff jerked his thumb at a kid in a Brandon Buffalos sweatsuit on the front porch. "Recognize the kid?" Kendall asked Marty.

"Cameron Taylor. I went to school with his mother." Marty fished his cell phone from his jacket pocket. "I saw his folks at the church. I'll tell 'em to come over here."

"Good idea. See what you can find out from the boy." The sheriff tipped his head toward the house. "I'm goin' inside."

Marty said a few words into his phone and then sat down next to Cameron Taylor on Coach's front steps. Teardrops clung to the soft mustache hairs along the teenager's lip and sparkled in the pulse of the ambulance's flashing lights. The boy who had made the winning basket four hours earlier rocked back and forth. Marty had seen folks at car accidents do the same thing. Like they hoped the motion would erase the terrible things they'd seen.

"I called the church." Marty folded his hands. "Your daddy and mom are on their way over to get you. I talked to Grandma Titus. She's sendin' a plate of flapjacks with 'em."

"I'm not hungry."

"We'll see." He shouldn't have said anything about the pancakes.

Cameron sucked in a breath. "Coach said if I could just make my free throws, he'd let me suit up with varsity on Thursday. I didn't miss any today. Hit two with three seconds left. That's why I came over here. I wanted him to know." The boy's voice broke, and he stared at the ground. A cry he didn't want to let out escaped.

"Coach still leave that house key in an aspirin bottle under that rock by the corner of the house?" Marty tilted his head.

"Yeah," Cameron whispered.

"He kept it there for Chase and me. Chase, mostly. A lot of nights we'd let ourselves in and watch games on TV. Coach'd come home, find us there, and cook up some hamburgers and watch the games with us."

"Who's gonna do that, now that he's—" Cameron's head fell forward and sobs flowed.

Cameron's parents' car pulled in next to the ambulance. His mother hurried around the car with her arms out. Cameron met her, and she held him close. Though Cameron was taller than she was, Marty knew that in that moment, he was her baby again.

Cameron's father touched his boy's shoulder and then stuffed his hands in his pockets. He walked over to Marty. "Know what happened here?"

"We're thinkin' Coach fell in the bathroom. Hit his head." Marty looked over the man's shoulder and watched Cameron get in the car. "It's not pretty in there. A lot of blood. He'd been layin' there most of the day."

"Accident, huh?"

"That's what it looks like. Could be a heart attack or somethin' like that. We'll get his body over to the coroner in Comanche Springs to tell us for sure."

"Jimmy Riley gettin' shot. Now this. It's not right for a man to die alone. Those things shouldn't happen in Brandon, you know that?" The boy's father shifted from foot to foot.

"Yeah." Marty licked the syrup from his lips. The sweet taste reminded him of better times. "But they do."

"And bad comes in threes, deputy. Mark my words."

Marty held back. Paco had told him not to say anything about religion or superstitions or omens or any of what came out of folks when evil struck. Folks who had been hurt needed something to hang onto when nothing made sense. He looked back at Coach's house and wished Paco had told him what to grab on to.

He watched the Taylors drive off. He called Deb's cell phone and told her he would be late. One of the paramedics came out of the house and motioned for Marty. He followed her into the house. A late-night pro game played on the giant TV screen. Marty switched it off.

Sheriff Kendall stepped out of the bathroom and let the paramedic by. He looked at Marty. "Cameron say anythin' more?"

"Just what he told you. He came over after the bus got back to tell Coach about the win. Saw the blood. Found him on the floor and called nine-one-one."

"Did he say he went into the bathroom?"

"He saw the body and called. Why?"

"Put your gloves on, Marty. I just called the state. We got a crime scene here." Sheriff Kendall's jaw muscles worked. "I didn't want the boy to hear this. But when we turned him over, Coach had a kitchen knife stuck in the middle of his chest."

When Marty's tongue touched the sticky place on his lips, the sweet turned bitter. He thought of Cameron's father warning that bad comes in threes.

What would happen next?

CHAPTER TEN

All around the church basement, the whispers changed. Chase didn't hear his name murmured after Marty and the sheriff left.

"Ambulance?" The question was spoken softly as flashing lights passed outside.

"Coach's house," a teenage girl at the next table whispered to her parents.

"There's been an accident." The church's pastor took his coat and hurried up the stairs.

The warm pancakes turned to an icy lump in the pit of Chase's stomach. Coach's house? "I need to go see if I can help," Chase told Mercy as he stood from the table.

"I'll come with you."

He took her hand and as she followed, the heels of Mercy's cowboy boots clattered up the stairs behind him.

Birdie tilted her head at the clack of Mercy's boot heels. She snuck a quick glance under the table at Deb's boots.

How many other women in this church basement were wearing Tony Lama shit-kickers?

When she lifted her head, Mercy was gone and the same cadence of boots kicked across the cement floor. A woman with a baby on her hip walked to the table with the coffeepot.

Maybe that boot print in the parking lot didn't mean anything.

Birdie looked at the basement stairs again.

But maybe?

"Deb, I better go with 'em." Birdie swung the little boy in her lap to his mother. "I might be able to do somethin'." She hustled from her place at the table.

Outside the door, Birdie saw Chase's truck pull away. She crossed the parking lot to where the Dodge had sat, pulled a mini Maglite from her jacket pocket, and shined its beam at the dirt on the ground at the passenger side.

Crap.

Wind-skittered grains of dust fell one by one into the boot print. In a few minutes the impression would be blurred, but it was plain now. A chill ran up Birdie's back.

What to do?

The state crime scene techs had laid a ruler next to the tracks she'd found in the field before they took pictures and poured the plaster of Paris for the molds. Birdie needed something to give an idea of the scale. She thought for a minute and then plucked her ballpoint pen from her uniform pocket and laid it next to the fading boot print. She snapped two pictures with her cell phone.

God, would it be good enough?

She stared down at the pictures in the glow of her phone. Not the best. But it was all she had. When she looked at the ground again, the breeze had rounded the sharp edges and the logo was blurred.

She was still shaking her head as she climbed into her truck and drove toward Coach's.

Birdie parked her truck at the corner of the block, three houses down from Coach's home. She sat for a minute to take in the scene on the street. Headlights from the ambulance bathed the front of the white frame house. Chase's Dodge nosed in close to the sheriff's truck, next to the ambulance.

It's bad. Birdie felt sick to her gut.

The two paramedics stood on the porch. One scribbled on a clipboard. No urgency. No one hurried. Worst of all, the flashing lights on the ambulance were off. There would be no lights-and-siren dash to the hospital in Hugo.

Marty came down the steps and went to Chase's truck. Chase opened the door and stepped out. Marty shook his head. He half turned back toward the house. Birdie could see his mouth move as he talked.

Chase must have asked something. Marty shook his head. Chase's shoulders drooped, and he leaned back against his truck.

Too late. Whatever had happened here, everyone was too late to help Coach.

Sheriff Kendall and the pastor from the Methodist church stood by a tangle of rosebushes that crowded the chain-link fence that divided Coach's yard from his neighbor's. A white-haired woman with a little dog in her arms looked up from her side of the fence at the two men. Suddenly, she raised her hand and pointed toward Chase's truck. Kendall's head bobbed up and down as he spoke to her. Then the sheriff turned and walked toward Chase.

Birdie pulled up on her truck's door handle.

Don't want to miss this.

"Tell me what happened, Marty." Chase looked at his friend's face, wanting everything he had just been told to be a lie.

"I can't say anythin' more." Marty turned away. His eyes sank into dark shadows from the glare of the truck's headlights. "I said too much already."

"Marty, you got to tell me. What happened in there?" Chase demanded.

"We're not sure. Let us do our work. I'll tell you what I can later. I promise."

"You just told me Coach is dead, and you want me to leave?" Chase felt his voice rise.

"Take Mercy and get out of here, Chase."

Dry leaves scattered away from Kendall's footsteps, and the wind chased them down the sidewalk. "Ford, I need to talk to you." The sheriff stepped between Marty and Chase. "Neighbor lady just told me she saw a truck that looks a lot like yours parked in front of Coach's house this afternoon."

Chase's mouth went dry.

"She also said," Kendall continued, "that she saw somebody peerin' in the windows and actin' like they was trying to get into the house. That you?" The thread of the shiny scar beside his left eye pulled tight.

"What are you askin', Kendall?" Chase held the lawman's stare.

"Was it you?" Kendall eyes tightened to cruel slits.

"Yeah." Muscles coiled rattlesnake tight in Chase's neck, and his hands balled into fists. "I stopped by to see my friend. The door was locked, and the TV was on. Coach always left the TV on."

"Chase didn't kill Coach," Marty blurted out. "No reason to think that, Sheriff."

Marty's words hit Chase in the belly like a sucker punch. He fought for his breath until words seeped out. "Killed? Are you sayin' he was murdered?"

Kendall never blinked. "Ford, I want you to give your statement to Marty. I want to know why you were here and when. Go back to wherever you're staying, and don't even think of leavin' my county without askin' me first." He turned to walk away. When the sheriff saw Mercy in Chase's truck, he tipped his hat.

Mercy climbed from Chase's truck to the street. She struggled into her jacket and crossed her arms under her breasts at the chill of the night. On the other side of the truck Chase was talking to Marty. The deputy had a pocket-sized notebook in one hand and a pen in the other. Chase's hands made fists, and it seemed every word he said to Marty caused him pain.

She walked down the sidewalk to the gate in the chain-link fence that surrounded Coach's house. Something terrible had happened inside, she knew it.

Sheriff Kendall talked with the two paramedics on the porch. He took his ringing cell phone from his jacket pocket and held it to his ear. She'd worn the tight jeans, and he never turned to look her way.

Birdie hurried up to where Chase and Marty stood.

"You heard the sheriff, Chase." Marty touched the back of his hand to his mouth. "Look, I'm off tomorrow. But what with all that's happened, they'll probably need me. If they don't, I'll come out to the ranch and find you. Just go on now. There's nothin' anyone can do here."

Chase looked down the street. He nodded his head. "Birdie, can you see to it Mercy gets home?"

"Count on it, Chase," she told him.

When he nodded again, Birdie bit her tongue to keep from gasping at the color of his face. Even in the light from the headlights, it was ghostly white. As pale as it had been on the day she had told him his mother had died.

He got into the Dodge and started the engine. Then he slumped forward until his forehead rested on the steering wheel.

"Should we do somethin'?" Birdie asked Marty.

"Just wait."

They both watched the truck. In a moment Chase sat up, slipped the pickup into gear, and backed into the street.

"Coach's dead, huh?" Birdie's tongue touched her dry lips.

"Somebody killed him."

Birdie had known it was bad. *Killed?* Not this bad. "Think it has anythin' to do with Jimmy Riley?"

"Lord only knows."

Birdie followed Marty up onto the porch with the paramedics and Sheriff Kendall. From the way he was talking she knew the sheriff was on the phone with the state police. The white car she'd seen that morning pulled in behind the ambulance. It was the coroner's car.

Kendall met the coroner at the front gate. The two talked for a minute. They kept their voices low enough that Birdie couldn't hear. One of the paramedics joined them. More hushed conversation, and then the coroner and paramedic went into Coach's house.

Sheriff Kendall walked to the corner of the yard. The neighbor lady, the pastor from the church, and Mercy stood there at the fence. The sheriff told them it was best if they would all go home. Mercy unfolded her arms and touched the ends of her hair.

Damn, Mercy. Just like high school. Never miss a chance to show off for the boys.

From the porch with Birdie, Marty and the other paramedic watched Mercy stretch and primp. Birdie glanced down at her short legs, green uniform, and stained Carhartt parka, then shook her head.

And sixteen years later Mercy still has more than clothes to show off.

Sheriff Kendall came back to the porch. "Officer Hawkins," he said, "you talk to Ray-Ray this afternoon?"

She shook her head. "Never caught up to him. Went by his place. No sign of him." All the pancakes she'd eaten in the church basement somersaulted in Birdie's stomach. "You're not thinkin' he had somethin' to do with this?"

"Two murders in my county on the same day. I gotta think about everythin'." He looked from the house back to the yard.

When Birdie followed his eyes, Mercy was still by the fence.

"Hawkins, I want you to check Ray-Ray's house once more on your way home. If he's there, call me, and we'll decide what to do. Otherwise there'll be a meetin' at my office, nine o'clock tomorrow mornin'. I want you to be there. Go on now."

"I promised Chase I'd take Mercy home."

"You do what I say. I'll take care of Mercy."

Marty had just finished stringing yellow crime-scene tape around Coach's house when two cars from the state police showed up. An hour had passed so he called Deb again to tell her where he was and let her know he had no idea when he'd be home.

Paco Martinez's patrol car pulled in behind the boys from the state. Instead of following them into the house, the old deputy came to Marty. He had two cups of coffee from Town Pump in his hands and a paper bag tucked under his arm. He handed Marty one of the cups and opened the bag. "Breakfast burritos. Take one," he said.

"We've had long nights before," Marty said, reaching into the sack, "but none like this."

Paco gave a head jerk to the paramedics. They joined Paco and Marty at the fence. Paco had burritos for them, too.

"Anythin' yet?" Marty asked.

The lead paramedic shrugged. "We could be here a long time. It'll be up to the coroner how soon we can take the body."

"Do we know anythin' more than when we got here?" Marty sipped his coffee.

"Coroner had me take a liver temp. I'm guessin' time of death was late last night." The paramedic took a bite of his burrito. "Did you see that gash on his forehead? Before we found the knife, I thought he fell and hit his head. Now I'm thinkin' someone hit him and then stabbed him. Hit him hard. No sign of a struggle. He could have laid there for three or four hours before he bled out."

A chill crept down Marty's back.

The paramedic chomped down another bite. "Helluva way to die. All alone like that."

Kendall crossed the yard to join the others. Paco held out the bag with the burritos. Kendall shook his head. "There's nothin' more for me to do here. Paco, you and Marty hang tight and help the troopers with anythin' they need. I want you both in my office at nine in the mornin'." He zipped up his coat and adjusted the brim of his cowboy hat. "Earned your money today, didn't you?"

The sheriff let himself out of the front gate and opened his pickup's door. In the light from the dome lamp, Marty spotted Mercy Saylor in the passenger seat.

Birdie knew Ray-Ray wouldn't be home. He damn well knew they were looking for him and was holed up somewhere waiting for things to blow over.

If he was still even in the county.

But her oath as a Division of Wildlife officer was to uphold the laws of the state. That meant even if she didn't like Sheriff Kendall, she had to do what she was asked.

There was no sign anyone was home at Ray-Ray's when Birdie pulled into the yard. A dog came out from under the porch and barked. No lights came on in the house. She sat for a long minute more and then slipped the truck into reverse and headed for home.

Damn it, she hated taking orders from high-and-mighty Sheriff Lincoln my-shit-don't-stink Kendall.

She could complain to her boss first thing in the morning. But he'd tell her that the state of Colorado paid her to enforce the law. Not just when it came to game and fish. And if the locals needed her help, she was to do what she could.

It should have been a good day. Seeing Chase again. But two dead bodies . . .

Birdie opened the back door to the old house she rented a mile south of Brandon.

Chase looks just like he did.

Birdie kicked off her boots on the throw rug just inside the kitchen door. She hung her jacket and gun belt on the hooks next to the refrigerator. She took a water glass from the dishes left to air dry on the rack next to the sink.

Birdie opened the cabinet over the sink, took down a bottle, and filled the glass half full of Crown Royal.

Chase Ford. She still dreamed about him after all those years. But Mercy still had his attention. Always would.

Birdie took a drink. And the tears she thought were gone poured down her face.

CHAPTER ELEVEN

If any house in Comanche County was haunted, it was the ranch house where Chase was raised. Not by ghosts or spirits, but by his memories. No matter how far he took himself from the Colorado prairies, no matter how much money he had, and no matter how many people knew his name, he could not forget the things that had happened in that house.

He had promised himself he would leave it just the way it had been on the day he walked away. After his father's death, he had paid people to take the food from the kitchen, give his father's and mother's clothes to charity, drape the furniture, and pull the curtains. He never wanted anyone to live there again.

Drawn to the house because of the two dead men—one who had been his friend and the other who was so much like Chase himself as a boy—Chase did something he had told himself he would never do.

He opened the door.

The beam of his flashlight pierced the midnight darkness. A spiderweb, filthy with years of trapped flies and moths, curtained the opening. Chase reached up and brushed it away. He held his breath, fearing that the betrayal and evil he remembered would reach out their talons and draw him in.

But it was just an old house. Swirls of dust floated in the column of light. Piles of stuffing the mice had torn from the furniture were strewn across the floor, and rodent droppings crunched under his boots.

It was the good times he remembered first.

The smells of all the dinners from his mother's kitchen. The warmth the house offered on cold nights. The times they laughed together—his father and his mother. The times before the accident.

Big Paul never said it was Chase's fault. He never said it with words. But his father's eyes and the things he didn't say made it clear to Chase that his father held him accountable for that terrible day.

It was Chase's sophomore year of high school. The basketball team had a game in a town a half day drive from Brandon. Big Paul was busy with the harvest and needed his help. Chase pleaded to go with the team, and Big Paul only relented when his mother said she would drive the truck.

She'd done it before, and that day should have been like all the others. But it wasn't.

When Chase got to the hospital in Hugo, she looked small. Bruised and cut, plastic tubes taped to her arms. A helicopter was on its way to take her to Colorado Springs, where they could better care for her.

"Her back's broken," the doctor told him. "She might never walk again."

But Chase's mother was strong. She had faith. He loved her. He would help her.

After weeks in Colorado Springs, they moved her to the rehabilitation center in Denver. Chase drove there each weekend. To see her, to help her, to tell her how much he loved her.

Big Paul never visited, and his mother never walked again.

In the beam from his flashlight, dingy bed sheets hung over the hospital bed Big Paul had brought from Pueblo. When his father finally brought her back to the ranch, he put the bed in the dining room. His mother stayed there. While Chase was at school and Big Paul worked the farm, she lay in her bed alone. A nurse visited each day. But his mother was alone.

Then Isabel came. Big Paul said he hired her to cook and clean. Take care of the house. Do what she could for his mother.

At first everything had been fine. Then instead of coming each day, Isabel moved in. It would be easier that way, Big Paul told him. She took a bedroom upstairs. And then she shared Big Paul's bed.

His mother had to know. But she smiled and pretended everything was fine.

Chase pretended, too.

For two years he pretended. When the people in Brandon talked, he pretended he didn't hear. When alcohol fueled Big Paul and he bellowed through the house that his mother should do them a favor and die, Chase pretended he didn't mean it. When Isabel swelled with the baby, he pretended that he couldn't see.

His world became basketball. The people in town praised him. He led the state in scoring. Everyone in the county came to the games. Everyone but Big Paul.

And when they played for the championship in Denver, his mother listened on the radio by the hospital bed in the dining room. Big Paul and Isabel never made it to the game. They stayed in the hotel. Together.

And his mother died. The favor his father demanded happened three days after the championship game. And Chase quit pretending. He moved in with Coach and promised himself he'd never go back to the ranch again.

What do seventeen-year-olds know about forever?

A full-ride scholarship took him to college that fall. Then four years in the pros. A year trying to make it back and three more on TV. And four lived in a blur. Billee left him, and he was alone. As alone as his father.

He heard that Isabel moved out. And that she had a baby girl she named Dolly. Years later she married an older man named Victor and lived in Brandon until she died.

Like the old house, Big Paul stayed alone on the prairie. Worked the farm and raised his cattle, and folks in town said he partnered up with Jim Beam. Driving by the homeplace, anyone would think it just like every other farmhouse and would never know about the filth and darkness inside.

Chase climbed the stairs to his room. He sat on his bed and switched off the flashlight. Darkness wrapped around him. Outside an animal screamed. A barn owl swooped by the window carrying a struggling rabbit in its talons. Down the hallway, Chase heard bedsprings groan and his mother cry downstairs.

He left the house and locked the door behind him.

Sheriff Kendall jerked awake to the vibration of his cell phone on the table by the bed. He caught the phone as the next series of hums made the phone crawl over the polished wood. As sleep left his eyes he saw the incoming number.

He punched *receive* and pressed the phone to his ear. "Sheriff Kendall here."

He twisted in the sheets and touched the naked hip of the woman next him.

"Good to hear from you," he whispered into the phone.

"I've cleared it with my boss. I'll be there tomorrow, and I'm bringing a camera crew with me. Anything I should know?"

Kendall enjoyed the woman's voice. "Meetin' tomorrow mornin' at nine. Can you be there?"

"I'll do my best."

He liked the purr in her voice. "Okay. County buildin' in Comanche Springs. See you there."

Kendall swung his legs out of bed and sat up. He squeezed the cell phone until his fingers hurt.

"What it is, Linc?" the woman beside him asked.

"Just a reporter from a TV station in Colorado Springs. Wants to interview me. About the murders."

"Oh, no. Don't you have enough to do?"

"It goes with the job," he told his wife. *And voters remember a man who's been on television.*

CHAPTER TWELVE

Most times a shower washed away the day's troubles and put Marty at ease. This night, he stood under the stream of water until he had used every drop from the double-wide's tiny hot water heater. He let icy cold water pound his back and shoulders while the faces of the two dead filled his mind.

Murders didn't happen in Comanche County.

The last one Marty remembered was two years before. A farmworker with too much liquor in him had stuck a knife in his brother's back. Over a woman. Paco found the killer behind the bar, cradling his dead brother's head lying in his lap, bawling over what he'd done.

That killing happened in a blur of whiskey and machismo. It wasn't cold and calculated like what had happened to Jimmy Riley and Coach Porter.

Marty padded barefoot past the room where his two boys slept in their bunk beds above a tumble of toys and clothes. He whispered a prayer to keep them safe as he looked in. Marty dared not turn on the light in the master bedroom, but pushed Deb's cowboy boots out of the way with his foot and eased into bed beside her.

Her eyes never opened. She mumbled to him, turned, and

curled up next to his side. In his wife's belly, the weight of their unborn little girl rested between them. Marty's eyes wouldn't close. Too much to think about.

Jimmy and Coach.

Marty replayed the day over and over again in his mind. Each time it came back to Jimmy's father. He never went to see his son play. Worried about the truck and how much a funeral would cost. Then Marty had found the cartridge box on the table in the apartment.

Did Jimmy's old man have something against Coach for the attention he gave his son? And what had he said about Jimmy's girlfriend?

Sniffin' after that Mexican girl.

Would he kill his son over that?

Marty shifted in the bed and balled up his fists.

Dead buffalo. Dead boy. Coach on the floor. Blood. And his best friend, Chase Ford, back in town.

No way Chase had anything to do with any of it. But Kendall hated Chase. What might the sheriff try?

Don't even think it.

Marty's eyes flew open again. A scream caught in his throat. *Keep it in. Don't let it out.* Paco had said, *Don't let it get to you.* But it had. Every image had climbed into his brain and threatened never to leave.

Kendall tugged the bed sheet over his chest. He shook his head.

A dead boy in the morning. Then Coach.

He hated having to call the state for help. Come election time, some might think he couldn't do his job.

And what about Mercy? She gave off all the right signals. Called him and purred like a kitten when she asked if she would see him at the church supper. But she showed up on Chase Ford's arm. Strutted her tight little self in those tight jeans and looked over her shoulder to be sure he noticed.

He noticed. Even licked his lips.

At Coach's house, when he'd sent Ford on his way, Mercy

jumped up into his truck and even snuggled up to him once they were down the road and out of sight. When he'd pulled the truck around to the back of her house and killed the headlights, she jumped right out of the truck, ran for the door, and said over her shoulder, "See you next time."

Next time? Hell. She was still the same pricktease she'd been in high school.

On top of it all, Chase Ford shows up in my county for the first time in fifteen, sixteen years. Wouldn't it be something if Chase had something to do with this? Catching him would make re-election a sure bet.

He slugged his fist into the pillow and settled his head into the mark it made.

In the morning he'd float the idea by the state cops that they should take a hard look at Ford. For now he let the images of what might have happened with Mercy warm his thoughts. In a few moments sleep closed around him.

A tendril of smoke from the burning toast teased Chase's nose. He reached across his trailer's stovetop to flick the bread off the rack, and tiny drops of sizzling bacon grease splattered his wrist. He cursed to himself, but the pinpricks of pain reminded him that in spite of everything that had happened the day before, he still could feel.

Coach was dead. Murdered. Like the kid they found with the buffalo.

It would be light in another forty minutes. Not that it mattered. He hadn't slept. After breaking his promise never to go inside the ranch house, he'd lain awake in the trailer and counted the sounds of trucks on the highway, listened to the swoop of the wind around the old building and the coyotes' howls. Anything to keep his mind off Coach.

Chase cracked two eggs into the skillet. In the years since Billee had left, he still had not learned to fry his own eggs. He could do his own laundry and make his bed, but mastering breakfast never came to him. He picked at the pieces of shell that mixed with the egg in the pan.

Why Coach?

The man never had an enemy Chase knew of. Players and their parents would do anything for him. Coach Porter just wanted to help the kids and coach basketball.

Why was he dead on his bathroom floor with a knife in his chest?

Greasy, gray smoke from the burning eggs filled the trailer. He scooped them from the pan onto a paper plate with the bacon and burned toast, sat down at the table, and stared at the plate.

Outside, dawn blushed new and pink on the ragged eastern horizon. Chase stepped out of the trailer into the cold of the morning and slipped into his jacket and orange vest. He thumbed three cartridges into the old Weatherby and closed the bolt on an empty chamber. He put on his gloves and orange cap. He'd hunt close to the ranch this morning. Until he could talk with Marty and find out more about what had happened to Coach, maybe searching for the old buck would keep the bad thoughts away.

Later he'd drive to town and try to find Dolly Benavidez. He'd heard she'd be working a breakfast shift at Saylor's. The same blood that flowed in his veins ran through hers. Coach had sent him pictures. He knew she was a pretty girl, but he'd never seen his half-sister in person.

He slipped the rifle's sling over his shoulder and walked out through the fading night, past the corrals and onto the prairie.

Cecil pulled the full trash bags from the cans near the gas pumps. He tied the bags shut and put new plastic liners in each of the barrels. A mud-splattered SUV pulled in to the pump closest to where he was standing. The driver, wearing a blaze-orange hat and vest, climbed out, fed his credit card into the reader, and began to fill his vehicle.

"Mornin'." Cecil nodded to the man. "Do any good?"

"Could have had a doe, but I'm holdin' out for a decent buck," the hunter answered.

"Where you huntin' at?"

The man motioned with his head. "Irv Brown's place."

Cecil nodded. "Got mine yesterday just at first light," Cecil told him. "Big four pointer. Damn nice deer." Cecil didn't know why he lied to people.

"Where?" the hunter asked.

"My place." Cecil thought for a minute. Irv Brown's place was south of town. "North. I own four sections up there."

"Must keep you busy."

"I farm 'cause it's somethin' I've always done." Cecil jerked a thumb toward the gas station office. "Own this place to make a little money."

None of it was true. Cecil lived in a rented trailer parked in the lot down by the railroad tracks. He could no more run a farm than the man in the moon, and he was low man on the totem pole at Town Pump. That's why he was emptying trash and working the Sunday morning early shift. But Cecil would never see the hunter again, so why not let the man think he was more important than he really was?

The hunter waved as he drove away. Cecil carried the trash to a Dumpster around back. Inside Town Pump, he poured a cup of coffee, slipped onto the stool behind the counter, and adjusted the volume on the TV set. He wished the boss would put in a satellite dish. The only thing the rabbit ears picked up was the Fox station from Colorado Springs, and all that was on was news.

Outside, Brandon was waking up. Lights came on in the homes. Cecil guessed this Sunday morning would be like all the others, except for some extra business from the deer hunters coming in for gas and beer. Townsfolk would drift to church. A few might stop in for a cup of coffee on the way. After church, Saylor's would fill up, and those who hadn't made their Saturday trip to the Walmart in Lamar would head that way in the afternoon.

Mercy's Lincoln sped down the highway and turned into the gravel lot at Saylor's Café. He watched her pull around back. In a minute, lights in the little restaurant came on. Mercy was a woman he'd told himself stories about. Imagination was a good thing. It helped him pass the time.

Cecil sipped his coffee and settled in for a boring morning. He fished the *Hustler* magazine he'd squirreled away out from under the counter. He checked to make sure no one was watching before he thumbed open the slick pages.

He'd almost gotten caught a couple weeks ago. Late one night, he hadn't heard the basketball coach and the kid, Jimmy, come into the store to buy chips and pop. Cecil had needed to move real fast to tug up his zipper and hide the magazine under a newspaper. The kid had a smirk on his face when he paid for his Coke. Both of them were laughing when they climbed into the kid's truck with that cute little Mexican girl he was always hanging around with.

But folks like that got what they had coming to them. He was sure of that.

At the edge of the corrals, Chase propped his binoculars on the top rail and scanned the prairie. The field glasses gathered in the new daylight and sharpened the wrinkles and creases in the pasture ground. Three pronghorn antelope stood atop a hillock about a mile out. Two of them had already spotted Chase. The third's attention was fixed on something down along the creek.

Could be anything. Antelope were naturally skittish. An old coyote could be hunting jackrabbits for breakfast, or a prairie dog might be peeking out of his burrow.

Chase ducked down and eased out farther along the fence line. Where the rail fence met the barbed wire, he squatted down behind a clump of tumbleweeds caught in the fence and studied the place where the antelope was looking. Out about six hundred yards a puff of steamy breath floated in the calm, cold air. He looked closer and found a deer at the edge of the faded red tamaracks. It was a buck. And when it turned its head, through the binoculars Chase could see the broken antler tine. It was the big buck he'd seen the day before.

He huddled back, closed his eyes, and tried to remember all he could about that pasture. He'd played out there as kid, rode horseback across it more times than he could count, and bounced a four-wheeler across it chasing cows and calves. If he was going to get close enough for a shot, he'd have to remember each hill and gully that would hide him from the deer.

Birdie turned onto the lane that led from the county road to the Ford ranch house. Marty had called and told her to find Chase and not let him come to town until he could figure out what to do next. The murders had Sheriff Kendall fit to be tied, and Chase would only stir things up.

Marty had told her that Chase wasn't answering his cell phone. He probably had it turned off or had left it in the trailer and gone hunting.

Golden sunbeams slanted through the farmyard and sparkled on the aluminum trailer that Chase had parked in the empty corral out by the big barn. A cottontail rabbit dashed in front of her truck and dove for cover in a tangle of weeds near some rusted farm equipment. Before Chase's mother died, his father had kept the yard mowed and the buildings painted. Each tractor and piece of equipment had been parked in its own place.

Now overgrown weeds crowded sagging fences. What equipment hadn't been sold at auction was covered with rust. Paint peeled from the outbuildings, and the ranch house was as gray as the dirt in the corrals.

When Birdie stepped out of her truck, specks of sunlight glittered from a glass bottle hidden in the weeds. She looked closer. It was a whiskey bottle. Jim Beam, she guessed. Big Paul's best friend.

"Chase," she called. When he didn't answer, she pounded on the trailer's door and called again. "Chase, it's me, Birdie."

She dialed his number. Inside the trailer she heard a phone cackle. Marty was right. Chase was out hunting.

Unless. Don't think it, Birdie.

But the thought filled her mind.

Unless the same one who killed Jimmy Riley and Coach had murdered Chase, too.

She tried the trailer door. It was unlocked. She pressed her eyes shut and opened the door.

No. No. No.

When she opened her eyes the trailer was empty. A paper plate filled with cold eggs sat on the little table, and the trailer smelled of burned eggs and cold grease. The cell phone lay on the table beside the plate. She didn't see his heavy coat anywhere, and his Lakers cap hung from a hook on the wall. She plucked it down and held it to her face.

It smelled like Chase. Big, strong Chase.

She stepped out and studied the ground around the trailer. Fresh boot prints in the dust led out toward the corrals. Marty was right.

Chase had gone hunting.

The cottontail peered out from its hiding place under the rusted junk. Lacy films of ice filled the petrified hoof prints in the corral's dried mud. The new sun inched higher above the horizon, and the golden sunbeams melted away.

Birdie stepped back into the trailer and hung Chase's Lakers cap back where she had found it.

Good boy. You're wearing your orange hat. I won't have to ticket you.

For once, Birdie didn't mind walking. The back of her shirttail had worked its way out of her pants. She tucked it in and started off across the corral, following Chase's tracks. She found where he'd knelt down behind a bunch of tumbleweeds tangled in the fence. Saw the place where he'd shimmied under the barbed wire and guessed he eased down into the crooked gully that led down to the creek. Chase must have had something spotted.

Three antelope, nearly a mile away, stood on a high point. All three's ears were up, and their eyes were fixed on Birdie. In the next instant, the pronghorns sprinted off the hill and hauled ass for the next county.

Then Birdie spotted Chase.

The sun at his back painted a long shadow over the prairie and hid his face in the glare. But she knew his easy, graceful stride. She had memorized it so many years before.

She wriggled her short legs and wide backside through the barbed wire and started out to meet him. Her heart bounced inside her chest when he raised his hand to wave at her.

"You here to check my license, Warden?" he asked when they were close enough to see each other's faces. "There's a big buck hangin' out down along the creek. Saw him yesterday mornin' from the other side. Thought maybe I could get close enough for a shot, but he gave me the slip." He smiled at her.

Birdie felt her face cloud over. "Chase—" She wanted to tell him she was sorry about Coach, and tell him she was glad he'd come back to Brandon, and tell him that thing she kept so secret. But she couldn't tell him any of that.

"What's wrong, Birdie?"

"Damn it, when you wouldn't answer your phone this mornin', Marty called me and made me promise to come out here and be sure you were okay. So that's why I'm here, and now I'm gonna be late for the meetin' in Comanche Springs, and I got better things to do." She pushed the words out as fast as she could so he wouldn't hear what she felt. "One more thing: you keep your ass out of Brandon until Marty tells you it's okay. Don't even think about tryin' to find Dolly 'til things settle down. Kendall's on the war-path, and you're apt to cause a whole shitstorm of trouble, and the county got enough with the murders and all."

"Birdie?"

"Damn you for comin' back here, Chase Ford." She left him on the prairie and stomped away.

CHAPTER THIRTEEN

The aroma of baking cinnamon rolls and pancake batter blended with the rich smell from the morning's first pot of coffee at Saylor's. One cook put a gallon of maple syrup on to warm and the other man mixed milk with eggs to handle the coming orders for scrambled eggs and omelets.

Mercy filled her coffee cup and left the cooks to do their prep work. She flipped on the lights in the dining room and did a quick check to be sure the night crew had cleaned up like they were supposed to. They had. Mama had trained them well. She set her mug on the counter, opened the cash register, and filled the tray with bills and coins from the vinyl bank bag she'd taken from the safe in back.

Outside, an over-the-road rig pulled into the gravel parking lot. The fat dwarf of a driver stopped in twice a month, usually at opening time on a Sunday morning. He'd grab a stool at the counter, order eggs and hotcakes, and stare at Mercy while she did her morning chores and he tried to tell her about his adventures on the road.

Mercy clenched her teeth. *How did Mama stand it all those years?* The coffee that had tasted so good minutes before turned to warm dishwater in her mouth.

The little man climbed down from the cab. His belly jiggled as he jogged to the front door, and he had to stop to hitch his britches up over his narrow hips. He pulled a comb from his back pocket and ran it through a face full of beard.

Yeah, like that's gonna make me fall in love with him.

The trucker burst through the door, ordered two over easy and a stack of buttermilks, and plopped onto the stool closest to the cash register. "I like my coffee like my women," he said with a grin. "Hot, black, and with just a bit of sugar."

A real charmer, that one.

He stared up at Mercy all moonfaced.

She smiled back. At least this one had most of his teeth. Yellow teeth.

Diana tied on her apron and joined Mercy at the counter. "Mornin', boss lady. Isn't it terrible about Jimmy Riley and Coach?" She picked up a coffeepot from the warmer, filled a mug, and set it in front of the trucker. "Brandon's supposed to be safe. Not like Limon and La Junta and those other big cities. I might have to move."

"I know, Diana, I know." Mercy looked out the front windows. Bobby Jackson pulled his farm truck into the slot nearest the door. "That reminds me, I better make a phone call."

Diana slid a sugar jar in front of the truck driver, propped her elbow on the counter, and began to tell him about the murders. Mercy could tell his interest was on what was hidden inside the scoop front of Diana's blouse, not the story the waitress was telling.

Mercy grabbed the phone on the wall and stepped inside the office out of the noise of the kitchen. She dialed a number.

"Robin, it's me, Mercy. Listen, I need a favor. You heard about that Riley boy?"

"God, it's terrible," Robin said. "I hugged my babies tighter last night than I ever have."

Mercy went on, "Dolly didn't come in yesterday, and I don't think she'll make it today. I know you're not supposed to be in 'til lunch, but could you come in early?"

"Poor girl. I'll get there as soon as I can."

"Thank you." Mercy looked at the mirror on the back of the door and ran her fingers through her hair. Not one bit of gray was showing. "I'll find a way to make it up to you somehow."

Mercy hung up. A rush of cool air touched her face. One of Bobby's farmer friends held the door for three hunters. One man had blood on his camo pants. They talked about deer as they jostled through the open door.

Pots clanged in the kitchen, and the day's first pan of cinnamon rolls came out of the oven.

Mercy put a smile on her face and stepped into the dining room.

Birdie couldn't let herself worry anymore over Chase Ford. She had her own set of troubles.

It would take an hour and a half of fast driving to get to the nine o'clock meeting at the Sheriff's Department in Comanche Springs. Birdie had an hour. And she wanted to drive by Ray-Ray's for a look-see. Sheriff Numb Nuts would want answers from everyone, and he'd examine those answers real close. If she didn't have the latest on Ray-Ray, he was apt to crawl up her butt with a pair of rusty tweezers to find out why she hadn't stopped. And if she told him she'd been with Chase, there would be hell to pay.

As soon as she hit the county road, she gunned the truck and made for Ray-Ray's. His house was dark and the yard dog asleep when she snuck up. No sign of Ray-Ray anywhere.

When he was sure Birdie was gone, Chase headed for town to find his half-sister. The girl had to be hurting. He didn't know what he could say or do. But something made him want to be with her. He didn't drive to the highway. Instead he took the back roads.

Friday night, he'd caught Jimmy and the girl parked under the trees. Even though Chase knew the two were dating, he didn't want to think the girl in the truck was Dolly. Birdie had said the alfalfa bale used to lure in the buffalo came from ground Bobby Jackson leased from Chase. He'd check that out first.

Chase had learned from playing basketball that big games were won with preparation and patience. Coaches would spend hours studying game films, looking for that one small tendency that could be used to an advantage. Whoever killed the Riley kid, and Coach, had a weakness somewhere. Something insignificant that would make the difference. Chase was going to find it.

There was a butt in every chair in the conference room in the Comanche County Building except for two folding chairs smack dab in the middle of the front row. Right in front of the podium where Sheriff remember-I'm-the-boss Kendall was standing.

The meeting hadn't started. Birdie had lucked out. Maybe things were turning her way for once. She was ten minutes late, expecting to be reamed in front of every lawman in the county. She slipped in the door, went to a back corner, leaned against the wall, and tried to be small. She'd answer any questions they threw her way. Otherwise, she'd keep her yap shut.

She counted Marty, Paco, and the eight other county deputies in the chairs in front of her. Even the women from the office were there. There were that many uniformed State Patrol troopers, the three techs she'd seen at the crime scene the day before, and two men in suits and ties. The suits were in the front row. Bigwigs from Denver aching to show how smart they were, she'd bet. She'd stay as far away from them as she could.

Kendall's big forty-five hung in a hand-tooled holster strapped to his hip. He'd even knotted the tie-down thong around his thigh. He was showing everyone he meant business.

"We're gonna get this meetin' started," the sheriff said, and the room went dead quiet. He tipped the brim of his cowboy hat back. Even from the back of the room, Birdie could tell his eyes were bloodshot. He nodded at the suits and then looked right at her. "Officer Hawkins, there's a chair up here in front. C'mon up and sit down."

Well, make me a shit sandwich and put pickles on it, too. Her face burned red hot.

Birdie got to the front as fast as she could. She knew the eyes of every man in the room were on her fat ass, and they weren't thinking about how cute it was. No way her butt would fit on that folding chair. The only question was if a half a cheek or a whole one would hang off.

Talk, Sheriff. Make 'em look at you, not me.

But the prick was polite and waited until she sat down before he said anything.

Only about a third of a cheek squished toward the next chair. She hid her relief.

Then Kendall started. "Two murders in my county." He paused and let his gaze sweep over those in front of him. Birdie puckered up when he looked at her. "To get the son of a bitch that's responsible, I've asked the state to throw every resource they can our way. My people will work side by side with them. What matters now is gettin' justice for the families and this community."

It was the first time in her life Birdie had any respect for the man.

From the podium, Kendall spotted the news reporter from Colorado Springs slip into conference room. The little blonde had called his personal cell phone an hour before and told him she was running late. That was why he held the start time.

Her pencil scribbled while he spouted all his bullcrap about "my county" and "justice for the families and community." It would make the news that evening and be on the cover of the county newspaper in the morning.

It was never too early to start the campaign for the next election.

Chase studied the neat rows of alfalfa bales in the stubble field.

All along he had thought that whoever had shot Jimmy Riley had been the one who brought the alfalfa to the buffalo.

Bits of yellow crime-scene tape knotted to the barbed wire fluttered in the wind. The ground around where the state police had made impressions of the boot prints was too trampled for Chase to see anything that would help.

Birdie had said the tracks in the dust were about the same size as hers.

If Chase was right and there were two . . .

Maybe two boys? Something to do with Dolly? Or any of those things that could set a teenage boy off? Maybe jealousy over Jimmy's talent on the basketball court?

That could be the connection with Coach.

He shook his head as he climbed back into his truck. The odometer showed it was 3.4 miles from where they'd found Jimmy to the alfalfa. Across the field was the natural seep that kept the field wet enough to grow the alfalfa. All around the quarter-mile-wide green island were sage brush, prairie grass, and cattle. On the high ridge between the field and town was the parcel of land that Ray-Ray Jackson's little brother owned.

Chase started the truck and headed for Bobby's place.

The road followed what was left of an old wagon road along Sandy Creek. Every other road in the county was gun-barrel straight. This was as twisty as a bull snake. On the south side was sage brush and prairie. On the other, dying cottonwoods, tangles of tamarack, and Sandy Creek—sand for three quarters of the year and a trickle of water for part of the spring and summer.

When Chase made a lazy curve in the road, he spotted a truck parked on the shoulder ahead. It disappeared in the turn, and he saw it again as he followed the winding road. He recognized Pop Weber's old truck. The driver's door hung open.

People in the county watched out for Pop. Marty said the old man still lived on his own, took care of his stock, but couldn't tell you whether it was Tuesday or Saturday.

Better check.

Chase pulled to a stop in front of the truck and got out. "Pop," he called. He laid his hand on the hood of Pop's truck.

Cold.

"Pop?" Louder. "Pop?"

The truck was battered and held together with rust, and there was no indication it had hit a deer or anything else. If there were engine trouble, Pop would have opened the hood.

"Pop?"

Chase looked between the open door and the windshield. A rust-colored smear stained the tired blankets that covered the rumpled seats. He hurried around the door and touched the spot. It was damp and cool to his touch. When he lifted his fingers they were brownish red.

Blood.

No. It couldn't be. No.

Whoever killed the others had killed Pop Weber?

Chase grabbed his cell phone and dialed nine-one-one.

Marty studied the image the state police detective's projector showed on the screen in the darkened conference room. Two colored lines, evenly spaced, ran from left to right. From the top down, twenty-four black lines crossed the colored ones. The black lines represented the hours of the day starting at 10 P.M. on Friday night. The colored lines were for each of the murder victims. Red for Coach and green for Jimmy.

"We're starting at ten o'clock because that's when we know both our vics were alive," the detective said. "Coach Porter and Jimmy Riley were leaving the high school in Brandon after the basketball game. The next time we know anything for sure is at six fifteen the next morning when the Riley boy's body is discovered. The coroner has estimated time of—"

"Wait." Marty waved his hand. "Someone told me they saw Jimmy and his girlfriend close to midnight."

"Who?" Sheriff Kendall called from the back of the room.

Marty turned. "Chase Ford, Sheriff."

"What?"

"Hear me out. I forgot all about it until now." Marty turned to face the detective. "Chase told me he went to the ball game on Friday. He slipped out before the game was over and drove over to Cheyenne Wells for some groceries. On account of he's stayin' out at his ranch to do some deer huntin'. He got back about midnight. He told me he saw Jimmy's truck parked under the trees on the road into the ranch. He flashed his headlights and saw Jimmy's face." Marty took a breath. "Jimmy and the girl were, uh, havin' sexual relations." He looked back at the sheriff.

"Anythin' else?" Kendall asked.

Marty bit down on his lip and turned back to the screen. "Not that I remember."

A black star appeared at midnight on Jimmy's line on the detective's chart. "Chase Ford?" the detective asked. "The basketball player?"

"Yes, sir. He's from down here," Marty answered before the sheriff could.

The state cop's eyes narrowed. "Wasn't he accused of assaulting his wife?"

Marty fought to stay in his chair. "That ain't fair. Those news people blew that up into a big story. His wife took all that back." Marty was nearly shouting. "No charges were ever filed."

The detective looked at Kendall. "I think I'd like to talk to Mr. Ford."

The door to the conference room swung open. Marty squinted in the bright light.

"Sheriff." He heard Arlene's voice. "We just got a nine-one-one you should know about. Just came in."

"Not now."

"But, Sheriff, we might have another victim." She told him about Pop Weber's truck and the blood on the seat.

The sheriff rubbed his face with the back of his hand. "Who called it in?"

"It was . . ." Arlene hesitated. "Chase Ford, Sheriff."

CHAPTER FOURTEEN

Dawn's first sunbeams filtered over the prairie and stirred Ray-Ray from his rest. He woke hungry, planning to get to his farmhouse and cook up a big breakfast. Caution persuaded his stomach to go slow, and that's when he spotted the dome light in Birdie Hawkins's pickup. Just a blink of bright in the gray, fading night. She'd parked on the road near his gate and was sneaking out on a high roll of ground so she could see his house.

He watched as she put her binoculars to her eyes and studied his place. Smart woman, she was. Others would have blundered in and got the dog all riled and caused the guinea hens to kick up a ruckus. But Birdie just sat out there and watched. She just wasn't smart enough to look about a half mile back to the west. That's where she would have seen him, belly down on a high spot watching her with his binoculars. If she were listening real close she might even have heard his stomach growl. It was that quiet.

His homegrown mellowed a man out just fine, and sleep came easy, but it made one awful hungry.

Going back to his house wouldn't be wise, so as soon as Birdie went to her truck and headed off toward Comanche Springs, Ray-Ray lit his can of Sterno and fried up fresh deer liver and what onions he had left. Between mouthfuls and gulps of water from his canteen, he planned what to do next.

Ray-Ray followed the creek bottom back to the fence line that divided his ground from the Butt Notch, hopped the fence, and worked his way through the gnarliest of the brush and tamarack until he found Sandy Creek on the other side. He could follow the creek to his brother's. It would take him until noon to get there, and if anyone saw him they'd think he was just a hunter.

He'd borrow a truck and get out of the county for a while. Ray-Ray had friends who thought his way across the Kansas state line. They'd hide him for a while. If need be, there were others of his mindset in places like Idaho and the hills of Arkansas, and if things stayed bad he'd always wanted to see Alaska.

There were a few folks like him still left in the world. Those who didn't need to hear some mush-head say you had to wear a helmet when you rode your Harley, or what kind of lightbulb to buy, or how much you had to pay a man for an hour's work. Men should decide those things for themselves and be responsible for their choices, he thought. If two disagree, let them work out their squabble between themselves. If they can't talk it out, they should use their fists. If fists don't settle things, that's why God created guns.

He'd said as much to that little pecker whose buffalo broke down his fences and to the high school kids who left their beer bottles and trash in his fields. No one understood about respect and liberty.

Ray-Ray's anger boiled hotter with every step he took until he stopped and raised his rifle over his head with both hands and bellowed out his creed.

"Leave me alone."

"Wait for the truck." Jody Rose cupped one hand over her head and lifted a sheet of paper with the other. Wind from the passing semi rattled the paper and teased the tips of her long blond hair. She studied her notes, committing the thoughts to memory.

The speeding truck followed the four lanes of blacktop away from Brandon. As Jody ran her fingers through her thick mane each strand of hair fell back in place. "How's the makeup look?" she asked the man with the camera, and pursed her lips.

He made an "okay" sign with his thumb and fingers.

Jody shut her eyes and ran her tongue over her lips and teeth. "Tell me when."

"Okay." The cameraman started.

Focus, Jody. This could be the one. My agent will get a demo out, and the networks will be calling.

The cameraman nodded, and the light on his camera blinked on.

Jody pressed her pretty face into perfect, practiced concern. "The same theme begins every conversation in this small town," she said in the most professional voice she could muster. "In hushed tones, citizens of Brandon tell each other, 'Things like this don't happen here.' You hear it again and again. While buying supplies at Murphy's Feed Store, filling the truck at Town Pump, and talking over coffee and pie at Saylor's Café. 'Murders don't happen in Brandon.'"

The reporter tilted the top of her head ever so slightly. "But two people are dead. And this town that still celebrates their 1992 high school basketball championship now mourns the death of a beloved coach and this year's star player. Both were killed Friday night. Sources tell this reporter a third person has gone missing." She straightened her head and looked directly into the camera. "Is there a serial killer on the Colorado Plains? This is Jody Rose reporting."

"Got it, Jody. Good job. Now I'm getting cold. Let's get out of here."

She pulled her cell phone from her pocket and checked to see if there was a message from the sheriff about the third victim. She's made him promise he'd let her know.

Nothing yet.

She looked back at the man with the camera. "No." Jody gritted her teeth. "I want this to be perfect. We'll shoot it again."

By the time Marty, Paco, two county deputies, and four state troopers arrived at Pop Weber's truck, Chase had walked half-mile loops on both sides of the road looking for any sign. But the hard-baked prairie ground had no secrets to share, and tracks around the truck made it seem that Pop had just disappeared. Wherever he had gone, he was hurt. The blood on the car seat showed that.

Chase told Marty and the others what little he could and pointed out where he had searched. He didn't tell them he'd taken pictures of the truck, bloodstain, and tracks with his cell phone.

"Look, Chase," Marty said as the other lawmen spread out to look for Pop. "Kendall wants you to meet him in Brandon. They're settin' up a command post at the high school to coordinate the investigation into the deaths."

"Murders, Marty," Chase said. "Coach and Jimmy were murdered." He swallowed. "Maybe Pop."

"I know." Marty face twisted with worry. "But listen to me. I told Kendall and the head cop from the state what you told me about seeing Jimmy and Dolly at your place Friday night, and they want to talk to you."

Chase rocked back on his heels. "Kendall thinks I have something to do with this?"

"No." Marty looked away. "I don't know what to think, Chase. The guy from the state brought up your trouble with Billee, and you know how Kendall can be. One little thing can set him off and he won't let it go, no matter how hard it bites at him. And you know the sheriff." Marty scuffed the toe of his boot in the dirt. "He's never liked you at all."

"This isn't a schoolboy's basketball game, Marty."

"I know. But there's one thing about Kendall for sure. He don't forget."

Cecil watched the reporter from the Springs TV station go through her little act for the sixth time. Not that he minded.

She'd asked permission to set up in the lot just out past the diesel pumps. She told him that spot would give a good perspective of the town. The camera could see the water tower, Main Street, the high school, and the cars in the parking lot at the Methodist church. She even promised him the Town Pump sign would be in the shot. He'd let her think he was the manager.

The stool he perched on behind the cash register had to be kicked six inches closer to the front door so he could watch her over the Doritos display. It made it harder to reach the register, but it was worth it. Jody Rose was quite a package.

She couldn't be but barely five foot tall and weighed maybe ninety pounds. But each one of those pounds had been placed on her in just the right spots. Her back was to him, and in those tight black pants she had one fine pooper.

Jody pumped her fist and dropped the microphone to her side. The guy with camera let out a whoop Cecil could hear through the closed doors of the convenience store. Jody plucked a cell phone from the pocket of her ski jacket, looked it over, and tucked the phone away, and then both she and cameraman started toward the store. Now he'd get another look at the front side of her. He hoped she'd unzip that winter coat.

Cecil had two cups of coffee on the counter when they came through the door. He smiled and nodded. "They're on me." Like he ever paid for coffee. "Sugar and cream are over there."

The cameraman went off to use the restroom and left Jody alone with Cecil.

"Like a doughnut to go with your coffee?" He pointed at the tired Krispy Kremes that had been delivered on Thursday.

Jody shook her head. "But you could help me." She pulled down the zipper of her parka about halfway.

Cecil leaned forward. "Sure can. I know a lot of what goes on here."

"You know why I'm here in Brandon?"

He liked the way she smiled when she looked at him. "Yes, ma'am. I figured that one out. Murders, right?"

"Did you know either of the victims?" She sipped her coffee and looked up at Cecil with big blue eyes.

"Good friends with both of 'em." Cecil lifted his Town Pump ball cap and smoothed the few strands of hair still left on the top of his head.

"You were good friends with a high school boy?"

Cecil had to think fast. "Sure I was. Coach would have me help some of his boys"—he thought for a second—"uh, with their, uh—what you call it, uh, free throws. Yeah, free throws. On account of I was real good at them when I played for him."

"You played on the school team here?"

"Sure I did." He stretched up all five foot seven of him.

"Oh, were you on the team that won the championship?" Jody set her coffee cup down, propped both elbows on the counter, and rested her chin in her hands. She was as pretty as the girls in his magazines. Even with clothes on.

"What'd you say?"

"The championship team. When was it? 1992?"

Cecil thought a second. He hadn't been on the team. He hadn't even lived in Brandon back then. And he dropped out of high school halfway through his junior year. But he was in too deep now.

There was probably a way she could check to see if he was on the team. He plucked at a whiskery hair anchored to his earlobe while he thought. "Naw, that was after I graduated." It was all he could think of. "But I knew those boys. I even helped Chase Ford learn to shoot his free throws. Coach asked me to help him on account of I was so good."

Jody stood. "Chase Ford, the basketball player? The one who was just divorced from that country singer, Billee Kidd?"

"That's him. He grew up not five miles from here. Out near my ranch." Sometimes Cecil just couldn't stop the lies. "He was damned good. Played for the Los Angeles Lakers before he got hurt. I taught him to shoot free throws, you know."

Cecil could tell Jody wasn't paying attention to him. She was thinking real hard. He had to get her back.

"Let me tell you somethin'." He looked around. There weren't any cars at the pumps, and the cameraman wasn't back from the crapper. "That boy that was killed . . ."

Jody whispered, "Jimmy Riley?"

"Yeah, that's right." He took a bag of Flamin' Hot Cheetos from the rack on the counter, opened it, and offered one to Jody. She shook her head. He stuffed two in his mouth and crunched down. "Jimmy's girlfriend is Chase Ford's half-sister. And he's here in town."

"Ford's here in Brandon?"

"He is." He had her attention now.

"Tell me more."

Cecil grinned. He'd have to be careful. Sometimes he said too much. He popped two more Flamin' Hot Cheetos into his mouth and began, "Seems Chase's mother got hurt real bad in this car accident. His daddy hired a pretty little Mexican girl to keep house. . . ."

Jody stepped out into the cool fresh breeze and away from the smell of stale coffee, bad breath, and Flamin' Hot Cheetos. She felt as if she needed a shower to wash away all of that vile man's leers. She took her cell phone and dialed Colorado Springs.

"Hey, Rhonda, need some help here. Find everything you can on Chase Ford."

"Chase Ford, the basketball player?" Rhonda asked through the crackle of the cell phone.

"Yeah, that Chase Ford. He's from this little town, Brandon or whatever. And he's here now."

"What are you thinking, girl?"

"I'm going try for an interview."

"He hasn't talked with anyone since that country singer divorced him."

"He'll talk to me." Jody's cell phone vibrated with an incoming text message. "Listen, I got to go. Get that to me as soon as you can."

She cradled the phone in her hands and looked at the screen.

Possible 3rd vic Alfred "Pop" Weber
Old farmer—more when I get it

The sheriff had kept his word. Now she owed him.

She pulled up the zipper on her jacket and turned to the window of the store. The gross little man was still staring at her.

As much as she hated to think it, Jody had to stay close to Cecil. She fluffed the ends of her hair and smiled at him.

CHAPTER FIFTEEN

Sheriff Kendall needed a man like Jim Doyle. He'd met the Colorado Bureau of Investigation agent at a law enforcement conference in Estes Park the year Kendall took office. Doyle's credentials were some of the best. He'd led teams that had solved crimes all across the state. Murder investigations were his specialty. When it came to solving multiple murders, there was none in the state better.

But what Kendall liked about the man was that in almost thirty years, Jim Doyle had never once sought recognition for himself. Solving the crime and seeing justice done was all that mattered to him. With eleven months until he could begin drawing a nice, fat state pension, Kendall didn't think Doyle would change his ways. All Kendall needed to do was stay close, follow Doyle's lead, and take the credit when this thing was over.

It was Doyle's idea to use the high school in Brandon as a command post. Tables were set up in the gymnasium, and Doyle put the county office staff to work entering information from the evidence that had been gathered into a database. He took over one classroom as his office and had whiteboards brought in. He labeled each board with the name of one of the victims and made notes in neat block letters across the board. He'd even color-coded the notes, and when he explained his method to Kendall, the sheriff had just nodded.

By one o'clock he'd scheduled interviews with teachers and the principal, and written a script of questions for Kendall's people to ask students who were friends of Jimmy's.

The white-haired man never undid the top button of his frayed blue oxford shirt, never uttered a cuss word, and kept his reading glasses on a string around his neck. He didn't wear a gun, and when Kendall asked if he wanted to see the crime scenes, Doyle told him he wasn't that kind of cop.

Kendall liked that. Little chance that Doyle would be doing TV interviews with Jody Rose.

The thing that Kendall liked most about Doyle was that he wanted to talk to Chase Ford.

Kendall stepped into Doyle's office. The agent had kicked his shoes off. Threadbare socks rested on the table in front of him. His laptop sat across his knees, reading glasses hung on the end of his nose, and there was a Diet Coke in his hand.

Doyle waved with the Coke. "You should see this. First report on the Riley boy from the ME."

The printer on the table whined to life and spit half a dozen pages into the tray. Kendall picked them up and began to read.

"Go to page four. About halfway down," Doyle said. "See what it says?"

Kendall found the spot and read slowly. He raised his face and looked at Doyle. "Nothing new here."

"Go on, read."

Kendall looked back at the page. He skimmed a few words and then read the next out loud: "Evidence of recent sexual activity."

"That means what your deputy said about Ford seeing Riley at midnight with a girl . . ."

". . . was the truth," Kendall said, finishing the sentence.

Doyle took a sip from the can. "I suggest you find that girl." He let the carbonation sizzle on his tongue. "Any word on when I'll get to speak to Mr. Ford?"

"He's supposed to be on his way now."

"Good," Doyle said. "And, Sheriff, if you look a little farther down in the report you'll see something else about the boy. Ford wasn't lying. ME found traces of lipstick on the boy's neck and . . ." Doyle paused. "Read it for yourself. There was lipstick found other places on the body."

Mercy finished putting pots, pans, and dishes in the washer, pulled off her rubber gloves, and ran her fingers through her hair.

Busy day.

Every table had been full with customers waiting since the churches let out. It was as if Saylor's Café became a refuge from the tragedy that had visited their community. Farmers and ranchers who lived in houses miles apart huddled close together around cramped tables in the little café. The conversations were quiet, and two names could be heard whispered again and again: *Jimmy, Coach.* Comfort on this Sunday came from fried chicken and meatloaf, mashed potatoes and green beans and hot peach cobbler, not their pastor's prayers. Mercy would have never thought that murder would be good for business.

Should have come in today, Dolly. Tips would have been good.

"Hector, is that carry-out order for the sheriff ready?" Mercy called to the cook.

"Packin' it up right now, *señora.*"

"I'll drive it to the school myself," Mercy said. "I need to get away from here for a few minutes." She stepped into the office, took her coat from a hook behind the door, and checked her lipstick in the mirror. "Don't put the food in the trunk. Just set it on the back-seat. And, Diana," she called as she went out the back door, "add rubber gloves to the Sam's Club list, we're almost out."

Kendall shut the door behind him and sat down on the edge of a table in Doyle's office. "I told that TV newswoman that we're trying to locate Jimmy's girlfriend."

Doyle turned in his chair and peered over the top of his reading glasses. "I suggested that you only provide written statements at this stage of the investigation."

"The word's out all over town. I had the office send out a written notice. The reporter was here in Brandon, so I told her."

"You might not want to do that. It will appear you're playing favorites."

I am playing favorites. I do something for her. She'll do something for me. It's called politics, Doyle. Kendall mumbled, "I'm not used to this. I'll be more careful from now on." *Like hell.*

Doyle turned back to his laptop. "Anything on the search for the old man?"

"Nothing yet. I took your advice. Fort Carson is sending two helicopters to help. They should be in the air by now. Your man knows and has sent the GPS coordinates. I've got everyone we can spare on the ground."

There was a rap on the door. The door swung in. "Sheriff, you need to hear this." A high school kid stood in the opening with one of Kendall's deputies behind him. "Tell the sheriff what you just told me, Allen. Just leave out all the f-bombs this time around."

The kid looked down at the top of his scuffed boots. His Wrangler jeans were faded and torn at the knees. He had on a bright red T-shirt under his Carhartt work coat. His shirt had the name of some music group or computer game Kendall didn't know anything about stenciled on the front. But it was the Nike cap on his head that made Kendall bite his tongue. It was brand new, and instead of curving the brim to keep the sun out of his eyes, Allen had left the bill of the cap flat with a shiny sticker still stuck to the top, and he'd cocked the hat a quarter turn. The farm kid was trying to show he was just as cool as some ghetto gangbanger.

"Go ahead. Tell the sheriff what you told me." The deputy pushed Allen into the room and pulled the door closed behind them both.

The kid shrugged his shoulders. "Don't I have the right to remain silent?"

"Nobody accused you of a crime. We're just gathering information." The deputy nudged Allen again.

"Shouldn't my parents be here?"

"A few minutes ago, you were real proud that you just turned eighteen, but I can call your mama. She'll be happy to hear about the drugs and drinkin'."

Allen looked at Kendall. And then at Doyle.

Kendall hooked his thumbs in his gun belt. "Take off that damn hat, or I'll take it off ya. Now start talkin', kid. I don't have all day."

Allen snapped off the cap and hid it behind his leg. "Like I told him. Everybody knows Ray-Ray Jackson grows pot out on his place."

Kendall's eyes shot Doyle's way. If the state man cared that Ray-Ray was growing pot, he didn't show it. "Go on, Allen," Kendall said.

"Me and a couple of other guys"—Allen glanced up from the floor—"I don't hafta say who, do I?"

"No. Get to it." Kendall tapped his trigger finger on his belt buckle.

Allen looked back at the floor. "Anyway, we went out there to see if he'd sell us any. It wasn't my idea. I just went along."

"And?"

"Ray-Ray went all ape shit on us. Pulled a pistol out from under his shirt and started wavin' it around. Hollerin' for us to leave him alone. So we got out of there."

"What's this got to do with anythin'?"

"There's more. We went there in . . . like August. A couple weeks later, just before school started . . . on this Friday, there was a party out at the Butt Notch. You know, next to Ray-Ray's."

Kendall nodded. "Get on with it. I'm not hearin' anythin' here."

"Okay, okay. The party was goin' good. Somebody brought a keg. And you know . . . stuff."

"Drugs?"

"Yeah. But I didn't bring 'em."

"Get to it."

"It was late. It was real hot. You know there were all these mosquitoes because of the weeds and shit in the Notch. So we kinda like moved the party onto Ray-Ray's. Somebody cut his fence so we could drive out there. Wasn't me, though." Allen took a step back. "Somebody turned up the music and maybe built a fire. You know, we were just hangin'. Everybody was there. All of a sudden Ray-Ray came barrelin' over the hill in his old truck. He jumped out hollerin' like he was crazy. Shitfire, he pulled out his shotgun. People were scared like he was gonna shoot us all." He looked at the sheriff. "You should do somethin' about him."

Kendall narrowed his eyes. "Keep goin'."

"Ray-Ray was wavin' the gun around. Girls were cryin'. Then, Jimmy Riley, he tried to play peacemaker or somethin'. He tried to talk to Ray-Ray. I thought he was gonna get killed. Ray-Ray just screamed louder. Then Jimmy sorta settled him down. And we all left. I mean fast, we got out of there. And as we were leavin', I think about then Ray-Ray saw the cut fence. He yelled real loud, 'I'll kill you all.' He pointed the gun at Jimmy's belly, and his eyes went all crazy. Like he blamed him or somethin'. He said somethin' to Jimmy I couldn't hear. That's all I know, and we hauled ass out of there."

Kendall looked at Doyle.

"Tell me a couple of things," the agent said to Allen. "Jimmy Riley? Was he one of the ones who went to try to buy the drugs with you?"

"No, sir. Jimmy don't hardly drink or nothin'. He thinks basketball is gonna get him a scholarship. He wants to be like Chase Ford. You know, play in the NBA." He looked away. "I guess he won't now." Allen exhaled, and his shoulders dropped. "Can I go?"

"A last question. Who supplied the beer?" Doyle flicked his glasses off his nose. They swung back and forth from the string.

"Jeez, I don't want to say."

"Call his mama, deputy," Kendall said.

"Don't do that. It was Cecil. Over at Town Pump. The dumbass thinks if he buys for us, we'll think he's cool or somethin'."

"Was he at the party?"

"Hey, you said one more question."

Kendall stood up. "Was Cecil at the party?"

"Okay, yeah. That's the deal. He buys, and he gets to come.

He likes lookin' at the girls." Allen blew out a breath. "It was almost funny, I thought he was gonna shit himself when Ray-Ray showed up with the gun. Now, can I go?"

Kendall looked at his deputy. "First, Allen's gonna write us a list of everyone who was at the party."

"Hey. They'll all think I'm a snitch."

"Your friend's dead, kid."

"Yeah, okay. Just tell everybody you heard about this somewhere else. Don't use my name." Allen bit his lip. "Please."

Kendall pointed to the door. "Take him out, Deputy, and give him a piece of paper and a pencil."

The kid lifted his hat to put it on his head, looked at the sheriff, and put it back down.

When they had left, Kendall turned to Doyle. "What you make of that?"

"Too early to tell." Doyle took a drink from a new can of Diet Coke. He leaned back in his chair and opened his lips. Kendall could hear the bubbles fizz in the agent's mouth. "I suggest you find Ray-Ray so we can talk with him. And when can we expect Mr. Ford? I'm anxious to ask him a few questions also."

Kendall started for the door when Doyle spoke again. "And, sheriff, this girl, Dolly Benavidez. As far as we can tell, there have been no posts on her Facebook page since Friday. No cell phone activity, either."

Two people had been killed, and Pop Weber was still missing. No one had seen Ray-Ray in two days, Chase Ford hadn't come to town yet, and he'd spilled the beans to Jody Rose about the black-haired Hispanic gal Jimmy had been dating. Kendall guessed that Doyle wasn't real impressed with his police work.

Mercy heard footsteps on the gravel parking lot. She looked up from the back door of her Lincoln.

"You're Mercy Saylor, aren't you?" Jody hustled from the TV van. "I recognize you. My cameraman and I had a quick breakfast at your café this morning." She stuck out her hand. "Jody Rose. KBBW TV Colorado Springs." She smiled.

"We served a lot of people today. Forgive me if I don't remember."

"No trouble." She looked down at the boxes of food on the backseat. "Need help?"

"Sure, if you want. The sheriff ordered food for those who are, you know, helpin' with the investigation. If this whole thing wasn't so bad it might be excitin'." Mercy lifted a box and handed it to Jody.

"You know, I heard something about your restaurant I'd like to ask you about. I might be able to use it in a story."

"What's that?"

"Is it true your mother shot a man trying to rob your restaurant?"

"Where'd you hear that?"

"Cecil at Town . . ."

". . . Pump," Mercy finished. "Cecil has most of it right for a change."

"Fill me in. It might make a good human interest thing, while everyone is waiting to find out about the murders."

The two walked to the school with their boxes. "I think I was only six or seven, so most of what I know is what I was told," Mercy said. "Mom was there at the café one night when this guy came in, pulled a knife, and demanded money. Mom kept a pistol on a shelf under the cash register. She grabbed it and waved it at the guy. He ran out. Mom followed him and shot a hole in the back window of his truck. That's how they identified him when he got pulled over in Comanche Springs. I think I have the newspaper story in a file cabinet back at the restaurant if you want to see it."

"I'd like that. Did your mom get in trouble for shooting?"

"Things were different back then. Sheriff Kendall's father was the sheriff, and he thought she'd done the right thing. The bullet hole is how they knew they caught the right man." Mercy laughed. "That pistol's still under the counter."

"Is it covered with dust and rust?"

Mercy winked. "Not at all."

"Great story." Jody opened the door to the school. "Could I ask another favor? Cecil tells me you know Chase Ford. I'd like to meet him."

CHAPTER SIXTEEN

Chase promised Marty that he would go to town and meet with Kendall and the agent from the Colorado Bureau of Investigation.

A dozen law enforcement officers scoured both sides of the road along Sandy Creek looking for any sign of Pop Weber. Marty let Chase know that two helicopters were on the way from the army base in Colorado Springs to help with the search, and a National Guard unit from La Junta would be there by nightfall. He told Chase that Kendall would be impatient and for Chase to get in his truck and go.

Chase agreed. But he didn't tell Marty that he was going to drive out to Bobby Jackson's first. He didn't know what he'd find at Bobby's, but if Ray-Ray had something to do with all this like Kendall seemed to think, Chase wanted to talk to the Jackson brothers.

The turnoff to Bobby's place was hidden by a jog in the road. Chase slowed his pickup, swung onto the packed trail, crossed Sandy Creek, and left a rooster tail of dust on his way up the hill to Bobby's. If Marty was watching he'd know where Chase was headed.

Bobby lived in a double-wide he'd towed to the hilltop ten years before. The front door faced south and east so that morning sun would melt the ice on winter days. There were two metal buildings, better kept than the trailer, for Bobby's tractors and machinery. Half a dozen old rusted cars sat in the yard, and where pickups and tractors hadn't mashed down the vegetation, the weeds stood three feet tall.

In the shade of one of the buildings, a skinned fork-horn buck hung from the bucket of a Bobcat front-end loader. Hunters from the city would have hoisted a deer onto a tree branch with rope and had fun doing it. Farmers let machines do the lifting and saved their backs. It was things like that Big Paul had pointed out to Chase.

Bobby led a pinto saddle horse to a trailer he'd hitched to the back of his pickup. He tied the horse's lead rope to the trailer and walked out to meet Chase. "Whatcha think, Chase?"

Chase climbed out of his truck. "Nice deer, Bobby. Where'd you get him?"

"Don't tell Birdie this." Bobby grinned, bent forward, and let a mouthful of tobacco juice dribble onto the ground. "Comin' back from breakfast at Saylor's this mornin', and that little deer was standin' in the creek bottom where my road crosses Sandy. I stopped the truck and he just stared at me. Popped him out the window with my aught-six."

Chase smiled. "Which way you come from town?"

Bobby's grin left his face. "From the highway. Why?"

"They found"—Chase didn't want to say it was him—"Pop Weber's truck about half a mile from your turnoff. Nobody can find him. Sheriff's boys and state troopers are lookin' now."

"I know. That's why I'm loadin' this horse up. Got a call from town. We're gonna make our own search party and comb both sides of Sandy from the highway to Butt Notch. About twenty men volunteered so far."

"Kendall know about this?"

"I ain't told him. Don't think anyone else has. He's too busy with the murders." Bobby spit again. "What's he gonna tell us to do? Not look?"

"He might."

"Piss on him if he does." Bobby reached back to rub his horse's ear. His jacket rode up his hip, and Chase spotted a holster on the farmer's belt.

"What's the pistol for, Bobby?"

"People been killed in this town. Man should be careful. That's what it's for." Bobby cocked his head. "Why you askin' so many questions, Chase?"

"One of the dead was my good friend."

"We're all gonna miss Coach. But you didn't come out here to tell me that."

Chase bit his lip. "The boy was killed three miles from that alfalfa field you lease from me. Thought maybe you might have seen somethin'. If you didn't, maybe your brother did. He around here?"

Bobby tangled his fingers in the horse's halter. The horse pulled away, but Bobby wrapped his hand tighter until his knuckles turned white. "You think your shit don't stink, Chase Ford. You go away to college and play basketball on TV, marry up to that pretty little country singer, and never come back here even once. Now your world turns to shit. Can't play ball no more. Wife left you, and you show up here. And Coach's dead." Bobby yanked on the halter. "You're not the big man you used to be." Bobby's jaw muscles bunched. "Maybe you should quit askin' questions and get off my property."

"The murders have us all on edge, Bobby."

"Leave, Chase."

Chase nodded, backed to his truck, and got in. Bobby stood stock-still. When the horse struggled and tried to pull away, Bobby held firm. Chase dropped the truck in reverse, backed away from the trailer, slipped it into drive, and swung a wide circle in Bobby's yard on his way back to the road.

Which question didn't Bobby want to answer?

There was no sign of Ray-Ray around the trailer or barns, but he could have been hiding anywhere.

With his deer rifle pointed at my back.

But Bobby was on his way to help with the search for Pop. Would he do that if he had something to hide?

He would if he thought it would throw the suspicion off him and his brother.

No.

Chase hadn't learned anything at all. Bobby and Ray-Ray liked to keep people at a distance. In Bobby's mind, Chase had asked too many questions. That was that.

Unless—

A flock of magpies cawed and hopped around something just inside the fence line at Sandy Creek. Chase slowed his truck and swung to the edge of the narrow trail road. The black and white birds crowded together and pecked at the ground.

Something's dead.

When Chase rolled down the window, the birds never spooked. He hollered, and they stayed fixed on their free meal.

Could it be? Pop?

Chase opened the door.

He snatched a stone from the road and hurled at the greedy birds. They hopped away. The pile was shiny and slick pink, bulging with purple and red.

Gut pile from Bobby's deer.

Chase let himself breathe. He was as edgy as everyone else in Comanche County.

Chase needed more time before he went to talk to Kendall. He wanted to find Dolly. If for no other reason than to tell her he was sorry about Jimmy.

There was a shortcut he remembered. He had passed the gate into Bobby's neighbor's pasture. A rutted trail angled across four fenced sections. In about the center of the pasture sat a windmill and stock tank. From there, the path crossed to the far corner of the property and met a county road about a half mile from town. The road crossed the railroad tracks and led into Brandon just behind Saylor's Café. He'd stay away from the highway, weave through town on his way to where Dolly lived with her stepfather, and hope Kendall or one of his deputies didn't see his truck.

Ray-Ray had one more road to cross before he made it to his brother's farm. There was a bridge over Sandy Creek four miles from Bobby's, but less than a mile from town. It had taken him longer than he'd thought it would to cover the distance between his place and his brother's. He'd been careful and tried to keep hidden along the creek bottom.

Once he'd stayed under a fallen cottonwood for a half an hour and watched two city-boy hunters try to get within a rifle shot of a herd of deer. The deer gave the boys the slip and walked close enough to Ray-Ray that he could count the flies buzzing around the deer's heads.

Another time, he held tight and watched a farmer's wife out checking stock in a field. He thought it better to stay still than risk her seeing him.

Ray-Ray was sure no one knew where he was. But he'd be cautious before he crossed the county road. He'd listen for cars and trucks before he made his dash under the bridge.

The prairie could be a quiet place. But quiet meant to Ray-Ray that something was on the prowl. A bobcat hunting at dusk hushes the night birds. Rabbits hunker tight when a coyote's about. Prairie dogs shush their chatter and dive deep into their burrows when a hawk's shadow crosses the ground.

Ray-Ray let himself down onto his belly behind a waist-high patch of weeds, watched, and listened. A meadowlark on the dead branch in a cottonwood tree trilled its song. A wild turkey scratched for grit and clucked to itself in the dry creek bed. In the sky, geese from the lakes at Eads *V*'ed up and headed out to feed before dark. He could hear the swish of their wings and their honking calls to one another.

Nature's noise was good.

Then he heard it. From the west. Coming his way.

Whump—whump—whump.

Ray-Ray rolled on his back and found two dark smears against the clouds.

Helicopters.

He squinted as they came closer. There were white markings on the chopper's side, and they were painted desert tan.

Army helicopters. He gritted his teeth. Government helicopters.

The copters parted. The lead swung away from the other, over the high ground south of Sandy Creek. The second swooped lower.

Maybe a couple hundred feet over the tops of cottonwoods in the creek bottom. Gusts of wind rattled branches. Dried leaves danced along the ground.

Ray-Ray scrambled into a tangle of tamaracks and fallen trees. *Leave me alone, you bastards. Leave me alone.*

And he raised his deer rifle to his shoulder.

Chase turned up the heat in the cab of his truck. The shortcut took away miles from the trip to town, but was probably longer in time. He bumped along over the two rutted tire trails across the sage-and-prairie-grass pasture. Dried cow pies peppered the ground, but the grass was high for this time of year. Whoever ranched here was a good steward. They hadn't let their cattle overgraze. There would be grass in the spring.

Twenty or more mixed-breed cows huddled around the windmill and stock tank.

When they were in high school, Marty and Chase used the tank on hot summer evenings after working the fields. They'd filch Coors from the refrigerator at home, drive a pickup out, and soak in the cool water of the tank after the sun went down. He'd told Mercy about the place and dared her to come skinny-dipping with him. They snuck out after dark one night, but when the moment came, Mercy had a swimming suit on under her jeans and Chase soaked his basketball shorts.

Like playing basketball. Some games you win. Some you lose. You don't know until the final buzzer. And close games are the best.

Chase found the trail on the other side of the trampled ground around the water tank and headed west toward the road to town.

With each bounce of the truck, he thought about the terrible scene at Coach's house. He was glad he'd left before they brought out the body. He thought about the kid, Jimmy Riley, and how basketball might have given the poor kid a shot at college. Coach had said Jimmy was that good.

But thoughts of Dolly crept back in. His half-sister. By a father he didn't understand. Just a high school girl working for tips at the café and thinking she loved the basketball star. Jimmy and Dolly could have been Chase and Mercy.

He felt the pulse of wind slap the side of his truck. Out of the side window he saw the helicopter over Sandy Creek.

And Chase heard a rifle shot.

CHAPTER SEVENTEEN

Birdie beat it out of the meeting in Comanche Springs as soon as she was sure she'd answered Kendall's questions.

Yes, she'd checked Ray-Ray's house. No, he wasn't there. And, no, she had no idea where he was.

She headed to the east edge of the county to do what they paid her to do during the opening weekend of deer season. Be visible, check licenses, issue citations to law breakers and keep the landowners happy. She liked her job, and driving the back roads was sure less stressful than tracking Ray-Ray and following Kendall's orders.

The breeze's cold bite chilled her fingertips, and by noon clouds bunched on the horizon to the north.

Weather coming in. And, God, the county needed the moisture. Let it snow.

It was a prayer, not a curse.

Birdie knew cold and snow would send most of the weekend hunters scurrying for home. The more serious would stay. Deer would need to browse to keep their energy up in the cold, so they'd settle in near the alfalfa and feed crops. Snow-covered ground made them easier to spot. The hunters could take advantage of that. Most would obey the rules. A few might be tempted to hunt where they didn't have permission or road hunt or any of a dozen things she was paid to watch out for. But that would be tomorrow. For now Birdie would do her job.

And try to forget the murders.

By noon, she'd mediated a dispute between a farmer and two hunters he'd caught on his posted ground. The hunters showed her written permission they'd been given to hunt on the farmer's neighbor's place. They explained they had got confused by the big open spaces and crossed a fence they shouldn't have; they apologized and offered to pay a trespass fee. Birdie was convinced the men were telling the truth. She talked it over with the landowner, and he agreed to forget the matter.

Score one for Birdie. It's always better not to write a ticket.

Later, she helped a man and his eighteen-year-old daughter load a nice four-point buck in their truck. The girl had shot it. The father was so proud he could hardly talk. With tears in her eyes, the daughter told Birdie that her mother had died of cancer four months before. The girl was headed off to some college back east after Christmas and wanted to do something special with her dad before she left him. He wanted to take his girl hunting. Now they had a deer to show for the hours they'd spent together. And memories of a pancake supper in a church basement and the wide-open Colorado Plains. Some days Birdie loved what they paid her to do.

But there were two dead bodies, and from what she heard from listening to the sheriff's band on her radio, she knew there was no word on Pop Weber yet. Her truck needed gas, so Birdie swung out on the highway and headed north for Brandon. Maybe she could do something to help.

The needle on the fuel gauge bumped the "E" when she passed a highway sign showing she was twenty-five miles from Town Pump. She fell in behind two semis and a pickup hauling a horse trailer. Birdie let her foot off the gas and slowed to follow them into town.

Another pickup, with three men, caught up to her. The truck's blinker came on just as they crossed Sandy Creek. It followed the first pickup and trailer through an open gate into the pasture on the north side of Sandy. Two more trucks and trailers waited in the field. Birdie recognized Bobby Jackson's pinto horse tied to the back of his truck.

What the—?

"You told 'em I bought the beer?" Cecil stared across the counter at Allen and gritted his teeth to keep from screaming at the kid.

"They kinda, you know, made me."

Cecil felt spit bubbles form at the corner of his mouth. "What else you tell 'em?" He dabbed his mouth with the tail of his T-shirt.

"Well, I said we went out to Ray-Ray's to buy weed." Allen backed away. "But I didn't say you were with us. Honest."

"You say anythin' about—" Cecil felt fear and anger bubble in his gut. "You know what I'm talkin' about?"

"No. You know you can trust me." The kid looked down at the floor. "Can I bum a cigarette?"

"No." Cecil spit the word out. "You wanna smoke, buy a pack."

Allen turned away from Cecil and looked out the front windows of the store. "Who's that guy?" He pointed at the driver of a mud-crusted truck.

"That ain't no man, stupid." Cecil shook his head. "It's that fat little game warden, Birdie Hawkins. Wonder what she's doin' in town."

"Maybe she came in for a Weight Watchers meetin'." Allen smiled, proud of himself. "Hide the Fritos."

"Shut up, Allen. I'm not through with you yet. You might've got us both in big trouble."

The cold handle on the gas nozzle stung Birdie's hand. She placed it in the fuel port on the side of her pickup, started the gas flowing, pulled her stocking cap down over her ears, and jammed her hands into the pockets of her Carhartt jacket.

Jeff Mason's pickup, towing a horse trailer, rolled past on the highway and swung south toward Sandy Creek. The dark tail and rump of Jeff's bay horse pressed up against the trailer gate.

That's five trucks and trailers.

Birdie didn't know what to make of it, but she didn't like it. Whatever it meant. She hung the hose back on the pump, plucked her receipt from the slot, and headed into the store for a cup of hot coffee.

The wind shut the door behind her, and Cecil pulled the tail of his T-shirt down over a hairy swath of white belly. "What's goin' on, Cecil?" Birdie asked. She snatched a cherry fruit pie from a counter display and tore the wax paper wrapper open with her teeth while she filled her Town Pump plastic mug. "That's the fifth horse trailer I've seen. All locals." She tipped the top of her head toward the windows. "Four more parked off the highway just this side of Sandy Creek. You know anythin' about it?" She pushed a five dollar bill across the counter.

Cecil looked around the store. Across the room, a high school kid picked a hot-rod magazine from the rack and began to flip through the pages. Cecil motioned for her to come closer.

"Vigilantes, Birdie," he whispered. "I heard some of 'em talkin' in this very store. The men of this county are fed up with the way Sheriff Kendall is goin' about solvin' these murders. They're gonna go find Ray-Ray, and if they do, they'll string him up."

"What are you talkin' about?"

"Vigilantes. Would I lie to you?"

"Yes, you would." She shook her head. "Damn it, Cecil, you tell the sheriff any of this?"

"Just good men worried about their families. It's not my place to go talkin' about it."

"Aw, crap, Cecil." Birdie jammed the fruit pie into her mouth and made for the door.

As soon as the door shut Allen hurried to the counter. "You're good, Cecil." A broad smile beamed from the kid's face. "I wish I could come up with stories like you do. They just, like, you know, flow from your mouth. You ought to write books or somethin'."

"Any fool can write a book, kid." Cecil watched Birdie drive away. "Listen, there's somethin' I gotta do. You watch things for me. Darla will be in at four. Tell her I told you to stay." Cecil zipped up his sweatshirt over his paunch and went out into the cold wind.

By the time Birdie got her truck started, she'd thought over what Cecil had said.

Vigilantes out to lynch Ray-Ray? Another of his stories.

But there was something to five trucks and trailers, horses and riders meeting up outside of town. She'd check on it to see what she could find out, before she told the sheriff anything.

Cecil left the engine of his rattle-trap Ranger pickup running. He climbed out and went into his trailer. A half-empty bottle of Bacardi rum sat on a folding tray across from his TV, and a Marlin thirty-thirty rifle was propped behind the door.

When he shut the trailer's door behind him, Cecil took both with him.

CHAPTER EIGHTEEN

Mercy took the plate from Jim Doyle. The investigator dabbed the corner of his mouth with a paper napkin. "Thank you, ladies," he said. "That was very good, but I need to get back to work now." He pushed away from the table and stood.

"We have peach cobbler for dessert." Mercy pointed at the pan at the end of the table.

"Perhaps later. I have a lot I need to do." He took his can of Diet Coke and crossed the gym to the classroom he'd turned into his office.

"Not much for conversation, was he?" Mercy said to Jody Rose after the man was gone.

"Not at all. I was hoping he'd give me some tidbit I could use." Jody moved the mashed potatoes from one side of her plate to the other, lifted a piece of meatloaf with her fork, and then set it back down from where she'd picked it up.

Jody hadn't eaten anything. Just toyed with her food.

No wonder she looks like that in those five-hundred-dollar jeans. Mercy felt the corners of her mouth turn down into a frown. She'd seen the way all the state troopers and deputies stared at the reporter. They should be looking at *her* that way.

"Cobbler, Jody? I've got a big piece here. All for you."

"No, thank you. I'm not hungry. I must be worried about not having anything new to report." She stabbed the meatloaf on her plate and left the plastic fork standing in the cold meat. "It was good, though."

Good? The little bitch never tasted one bite.

Mercy shaved off a piece of the cobbler, stuffed it into her mouth, and caught the syrupy dribble on her chin with a finger. Behind her the table creaked. Sheriff Kendall settled into the chair where Jim Doyle had sat. Right across from Jody.

"Save some for me?" Kendall asked.

Jody's face beamed with the same sweet smile she'd tried on Doyle. It hadn't gotten her what she wanted from the old detective, but from what Mercy knew about Kendall, the smile and tight sweater would start the flow of information.

Mercy unsnapped the second pearl button on her western blouse. She filled a plate with meatloaf, green beans, and potatoes, and when she set it in front of the sheriff she made sure her shirt fell open just a bit.

"Damn, looks good." He was looking at the plate, not her.

Jody laced her fingers together, rested her elbows on the table, and perched her face on top of her hands. She tilted her head just so and looked at the sheriff.

I should stab her with her own fork. Mercy gritted her teeth and sat next to Jody.

"Am I the last one to eat?" Kendall asked between forkfuls.

"Uh-huh." Mercy thought it was best not to say much.

"You made a good impression, Mercy. Doyle said to order food for supper. He's gonna keep the crew here 'til late." Kendall looked over his shoulder at the troopers hunched over the tables and computers on the gym floor. "I'm not sure what's he's got all them doing, but he's supposed to be the man that knows. So can you bring somethin' over at around six?"

"I'll have Hector make burritos." Another bite of cobbler would have tasted good right then, but Mercy remembered Jody's tight jeans. She left the fork on the table. "Any word on Pop?"

"Nothin' at all. The helicopters from Fort Carson are supposed to be here any time. Maybe they'll help, maybe they won't. At least the state's footin' the bill on this one."

Jody shifted in her chair just enough to press her breasts against the table's edge. "You've already told us more than Mr. Doyle." The reporter put a pouty smile on her lips.

"He's tight-lipped all right." Kendall swiped a biscuit through the brown gravy on his plate. "But there's really not much to say. No murder weapon with the boy. No fingerprints on the knife that killed Coach." He pointed with the biscuit. "And I wasn't supposed to tell you any of that."

"All you told me was what you didn't know. How can I make a story out of that?"

Mercy could see the wheels turning in the little blonde's head.

"Are you going to question Chase Ford?" Jody asked.

"We're waitin' for him to come in now."

"Oh."

The fool had just given Jody her next story. Chase Ford. Murder suspect. Or maybe the fool was a fox.

Kendall finished his meatloaf and ate two pieces of the peach cobbler. Jody helped Mercy gather up the leftover food and throw away the paper plates. When the table was wiped down, they put the serving dishes in the boxes Mercy had brought. Kendall picked up the boxes and followed the two women out the door.

"Look." Jody pointed at a helicopter low in the sky just south of town.

"Army chopper," Kendall said. "It's flyin' just over the trees along Sandy Creek. Maybe he'll see somethin' from up there that we can't from the ground. Let's all hope he finds Pop."

Sunbeams flashed off its whirling propellers, and then suddenly the copter flared. It lifted higher into the sky, and for the first time they could hear the strain of its engine.

"What the hell's goin' on?" Kendall shifted the boxes to keep from dropping them.

The sound of a faraway gunshot drifted in from the prairie.

Chase stomped the brakes and twisted his head to look back at the cottonwoods along the creek. Three deer bounded from the trees into the brown pasture grass. The third deer's legs wobbled. It struggled to keep up with the others. The animal stumbled once, fought to stay on its feet, stumbled again, and went down. Chase could see a red smear on its side. A hind leg flailed the air and went still.

A man in a blaze-orange hat and vest stepped from brush along the creek bottom. He looked to where the deer had fallen, slung his rifle over his shoulder, and walked to his kill.

I'll see if I can help, Chase thought.

That's what folks still do out here in farm country. They help one another. Not like the big cities where people don't even know their neighbors' names.

Maybe Chase could help gut out the deer. He could put it in the back of his truck and give the man a ride to where he left his vehicle. Neighbors should help one another.

Especially when a murderer was about.

Chase turned the truck and eased over the rough pasture ground to the dead deer.

At the sound of the shot, Ray-Ray put down his rifle. The helicopter banked higher and swung to the south.

"Leave me alone," he hissed, and looked back down the creek bed toward the sound of the shot.

Ray-Ray spotted the hunter just after he saw the deer.

Maybe it was luck. If it hadn't been for the helicopter, Ray-Ray would have crossed the road and could have run into the hunter. No telling what Ray-Ray might have had to do then.

Getting to his little brother's place was too risky for now, what with the helicopters and the law crawling all over this end of the county. Ray-Ray had known a day like this would come.

When laws were more important than the people they were made to protect, when a few high-ups decided what was best for everyone and didn't listen to the regular people, natural, God-given rights were forgotten.

But Ray-Ray was ready. He'd prepared for that day. He'd built his stronghold, and all hell could rage against him.

Let 'em come.

Cecil pounded both fists on the steering wheel.

"Damn him." He glugged down another swallow of Bacardi and chased the rum down with a swig of Coke. "Damn him! Damn him! Damn him!"

The little shit Allen had told the police everything. Now the sheriff knew about the weed, the party at Butt Notch, and Ray-Ray's threats. If Allen had spilled his guts about that much, what else had he said? There was one thing Allen couldn't have said. Allen didn't know about that. Only Cecil knew. But if the sheriff started nosing around . . .

Cecil didn't chase his next swallow of rum with the Coke. He chased it with more rum. He opened the door of his truck and staggered to the edge of road. He had to think of something quick. The sheriff would be knocking on his trailer's door anytime now. When Cecil wasn't there, they'd comb the whole county.

Where could he go? He didn't have enough money in his wallet to buy gas for his truck. If he could get to Limon he could pawn his rifle for a few bucks. But he knew his piece of crap truck wouldn't get that far.

"Shit, shit, shit," he called out, and quenched his curses with more rum. "Think of somethin'."

The edge of the road crumbled away under his boots. Dirt clods tumbled down the steep bank into years of dried, gray tumbleweeds stacked on themselves in the gulley. The wind stirred the treetops, and a shower of brown cottonwood leaves fell into the dry grass.

Cecil stared down at the tinder-dry weeds in the creek bottom.

That shit's a wildfire waitin' for a spark.

The alcohol's blur cleared for an instant.

What if?

Cecil cocked his head. What if?

What if a fire got started?

He smiled.

It would burn through the grass and weeds like a runaway train. Everybody in the county was on edge about how dry it was. A fire could start anyplace, and the wind would sweep it through the water-starved brush along the creek. If it wasn't stopped, stubble fields would go next. Then houses.

And the man who warned the town?

He'd be a hero for sure.

Cecil smiled at the story he played out in his head. What would it matter if Cecil sold a little pot to the high school kids and bought 'em beer for their parties? He'd be a hero. Jody Big-Tits would interview him on the TV news. Even Mercy Saylor would look at him as if he was important. Not like something to wipe off the bottom of her shoes.

Cecil took a last swallow of rum, grabbed a handful of old newspapers from the floorboards, and climbed from his truck. He sloshed some of the rum onto the papers in his hand and gulped down the rest. He sparked his Bic lighter and touched the fire to the wet papers. Yellow flames curled out and singed the hair on his arm. He tossed the burning paper into the tangle of dry weeds.

A fool would run for all he was worth. But Ray-Ray knew better. The helicopter was gone but could be back any minute. The hunter and the tall man in the Dodge pickup hadn't so much as looked his way. It'd be best to keep on just like he'd planned. But instead of the truck at his brother's place to get him out of the county, he needed to get to his stronghold and wait. And he'd do it slow and careful.

The Bible taught of men like Noah and Moses heeding God's command to prepare for bad times. Ray-Ray had done the same. A tithe portion of everything he'd earned was set aside to buy what he needed. That money bought rice, beans, sugar, and coffee. And what he didn't have money to buy, he did for himself. He canned the okra, squash, and corn he could grow on his own. Traded blacksmithing and welding for more. Put up the meat of a fat calf and salted his own pork. Dried deer meat, too.

Noah and his folk were on the ark for forty days and nights. Ray-Ray put away food to last for more than two months. He'd patched a hundred-gallon water tank he bought for next to nothing and filled it to the brim, a bucket at a time.

For every mouthful of food and each sip of water, Ray-Ray had a bullet for his deer rifle stored in the stronghold. Others could beat their swords into plowshares. Ray-Ray would stand for what was his.

Let 'em come.

They'd have to find him first. His stronghold was hidden where no one would think to look. And while he waited, he'd be comfortable. Hanging in the cool dry of his fortress, stalks of his best homegrown weed perfuming the air.

He waited until the hunter and the man from the Dodge had started gutting the buck. He checked the skies for the helicopter, and when he saw nothing, he climbed from his place in the brush. In a few running steps, he was out of sight of the two men. He dropped into a steady pace down the creek bed.

If Ray-Ray was right, there were four government agencies after him. He'd seen both county and state police vehicles on the roads. The markings on the helicopter showed it was US Army for sure, and if you threw in chubby little Birdie Hawkins from the Department of Wildlife, well, that made the fourth.

How much taxpayer money was being gobbled up by it all? Ray-Ray would wager that the decisions were being made by someone appointed to his job, not even duly elected. If some government muckety-muck had a mind to, they'd use all that tax money they collected from good people to hunt him down.

That was what this was. A vendetta. All because he hadn't bought a hunting license.

A man needed a license to hunt the deer that lived all the year on his land? Foolish. A man should have the right to manage the deer that ate his crops and drank from his well. The government couldn't stick their noses in everyone's business.

Leave me alone. He wanted to scream it.

But instead, Ray-Ray stopped stock-still. He cursed himself. In all his carefulness, he'd missed the one thing he could count on. Quiet hung thick in the air around him. Leaves rustled in the breeze. But there were no sounds from the birds. Not one chirp. No swish of wings.

Maybe the end times had begun.

The Book said that back in the beginning, when things got too out of hand, the Lord had used a great flood to destroy all the wickedness. When it came time to do it again, it wouldn't be water. The God of all creation would destroy the evil ones with fire.

Ray-Ray smelled it on the breeze.

Smoke.

Dry grass curled in the heat, and the flames raced into the leaves and autumn brush in the creek bed. It was almost beautiful. Cecil's breathed in the smoke. He laughed at the crackle.

I'll tell 'em I left work early to go hunting. Came out here. Saw the fire. Some city hunter must've tossed a cigarette out the window. That's what I'll tell 'em. By the time I get back to town, the fire will have burned up two miles of creek bottom.

But I'll be the hero who saved 'em all.

Fingers of smoke filtered through the gulley where Ray-Ray hid. Dry brush hissed and popped. Like a skunk caught in a snare, Ray-Ray's instincts told him to claw and bite and do everything he could to get out.

But he had hidden too well.

There was no way he could scramble up the sheer dirt sides, and the brush and trees that screened him threatened to burst into flame. Like bits of grit spun loose from a grinding wheel, and floating ash found its way onto the backs of Ray-Ray's eyelids. With each blink the texture of fine sandpaper tortured his vision.

He clomped down the creek bottom away from the cackle of flames, stumbling in the sandy soil. Creatures fled with him. A cottontail ran a dozen steps, froze for an instant under a fallen tree limb, and darted off again. A pair of squirrels bounded through the branches overhead. Magpies clattered past.

He gripped his rifle tighter, drew a deep breath, and pushed on. In ten yards, smoke caught in his throat, and he bent over, grabbed his knees, and coughed until he thought his insides would spill out.

A whitetail doe dashed past him. She turned and bounded up the grass-tinged crack in the steep dirt sides of the arroyo. The animal stumbled, slid back, and tried again. Her hooves found traction, and she struggled up, tossing dried clumps of dirt behind her.

Ray-Ray drew in another breath, saw his chance, and followed the deer. Boots slipping, hands grabbing for bits of weeds, he fought his way up the side of the gulley.

Behind him, flames took over the brush. Above the roar, the tortured scream of an animal that was too slow froze the blood in his veins.

The clump of dry grass Ray-Ray had tangled his fingers in pulled loose from the steep bank. He sprawled belly down across the slope, boot toes digging for a grip, to keep from falling to the fiery tangle below. He mashed the side of his face into the dirt, fought for breath, and turned to look below him.

At the base of the hillside, in an island of weeds the fire had not yet consumed, the crumpled form of a young woman lay still. Ashes from the fire all around her fell on the fan of black hair that haloed the girl's face. Her eyes were shut as if she was sleeping.

Ray-Ray loosened his grip and slid down the dirt toward her. Heat touched his face and each lungful of air scorched hotter than the one before.

"Miss?" he croaked. He grabbed her shoulder. "We gotta get out of—"

In spite of the fire all around, her body was cold to the touch. He knew in that instant all he could do was save himself. The hair on the back of his hands curled in the heat. He scrambled and clawed his way up the bank.

When he looked back at the girl, the wind drove a curtain of flames into the weeds around her. Her long hair turned to a thousand twisting curls in the bright orange flames, and the skin on her face melted like warm wax. In the next second the sweep of the fire was past her and her place of rest.

At the top of the gulley, he scrambled under the wire fence and onto the roadway. Tire tracks, which he guessed had been made last night, blemished the dust along the side of the road. He could see the marks where someone had dragged the girl's body to the edge of the road and let it topple over. Pointed toe prints from cowboy boots left the edge and returned to the car. The prints from boots so new that the Tony Lama logo showed in the marks left by the heels.

Ray-Ray watched the fire race away up the creek bottom. On the road without cover, the government men might find him.

Had the bastards lit the fire to smoke him out? And killed the girl, too?

He'd never put anything past them.

Ray-Ray sized up his surroundings. It was three miles across open stubble fields to the stronghold he'd outfitted.

Even in the smoky haze, he could still spot the deer that had led him to safety. Its white rump stuck out as plain as day even though the little doe was a long rifle shot out into the stubble. He couldn't wait. He had to follow.

Ray-Ray checked both ways on the road and coiled to run, but he heard the whirl of an engine struggling to turn over.

Ray-Ray ducked into a wrinkle at the edge of the gulley. He bit back the taste of smoke in his mouth and stifled a cough.

The engine spun again and came to life.

Cecil slid his fat belly behind the steering wheel. Ash fell on the windshield. He turned the key. The old truck coughed.

C'mon.

He hit the ignition again. The engine sputtered but wouldn't turn over.

Damn it.

Smoke filtered in from the cracks around the windows and doors. The stench came up through the vents. Every drop of alcohol in his body evaporated and fear rushed in.

Start, damn you. He turned the key.

Yes!

Cecil slammed the gearshift into reverse and backed into the roadway. He pointed the truck at Brandon and pressed down on the accelerator. At the edge of the burning gulley, tongues of flame as high as the top strand on the barbed-wire fence licked at everything that had ever lived. Grass, weeds, and fence posts shriveled in the heat. A jack rabbit burst from the inferno and raced for safety.

Standing in the middle of the road, an old man raised his hands.

Cecil jammed on the brakes.

Pop Weber?

Chase swung open his pickup's door. "Nice buck. Can I give you a hand?"

The hunter was about Chase's age. His rifle showed nicks and scratches from being carried, and there were old bloodstains on his orange vest. Sun flashed on the edge of the man's hunting knife, and Chase knew the man wouldn't need his help dressing out the buck.

"No sense both of us gettin' our hands bloody." The hunter grabbed a hind leg and rolled the deer on its back.

"That helicopter spook 'em?" Chase asked.

"No. I saw this guy midmornin' and spent the next three hours tryin' to get close enough for a shot. I finally spotted him in the trees down there." He jerked his head toward the creek. "Somethin' on the other side of the road had his interest. I thought it was another hunter. I took my shot just before I heard the helicopter. Any idea why it's here?"

"There's a search for a farmer who went missin'." Chase lifted his cap and smoothed his hair. "Old man with Alzheimer's."

"That's tough. I hope they find him." The man looked up at Chase. The lines around his eyes tightened. "Hey, I think I know you. That Lakers cap. Yeah. Sure." He tapped his knife on the deer's belly. "You're Chase Ford, the ballplayer. I was at CU when you played. Never missed a game. You were good back then."

Back then? Chase let himself nod. So much had changed.

The hunter went on, "I remember now. You grew up down here, didn't you? What are you doin' these days? Since all that stuff about your wife—I mean ex-wife."

Chase raised his hand. "Wait." Something in the air seemed wrong. He sniffed again. "Do you smell smoke?"

CHAPTER NINETEEN

The prairie grass bent in the gusting wind until the tips of the stalks touched the dust like faint brushstrokes. Each second the wind grew colder. The breeze beat the side of Chase's truck and breathy blasts whistled around his ears.

"Do you hear that?" Chase asked the hunter. Even over the wind, Chase could make out a faint wailing noise. No more than a distant whine.

"I do hear somethin'." The man raised his head. "But in this wind—" His face strained. "Is that a siren?"

Chase knew the sound. He turned on his heel and started for his truck. "I better go." And he left the man with his deer.

The siren was coming from town.

Calling for the volunteers.

The volunteer fire department.

It was smoke he'd smelled.

Chase scanned the skies over Brandon. Nothing. He looked west. Feathery wisps of gray formed an angry column, maybe five miles off.

Chase slammed the door of his pickup shut, turned the key, and bumped over the rough pasture ground. The fire truck from

Brandon barreled down the county road and over the bridge at Sandy Creek. By the time Chase made it to the pasture gate, two pickups had caught up to the fire truck. Chase leaped out of his truck, dropped the gate to the side, jumped back in the cab, and rolled through.

The fire truck turned south. The pickups fell in behind. A county sheriff's car with flashing lights caught up to the three. Chase checked the western sky again. The smoke pillar had doubled in size. Against the dark clouds, it boiled and tumbled back on itself.

Birdie was about to turn off the highway to the spot along Sandy Creek where she'd seen Cecil's vigilantes unloading their horses when the radio in her truck squawked to life. At the same instant her cell phone rang. She snatched the cell from her jacket pocket and pressed the phone to her ear. The automated voice of a prerecorded warning message began to play. She tossed the phone on the seat beside her and hit a button on the radio.

"What is it, Arlene?" Birdie said into the microphone.

"Fire on Sandy Creek ten miles south of town. It's already jumped up from the creek bottom. I just got a call from Connie Mason. She says it's bad, Birdie. We're gonna need all the help we can get."

"I'm on my way."

The speedometer showed seventy-plus when Birdie turned off the asphalt onto the dirt road along Sandy Creek. She knew she was ten miles from the Masons' farm when she saw the smoke in the sky.

"Holy hell."

She jammed her foot onto the gas pedal.

"Get over." Marty gritted his teeth and raced his patrol car up behind the pickups following the volunteer fire department truck. "Come on. Come on," he hissed through his teeth. "Get out of my way." He flipped the siren switch on the dashboard. The warning wailed, and the fire truck and its followers eased to the shoulder of the road but never slowed. "Good. Good. Stay there." He floored the cruiser and shot around the firemen.

Billows of dark smoke rose from the tangles of brush and cottonwoods in the twisted creek bottom a mile away. Flying ash pelted his windshield, convincing him of what he feared. The wind was from the west and would funnel the fire through the dry fuel along the creek toward town. He slowed enough to make the turn onto the single-lane bridge that led to the Masons' farm. In his rearview mirror, the fire truck and pickups sped past the turn.

Bill was the third generation of Masons to live in the frame house at the curve of Sandy Creek. Like every other farmer in the county, Bill was apt to be too stubborn to do anything but fight to save what was his. Marty knew he might have to knock Bill on the head and throw him in the back of his car to get him to leave his farm to the fire. But Marty had to get Bill Mason and his wife out.

Flames crawled through the dead grass up from the creek and then flared taller than the barbed wire in the knots of tumbleweed caught in the fence. Fire spilled from the fence into Mason's wheat stubble. Like falling dominos the fire moved from row to row through the knee-high stalks of cut wheat.

Marty bounced the car over the rutted road and into the Masons' farmyard. Clothes on the line popped in the wind. Ash mixed with tongues of wind-driven dust blasted across the hard-packed ground. The back door on the faded white house swung open. Connie Mason, wide-eyed and with her grandbaby on her hip, came down the porch steps two at a time.

"Where's Bill?" Marty yelled over the wind.

Connie met Marty at his car. "Bill's not here." She pushed the baby at him with both hands. "Take her. I gotta save the house."

"No, you're not."

A fiery bit of trash carried by the wind fell in the dry weeds near one the outbuildings. Flames crackled to life.

Marty caught Connie's arm and shoved the woman and baby into his car. "You're gettin' out of here now." She fought his grip. "Where's Bill?" he asked again.

"He's with the others. Lookin' for Pop Weber." The old woman's eyes pleaded. "The house, Marty. It's all we have."

Where the power lines crossed Sandy Creek, ugly flames climbed up a pole. The cable snapped like a rifle shot, and a shower of orange sparks arced across the sky.

"I'll do what I can, I promise." He pressed his car keys into her hand and pushed her and the baby down on the seat.

"Marty—" Connie's tears spilled from her eyes.

"Where does Bill keep his tractor keys?"

"On a hook. Just inside the kitchen door."

"Get outta here now." He shoved the car door shut.

Connie held the baby tight to her chest with one arm. She reached across the steering wheel with the other, turned the key, and dropped the sheriff's car into gear. The woman swung the car in a half circle and drove to the bridge across Sandy Creek and away from the fire.

Marty sprinted toward the farmhouse.

The back door wasn't locked. It probably never had been in all the years the Masons had lived there. From a shiny nail on the wall, Marty tossed a ring of house and car keys on the floor and snatched a braided piece of leather with a single key he knew would fit the Massey Ferguson he'd seen parked in the shade of the barn.

He bounded off the porch and ran to the tractor, wind and blowing ash peppering his face. As if each row of wheat stubble was a fuse to the next, the wall of fire had burned row by row to a third of the way across the field. A dozen fiery tumbleweeds cartwheeled ahead of the marching inferno.

Marty jumped up onto the tractor and jammed the key into the ignition. The engine rumbled to life. The only chance he could think of was to get ahead of the army of flames and plow up fresh dirt so the fire would run of out of fuel before it could reach the house and barns.

But Bill Mason's plowing discs sat in a tangle of dried weeds near the fence that separated the farmyard from the stubble field. The discs hadn't been hooked to the tractor since spring. Two men could hitch the attachment onto the tractor in ten minutes. It would take one man most of an hour.

He shifted the tractor into gear and rumbled across the farmyard to the discs. He cut a sharp turn, backed up, and leaped from the tractor. Smoke and grit burned his eyes and wind popped in his ears. He fumbled with a spaghetti tangle of red and yellow hydraulic hoses knotted in the stalks of dried weeds and began to hook them to the tractor. The wind took his Stetson from the top of his head.

Marty glanced at the fire. He didn't have an hour. And he wasn't two men.

Red road dust swirled in the gray smoke. Far ahead, in the haze, Chase could make out the flashing lights on the county fire truck.

He pressed down on the gas pedal and raced down the dirt road. From the turnoff to the Masons' place, a sheriff's car that looked like the one Marty had been driving swerved onto the road ahead of Chase. A gray-haired woman sat behind the wheel. Not Marty.

Chase hit the brakes, and his truck slid sidewise on the washboard. He fought the steering wheel, righted the Dodge a dozen yards from the patrol car, and was out of the door as it slid to a stop.

"Where's Marty?" he bellowed into the wind.

The window was down on the sheriff's car. Chase recognized the woman. It was Connie Mason. She'd been one of the few women in the county who visited his mother after the accident. She came almost every Tuesday and always brought something she'd baked.

"Oh, Chase. Thank God." Her face was wet with tears. She hugged a bundled baby close to her. "You've got to get him out of there. I shouldn't have let him make me leave."

"Who, Connie?" *Was she talking about her husband? Or Marty? Why'd she have his car?* The thoughts raced through his mind as fast as the prairie fire.

"It's Marty." She patted the baby's head and mumbled something comforting. "He's trying to save my house."

Smoke stung Chase's eyes. The flames had crawled up the creek bottom to within a hundred yards of the road to Masons' place.

"Get him out of there, Chase. He's goin' to die."

Chase bit down on his tongue. *Damn it, Marty.* "You go, Connie. I'll get him."

Like a cloudy sky that refused to let the wind take the smoke away, the terror came like a nightmare. Yellow flames in the distance. The whoosh of the wind. The cries of a frightened horse. And everything murky with gray smoke.

But dreams come in random bursts and float in one's mind without sequence. Everything about this horror had purpose. The wall of flames marched like an angry army across the field. Smoke clung to his tongue and teeth in grainy, bitter fragments.

He wheeled his truck into the yard in front of the farmhouse.

A chestnut mare tossed herself, wild-eyed, against a corral fence. Her lips drew back from her teeth, and her scream of pure terror iced Chase's veins. Chase jumped from the truck, threw open the corral gate, and slapped the horse's rump as she fled by him.

At least she'll have a chance.

Then he spotted Marty. His best friend was backlit by the wall of fire. He knelt behind a tractor and dug with his hands into the dry weeds around him—dry weeds that could explode with the next spark.

What the . . .

Then Chase saw the plow.

Damn him. He's going Eastwood.

Eastwood. That's what they'd dared each other sixteen years ago. Going Eastwood. Racing tractors, bull riding, surfing on the hood of a speeding pickup, or any of the dozen other stunts they did when they were seventeen and bulletproof, immortal. When a mistake meant a chipped tooth or scrapes and cuts, and anything worse happened to someone else. Back then Marty would never back down.

Damn him.

Chase ran to his friend. He grabbed Marty's shoulder and pulled him around. "We got to get out of here."

"No, Chase. Help me." Marty tugged away from Chase's grip. "It's no use."

With each second the fire gobbled up another stubble row. Now it was just fifty yards away.

Chase grabbed at Marty again.

Marty batted Chase's hand from his shoulder. "No. I almost got it." And he snapped the quick connectors of two hoses together. "Help me with the hitch."

"Leave it to burn, Marty."

"Chase, we can do it." He grabbed another set of hoses from the tangle in the weeds.

Chase shook his head. *We're both fools.*

But Marty scrambled up onto the tractor seat, jammed gears, and moved the tractor back a foot.

A burning tumbleweed somersaulted into the weed patch with the plow. Chase stomped the sparks before they could flare. He straddled the hitch and heaved up. The ball was still inches from the tractor. "More."

Marty let off the clutch and tractor rolled a few inches.

"Good." Chase dropped the coupler over the ball. Hydraulic hoses stiffened with life. Chase heard the whoosh of oil moving to the plow. He snapped the hitch lock closed. "I'll get the gate," he hollered.

"No time."

The tractor lurched forward through the weeds. In two running steps, Chase caught hold of a bracket on the tractor's rearview mirror and swung onto the machine's side steps.

"Hold on," Marty yelled, and he aimed the tractor at the fence.

A cedar fence post exploded into a thousand splinters at the front of the Massey Ferguson. Barbed wire stretched tight across the tractor's cowl and sang out as each strand broke away. A ragged end whipped by Chase's face.

With a jolt, Chase, Marty, and the tractor were in the field with the fire.

Chase held tight. Marty swung the tractor parallel to the coming flames. The deputy pulled a lever on the hydraulic pump. Behind the moving tractor, on the plow they'd worked so hard to hitch up, the silver discs began to spin. Marty jammed another lever, and the discs lowered to the ground and fought to cut into the dirt.

Marty edged the tractor closer to the moving flames. He looked over his shoulder. "Shit. It's not bitin'."

The silver discs danced over the surface of the drought-hardened ground, refusing to cut in.

Chase remembered how his father, in the dry years, had tied bags of cement, cinder blocks, anything that would add weight to the top of their plow just to make the sharp discs break through the hard crust and tear in. Sometimes just a few more pounds was enough.

"Slow down," Chase yelled, and dropped from the side of the tractor.

"What are you doin'?" Marty slowed the tractor to a crawl.

"Eastwood." As the plow rolled by, Chase sprawled his rangy length across the top of the machine. The toes of his boots dangled close to turning discs, and the fingers of one hand gripped just inches from a turning wheel. He turned his face to where the discs met the ground.

Damn it. Cut.

Brittle stalks of wheat stubble snapped as the plow passed. Just inches from his eyes, the discs carved through the crusty soil, churning up fresh dirt and biting deeper with each turn. New dirt churned into the air. He turned away and clamped his eyes shut. The tractor jerked as Marty shifted gears and moved faster.

Chase heard his friend bellow out, "Eastwood."

A chocolate stripe of fresh dirt, three plow-widths wide, separated the scorched field from the rows of wheat stubble the color of dirty honey. Here and there flames sputtered on the blackened, burned ground, and while the wind held its breath, thick dust hung in the smoky air.

Chase rolled off the plow. Bruises on his shins and thighs ached, and his fingers cramped into twisted hooks from clinging to the plow. He crawled to the back of the tractor and propped his head against the knobby tire treads so he could see where the Masons' farmhouse still stood. Safe and untouched.

Marty cut the engine and slid down beside his friend. He found a shaft of straw on the ground, hung it between his lips, and leaned back against the tire. "You know, if you hadn't gained all the weight after you quit playin' I don't think that would've worked, Eastwood."

"Shut up." Chase tried to spit out the dirt that caked his mouth. "I got a mouthful of cow shit."

Marty huffed out a breath and pushed his fingers through his dirty hair. "No, that'd be horse shit. If you came back home more often, you'd remember how the two taste different." He plucked a dirt clod from the ground and lobbed it out into the field. "We did it, didn't we?"

We did it, didn't we? The last time Chase had heard Marty say that was in the big-city locker room after Brandon won the state title. Everyone else was gone except the two senior boys. Chase and Marty couldn't let that minute end.

Brandon had been down five points with twenty-eight seconds left, when Marty was fouled making a layup. The guy who couldn't make three out of ten free throws in practice swished that one. Chase got a steal and hit a jumper to tie the game at the buzzer and then scored sixteen in overtime and was carried off the court on the shoulders of half of Brandon. The town still talked about that game, and Marty's three points had been forgotten by everyone but Chase.

He looked up at his friend, too sore and too tired to move. "Yeah, Marty, we did it."

The deputy brushed dust from the front of his shirt and leaned back against the tractor tire. "You know somethin' else?"

"What's that?"

"You let Mason's horse out of the corral, didn't you?"

"Yeah."

"You're gonna hafta catch it by yourself, Eastwood."

CHAPTER TWENTY

At the bridge to the Masons' farm, Birdie gave the finger to the volunteer fireman who waved for her to stop. She dodged around the back of his pickup and sprayed gravel at the man's truck. When she checked the rearview mirror he had his hands on both hips and was shaking his head. She didn't care. She had to get to Chase and Marty.

In the farmyard, the door to Chase's Dodge hung open and the wind banged a corral gate against a rail fence. Spirals of broken barbed wire stabbed the sky on both sides of a busted fence post. She pointed her pickup at the tire tracks from the tractor and drove through the opening in the fence out into the field.

Just where the wheat stubble met the plow-turned dirt, Chase stretched across the ground with his head resting on his folded arms. Marty sat on the ground beside him with his back against the tractor tire. Wisps of smoke from the dying fire drifted around the silent Massey Ferguson.

Her heart climbed into her throat.

One of 'em's hurt.

She pulled up close, opened the door to her truck, and before her stubby legs touched the ground, Birdie heard something that made her red-faced mad.

The two pricks were laughing.

"Damn it," she shouted, and slammed the door behind her. "I half expected to find you two all burned up, and now you're playin' in the dirt and gigglin' like two schoolboys who got a peek at their first *Playboy* magazine." She kicked a cascade of dust and dirt clods at Chase and Marty. "Damn you two." She rubbed her face to hide her smile. "Either of you hurt any?"

Chase raised up onto his elbows. "A little banged up, but we're fine, Birdie."

His knuckles were scraped and bloody, and when he smiled white skin showed through the dirt in the creases around his mouth. Right then Birdie didn't know what she would have done if he hadn't been okay. She wanted to cry but couldn't let him see her do that. She had to be Birdie, the tomboy. One of the guys. Just another friend. Not Birdie, the girl who had always loved Chase Ford. She couldn't look at Chase, so Birdie did what she always did when life confused her. She put on her tough act.

She snatched up a dirt clod the size of a hen's egg and heaved it at the side of the tractor. It exploded into a cloud of dust just over Marty's head. "Damn you, too, Marty Storm. Connie Mason is tellin' everybody how you made her take your car and promised you'd save her house. Playin' big hero, huh?" She stepped right up to where he sat and pointed her short, thick finger in his face. "Did you think for one minute about your wife and boys?" She stared down at him and trembled with what she wanted to be anger, but Birdie knew it was fear, or relief, or maybe it was love. "If I didn't care about your wife so much, I'd twist both your nuts off with a pair of fencin' pliers. And I'd do it right now." And she gritted her teeth because she needed to cry.

"Settle down, Birdie," Chase said.

"Settle down, my ass." She stomped back to her truck. Her hand shook when she reached for the door handle, and Birdie wanted long legs and blond hair and for Chase to look at her the way he always looked at Mercy. She wanted to be the woman standing next to him on the cover of the old *People* magazine that she kept hidden in a toolbox in the back of her pickup. But most of all, right then, Birdie didn't want to be Birdie. She stood with her hand on the door and stared across the prairie, so glad nothing had happened to him.

"Birdie," Chase called.

"What?" she snapped over her shoulder.

"Birdie, what about the fire? Did they get it under control?"

"Yeah." She sucked in a breath. "The boys decided the best place to fight it was 'bout a mile up the road." A dirty finger stopped a tear before it left her eye. "You know the place where there's that one big cottonwood and the creek bottom squeezes in real narrow-like? Seemed like every farmer in twenty miles was there with a chainsaw or shovel, choppin' trees and brush as that wall of fire came at 'em. Someone remembered where the county left one of their graders up the road. That Collins kid hotwired it, and they busted through a fence and scraped everythin' that might burn out of the creek bed for about a hundred yards."

She couldn't look at Chase. "The firebreak stopped it from movin' east. The road stopped it on the south and through the smoke, we could see you two turnin' dirt in Mason's field. The wind changed just enough to slow it, but I . . . ah . . . *we* couldn't see you through the smoke and dust you were churnin' up." She rubbed her mouth with the back of her hand. "If you two wouldn't have done what you did, it might still be burnin' fields and farms all the way to town." She wanted to see Chase's dirty face again and remind herself he was all right, but she couldn't let him see her wet eyes. "You did good. It was brave. Damn stupid, but brave." She rubbed her eyes.

Chase hauled himself up from the ground and started toward her. "What's wrong, Birdie?"

She waved for him not to come closer. "Damned smoke in my eyes, that's all."

From the way she said that, Chase knew it wasn't the smoke in Birdie's eyes. Something was wrong. It wasn't in her voice, the way she said it, or even the tone. It was the way the moment squeezed his gut when she spoke. So much like the way Billee spoke when the pills steered his life so far from hers.

When one pill eased the pain in his knee. The second numbed life around him. And the next took him hundreds of miles out of his mind. Until that day one too many pills turned numbness to rage.

Birdie glanced back. Her eyes searched deep inside him, begging him to speak to her. But his throat knotted, and he wanted those pills he had sworn to Billee, to the others in the room with that circle of chairs, and to God above that he'd never touch again. He clamped his eyes shut and prayed for something to rescue him from that moment, and when he opened them his rescuer was a GMC pickup.

Chase's throat opened, and he breathed out. "Look who's comin'."

The lights on the top of Kendall's new GMC flashed red and blue. The sheriff followed the tracks Birdie's truck had crushed into the stubble.

Chase turned, reached down, and took Marty's hand to pull him to his feet. With his next breath he swallowed away the need for the pill.

Marty brushed off the seat of his pants. "Just what we need."

The sheriff's truck veered off the tire tracks and pulled up next to Birdie's truck. Kendall jerked open the door and in two steps he pushed by Chase and was chin to chin with Marty. "Deputy, what the hell do you think you're doin'?"

"Sir?"

"You let a civilian take your car. Decided to fight the fire on your own?" Spittle sprayed from the sheriff's mouth, and the muscles in his jaws bunched. "Explain yourself."

"Sheriff," Chase said.

"Stay out of this, Ford."

"Sheriff." Chase pointed at the others who'd come to rescue him from Birdie. "If you wait a minute, Marty can explain it to everyone. They probably want to hear about it, too."

A string of pickups full of sooty-faced volunteer firemen drove through the farmyard and out into the field. Windows were rolled down, fists pumped, and men cheered. Near the end of the line was Marty's patrol car. As they came closer, Chase spotted Connie Mason still at the wheel. Someone had shown her how to turn on the flashing lights. Bringing up the rear of the parade was a van marked with the logo of the TV station from Colorado Springs.

Kendall tapped the front of Marty's shirt with his finger. "We'll talk about this later." As he walked around the side of his pickup, Kendall bent down and scooped up a handful of sooty dirt. He smeared some across his clean shirt and touched his face with his dirty fingers.

Birdie stepped up next to Chase—the old Birdie, the one he understood, not the one he'd tried to figure out moments before—and they watched the sheriff walk out to meet the newcomers. "You hold him," she said to Chase. "I'll get my fencin' pliers."

The men from the trucks rushed by Chase and Birdie to get to Marty. There was laughter and back slaps and as much noise as there had been sixteen years before when Chase was the hero of that basketball game in Denver. Chase half expected them to lift Marty onto their shoulders. Kendall leaned against the side of his truck, and his attention seemed more fixed on the van from the TV station than the celebration.

"Listen up," Earl Collins shouted out.

Chase recognized him from high school. Earl had been two years ahead of him in school and had the rounded shoulders and bull neck that a man gets from swinging eighty-pound hay bales onto the back of a flatbed trailer for most of his life. A white fire helmet smudged with black soot sat on his head. All the other helmets were red.

Earl threw his huge arm over Marty's shoulder. "Listen up," he said a second time. "Every one of ya did a great job out there today. I'm proud of ya."

"Does that mean you're buyin' the beer tonight?" A voice called from the circle. Thick laughter followed.

"Not hardly. I've seen all you can drink." He laughed with his men. "Besides, we still have work to do." He lifted his arm from Marty. "I want A and B squad to drive the perimeter and watch for hot spots. We don't dare let anything flare up again. Taylor's bunch needs to go back west, and the other swing north." He paused and looked over the group. "Rest of ya, we got an old man to find. There's still a girl who could be out there somewhere. Stow your gear, and let's meet back at County Road Seventeen and Sandy Creek. We only got a couple more hours before it gets dark. From the looks of this sky"—Earl raised his face, and every man in the circle looked at the dark clouds building on the horizon to the north—"we could be in for snow tonight. Y'all know Pop will never make it if it turns cold."

Chase tugged up the zipper of his jacket at the hint of chill in the air. Birdie fished a handkerchief from her hip pocket and wiped her eyes. When Chase looked at her, she glanced away.

"Sheriff?" Earl Collins called out. "Anythin' else you want these men to be doin'?"

Kendall had left the circle and was halfway to the TV truck. He turned back to answer. "You covered it all, Earl." Kendall touched the brim of his cowboy hat with two fingers in what Chase took for a mock salute. The sheriff raised his voice. "The county thanks each and every one of you."

"That dickwad sounds like he's makin' a speech for his next election," Birdie said just loud enough for Chase to hear, and she spat on the ground.

"Some things never change," Chase answered. "Look where he's headed."

Kendall walked up to a young, blond woman near the TV van. His stern look turned to a big smile.

CHAPTER TWENTY-ONE

Jody Rose lifted her thick hair and slipped in the earpiece. "You be sure that burned field shows in the shot," she barked to the man with the camera on his shoulder.

"Hey, I know what I'm doin'," he said. "Now let's get on with it, before what's left of the smoke drifts away."

"I'm almost ready." In spite of the cold, Jody wriggled out of her parka and let it drop to the ground. She tucked her shirttail into the top of her jeans and made sure the denim shirt pulled tight across her breasts.

She'd caught a break. The news manager had decided to give her this live shot at halftime of the Broncos game. Half the state of Colorado would be watching. Jody wanted this on the demo disc her agent had promised to send to the networks.

She stepped away from the van and motioned for Kendall. "Sheriff, stand here." Jody moved him beside her. She ran her fingers through her hair again and pulled the wind-whipped strands from the corner of her mouth. "Ready."

The man with the camera tapped his headset. "Going live in three . . . two . . . one . . . and you're on."

"Most regard Comanche County as a quiet place." Everything

slipped away but Jody's focus on the camera lens. "Take exit four-one-four from Interstate Seventy and drive thirty miles south on the two-lane road. It's a slice of yesterday's slower pace." She decided to drop the Andy Griffith Mayberry imagery she'd toyed with. Too sugary. "People here know their neighbors by name. Even if that neighbor's farm is ten miles down the road. No one locks their doors."

She could imagine what she looked like in the lens of the camera. Hair teased by the prairie wind. Behind her, rolling fields, some still smoldering from the fire. Standing next to the tall lawman in the cowboy hat. This was a once-in-a-career opportunity. Jody inhaled, and the smell of the smoke and fresh dirt fueled her.

"All that changed Saturday morning." Jody had to hold on to each second and make it work for her. She looked into the camera as if it were her friend. "The body of a high school student was discovered in a field just five miles from the sleepy town of Brandon. And when the sun came up this morning, Brandon High School's beloved basketball coach, Robert Porter, had been found stabbed to death in his home. Are the killings connected? Is a serial killer at work in Comanche County?"

Jody paused. "But there's more to this story. This morning eighty-seven-year-old local farmer Alfred 'Pop' Weber's abandoned truck was found on a county road. Friends, units of the National Guard, and helicopters from Fort Carson have joined the Sheriff's Department to search. You see, their friend Pop suffers from Alzheimer's." She stared at the lens and imagined viewers thinking of their own grandparents. "And within the last half hour, volunteer firefighters stopped a suspicious prairie fire that threatened farms and ranches." She touched Kendall's arm lightly and below the level of the camera shot—like she'd told him she would do. "I'm here with Comanche County Sheriff Lincoln Kendall to give us the latest on this series of unthinkable events." For the first time, Jody turned from the camera and looked up at the man beside her. "Sheriff, do I understand you're also looking for a missing high school girl?"

She knew Kendall was ready. No need to worry about that. Kendall was a man who used events and people to his own advantage. He wouldn't waste a few minutes in front of a TV camera. Right now, he thought he was using her. But she was way ahead of him.

"Thank you, Jody." Kendall touched the brim of his hat. "We are tryin' to find out what we can about the girl, but right now I'm more concerned about the old farmer. I told my team that Pop Weber is our top concern."

She smiled at just the right amount of cowboy twang in his voice.

Kendall fixed his eyes on the camera. "The volunteer fire department out of Brandon did a helluva job on this fire. They got it stopped before it could do any real damage. One of my deputies, Marty Storm, was a hero today. I'm proud of that boy."

Jody made a mental note to find out more about the hero.

"Right now," Kendall went on, "our priority is findin' the two missin' folks. I've asked the state for their help investigatin' the cause of the fire."

"Does that mean you think the fire was set on purpose?" Jody asked.

"The cause of the fire is yet to be determined. Let's just say I've asked them to investigate all possibilities."

Jody hid the tremor of excitement that coursed up her spine. The story just kept getting better.

"Sheriff, what can you tell us about the murders?"

"Hold on, little lady."

Little lady? No. Too much. Jody nudged his leg with her knee. For one second she turned her concerned look to a glare.

His eyes flashed with recognition that he'd crossed one of the lines she warned him about. No matter, she could edit it out of the tape going to the networks.

Kendall touched the shiny scar at the corner of one of his eyes. "The county has had two deaths in the last twenty-four hours. Both under suspicious circumstances. My department and the Colorado Bureau of Investigation are knee-deep in this. We'll have coroner findings sometime tomorrow. That's all I can say for right now."

"And the search for Mr. Weber and the girl?"

"Fightin' the fire took all our resources, but I've asked the volunteer fire department to help us out. Those boys'll be in the field shortly."

Jody moved the microphone from Kendall and held it to her mouth. "Thank you, Sheriff. We'll have more at six. Jody Rose, reporting live from Comanche County."

The camera man gave a thumbs up.

Jody touched Kendall's arm before he could walk away. "Thank you, Lincoln. I can call you Lincoln, can't I?" She used the head tilt that always seemed to work.

"Sure, if I can call you Jody."

She had him now. "I wouldn't have it any other way."

Near the Masons' house, the clothes that Connie had pinned to the line began to dance in the cold wind. Dark clouds boiled on the north horizon, and color faded from the blue sky like old Levi's.

Chase stepped up to Marty as the last fireman slapped a "good-bye and good job" on the deputy's shoulder. Chase tipped his head toward Kendall. "I overheard him tell that reporter that you're a hero. She'll probably be over here next wantin' to put you on TV."

"I'd better find my hat and get away before Kendall changes his mind and wants my job."

"Birdie went to look for your hat." Chase shifted his weight from one leg to the other. "Somethin's botherin' her. You got any idea what it is?"

Marty shook his head. "You're one dumb son of a bitch, Chase Ford."

"Huh?"

"You don't see it?"

"See what?"

"Birdie has—whatcha call it?" Marty mopped the dirty sweat from his forehead. "Uh—feelings for you. And she has since high school. Seein' you again, after you'd been away for sixteen years, brought it all back."

"What makes you think that?"

"My wife told me." Marty bit down on his lip. "Deb says she's always thought so and that she could see it for sure by the way Birdie was actin' when you were with Mercy at the pancake supper over at the church."

Marty's words hit Chase like an elbow to the ribs.

Birdie? Feelings for him?

He'd never thought of her like that. Birdie was just—Chase's mind stuttered. Birdie was just Birdie. Shooting baskets in the gym with the guys. Riding in the back of his pickup when Mercy was on the front seat between him and Marty. Birdie out in the parking lot after every ball game. With a cigarette in her mouth. She'd know how many points everyone had scored. Especially him.

But Birdie?

Chase always had an easy time with the girls. After Mercy, there'd been a series of pretty cheerleader types in college. Girls who liked a guy who was six feet seven with long blond hair, who had his name in the paper after every ball game. Girls who giggled at his polite country manners. Out in Los Angeles, after he signed with the Lakers, more girls. Models. Movie star wannabes, and even some for-real movie stars. Then he found Billee.

They were all good-looking, too. Every one of them. Not at all like—

Not like Birdie.

Besides, Birdie was just a friend. And she was a good friend. Didn't she know that?

Chase dug the tip of his tongue into the side out his cheek.

Oh, God, did I hurt Birdie?

Now all his doubts banged in his chest. And touched his heart.

Out near the torn fence, Birdie plucked Marty's Stetson from the sagebrush near where they'd hitched the plow. She dusted the dirt off the hat and started back to where he stood with Marty. Marching across the field all stiff kneed, just the way Birdie always walked.

Chase needed to say something to her. Maybe apologize. Maybe just tell Birdie that he'd missed her while he was away.

He looked at Marty.

Marty just shook his head.

Just then, another woman started toward them.

"Mr. Ford?" the TV reporter called out. "Chase Ford? I'm not sure, but you might remember me? I'm Jody Rose. We met seven years ago. In Los Angeles. You were doing the color for the Lakers broadcasts. I was an intern. It was my last year of college. We worked together for a couple of months."

Chase looked down at the woman. "Jody?"

"Actually, it was Janet Rosemont back then. I use Jody Rose as my TV name. Now most people call me Jody."

Seven years ago had been when the pills were the worst. Nights at the games blurred. So did the women from that time.

"I'm not sure I—"

Jody, or Janet, or whatever she called herself, smiled up at him. Thick blond hair framed big blue eyes and a pouty set of lips. She was pretty. Very pretty.

"No matter," she said. "I was just a lowly college intern. But you were always kind to me. I'm working for the TV station in Colorado Springs. On assignment to cover the murders." She tilted her head. "I was wondering . . ."

Birdie walked up and handed Marty his hat. Chase wanted to say something to her, but Jody Rose was there and before he could make his mouth work, Birdie walked away.

Jody was still talking. ". . . an interview. Maybe you could share a little bit about how things have changed since you've been gone. And I hear you stayed friends with Coach Porter." She paused and her lips turned down. "I'm so sorry about his death. Would you consider it, Mr. Ford?"

Chase watched Birdie's pickup pull away.

Some part of him knew he should run away from the reporter and stop Birdie's truck and tell her—

Tell her what?

Chase had no idea what he should say.

When he looked back at the reporter, the woman's face lit in the same kind of smile he remembered from when camera lights shined and microphones were shoved in his face by girls just like Jody Rose.

Jody tilted her head, and her smile moved from her lips to the corners of her eyes.

"Ma'am, you can call me Chase."

Jody Rose knew she was good at what she did. Chase Ford could be just the piece she needed to get out of Colorado Springs. A big market or a network gig was next on her plan.

And now the fallen hero was right in front of her.

Chase Ford, the cowboy from Colorado, had been a media darling. Tall, handsome, the white star in a sport dominated by black players. Didn't hurt that he married that country music sensation. People couldn't decide who was prettier, him or his wife.

Then one night, in front of the kind of a national TV audience that advertisers drool over, Chase Ford went rock-star famous. After scoring three dozen points and with the game on the line, Chase was knocked to the floor on a slashing drive to the basket. Hurt his knee, she remembered. After a long timeout, with no time on the clock, Chase limped to the line and made the first free throw to tie the game.

A hack sports writer couldn't come up with a more dramatic ending. If he made the next shot, the Lakers would win. A miss, and the game would go to overtime with Chase too badly injured to play. As the second shot dropped through the bottom of the net, he collapsed on the floor holding the knee. But the Lakers had the championship. The next morning everyone in America— maybe the world—knew Chase's name.

For the following year, his face was on billboards, magazine spreads, and TV commercials everywhere, selling Band-Aids, soda pop, and Levi's.

Chase never was the same after the surgery. There were rumors of drugs, domestic violence. The storybook marriage fell apart. When Chase was forced to retire from playing, he tried TV. He was an embarrassment as a sportscaster, and then one day Chase Ford just disappeared. What did they say? Fell off the radar.

Now Jody had found him in Cow Pie, Colorado. Right in the

middle of a serial murder story. Just what Jody needed to assure the next step in her plan.

She smiled at him again. "Thank you. Chase."

Chase Ford was no better than the hick sheriff. He fell for her full tilt. And even the lie about being a college intern.

Jody Rose knew she was good at what she did.

Kendall didn't like the way Jody Rose cozied up to Chase Ford. She batted her eyes, and he smiled down at her with the same *aw shucks, ma'am* way of his that the TV ate up. It made Kendall want to puke each time he saw one of those commercials, and it made him want to puke right then.

Kendall probed his wad of Skoal with the tip of his tongue. He thought things over and decided to send a deputy to pull Chase away from Jody and tell Chase that he was expected in Brandon for an interview with the state police. Marty Storm would be the right one to send.

Rub a little shit in both their faces.

But Marty was across the fence, helping Connie Mason put a horse into the corral. Kendall spotted Paco and started to motion for him to come over. But Paco was already headed his way.

"Sheriff?" Paco's breath turned gray in the cold, and Kendall could tell something was bothering the old deputy. "Sheriff, some firemen out puttin' out hot spots just called in. They found a body."

"Pop Weber?"

"No, sir." Paco shook his head. "It's a girl. They said she's wearin' a Brandon High letter jacket." Paco paused. "Jimmy Riley's name was embroidered on the inside. It could be—"

Kendall looked back at Chase Ford. "Dolly Benavidez."

CHAPTER TWENTY-TWO

Over the top of Jody's head, Chase watched Marty push his way into the huddle of deputies and state police crowded around Sheriff Kendall. The smiles and laughs from the victory over the fire had disappeared.

Pop. They must have found Pop.

Marty listened for a minute to whatever the men discussed and then looked at Chase.

It wasn't good.

"Listen, Jody." Chase had dodged the reporter's question about how soon they could get together for an interview. "We'll have to talk about this later." He left Jody and walked toward Marty and the others.

Marty nodded to the other lawmen, stepped away, and came to meet him.

"What is it?" Chase asked.

Marty hung his shoulders and looked at the ground between his boots. "Too soon to say."

"You know somethin', Marty. What is it?" His words were flat and measured.

"Damn it, Chase, I can't say 'til we know for sure."

"They found Pop, didn't they?" His mouth went dry. "He's dead?"

"No, it ain't Pop."

"Marty?"

Kendall's shadow filled the ground between them. "Go ahead and tell him, Marty." The sheriff stepped in close, as if he was about to enjoy whatever came next.

Chase's nerves stood on end.

"Not 'til we know for sure, Sheriff." Marty shoved his way between his friend and the sheriff. "It ain't right."

Kendall fingertips traced the shiny scar beside his eye, but his glare never left Chase. "I'll tell him then."

"No, Sheriff."

He pushed Marty out of the way with his forearm. The smile on Kendall's face turned cruel. "Chase, some of the volunteer firemen called in a few minutes ago. Seems they found a body not too far from where we think the fire got started." He paused and shifted the tobacco under his cheek. "A girl's body. They think it might be your half-sister, Dolly."

A pain worse than it had ever been stabbed through Chase's head and ripped its way down to his knee. He wanted to cry and scream, and his fists balled to lash out at Kendall.

Marty pushed him back. "We don't know that yet. It might not be her." He turned and looked at Kendall and then back at Chase. "I'm goin' out there right now. I'll find out. I'll call as soon as we know for sure. I promise you. I promise."

Thoughts tumbled in Chase's head. His fists tightened harder as he struggled to comprehend it all. *Coach. And now Dolly?* He craved the pills. And the place they made for him to hide and make himself numb to the hurt.

Kendall tapped his finger on Chase's chest. Chase slapped it away and cocked his arm to swing.

Marty pushed him back two steps. "Not now, Chase."

Kendall pointed with the same finger. "Get your ass into Brandon, Ford. You're gonna tell the state police everything you've done since you came back and every place you've been. And you're gonna wait until I get there, and then you're gonna tell me the same thing.

There's three dead bodies in my county on the first weekend you've been back in sixteen years." The smile faded. "I want to know why."

Birdie told herself she needed space between her and the sheriff. A whole lot of space. She unhitched her gun belt, tossed it on the passenger seat, and aimed her pickup for the far side of the county.

But it was a lie. It was Chase she needed to get away from.

She wanted to tell him how she felt. But Birdie couldn't put it into words because she had lied to herself since high school.

She left the Masons' place, made the curve on the road along Sandy Creek, and turned south on County Road Seventeen. A cock pheasant sprang from a tangle of weeds in the ditch. Birdie tapped the brakes. The bird sprinted ahead of her truck for two dozen steps before its gaudy-colored wings flapped and the rooster soared off into the wheat fields.

She emptied her lungs through her teeth in a long whoosh and dabbed her eyes. Something wild and free like that should make her forget Chase. Even if it was just for a few minutes.

She'd spent the days she should have been doing her own work chasing after Ray-Ray and running Kendall's errands. One side of her head told her to focus on her job and forget how foolish she looked sniveling over Chase. The other side said it was no use.

The dirt road doglegged west at an old homestead. What was left of the plank-sided building sagged, and the wood had weathered as gray as a sky full of coming storm. On that splash of prairie, the old house sat all alone and empty. As empty and lonely as Birdie was inside.

In three more miles, she topped a little knob in the otherwise flat nothing. Next to the road, an old pickup sat. The hood was propped up with what looked like a shovel handle, and the driver's door hung open. A man leaned on the fender, elbows-deep in the engine compartment.

The letters on the license plate meant the truck was registered in Comanche County. Hanging out of the top of the jeans of the man who fiddled with the motor was more butt crack than Birdie ever needed to see.

It was Cecil from Town Pump, and someone was in the passenger seat. That didn't sit right.

If they were having trouble, why wasn't the passenger helping out?

Birdie let off the gas and coasted up beside the stranded truck.

She powered down the window and shivered at the icy wind. "What's goin' on?"

Cecil turned around. "Birdie?" Shiny snot clung to the whiskers above his lip, and his face was red with cold. "God, I'm glad you're here. I found Pop." He jerked a thumb toward the pickup's cab. "Damn truck stalled, and my phone's dead." Cecil cleaned his lip with the end of his tongue. "I don't think he's feelin' too good. We got to get him to a doctor."

Birdie leaped out her truck faster than her short legs had ever moved. "Where'd you find him?"

"He was just standin' in the road a couple miles west"—he sniffled—"west of here."

She leaned in through the open door.

The old man huddled on the seat. Dried blood matted the few strands of hair that hung across his forehead. The wrinkled skin over one eye showed red and purple. He shivered like a dried leaf.

Pop turned toward her. Glassy eyes searched her face. "Alice?" he whispered.

"No, Pop. It's me, Birdie."

"Alice?" the old man said again.

Birdie turned to Cecil.

"That's all he'll say. I think he got knocked in the head a pretty good one." Cecil rubbed the back of his hand under his nose. "Do you know who he's talkin' about?"

"His wife's name was Alice."

Cecil bent down and looked in at Pop. "She dead?"

Birdie nodded. "Uh-huh."

"Long time?"

"She was gone when I met him." Birdie's gut tightened. "Almost twenty years ago." She looked back. "I'll get us some help, Pop."

"Tell Alice I'll be home soon."

"I will, Pop."

Birdie dug into her jacket pocket for her phone. "There's a slee-pin' bag behind the seat in my truck. Let's get him wrapped up in it. I don't want to move him if we can help it. I'll see how soon the paramedics from Comanche Springs can get here."

She checked the phone to be sure she had a signal. Only one bar showed on the little screen. She walked to the end of Cecil's truck as she stabbed at the keypad.

Birdie looked down at the tire tracks Cecil's truck had left on the dusty road. She spotted where his truck must have stalled and where he had turned for the side of the road. But further down, where the county roads crossed, she expected the tracks to trail back to the west. Instead, they turned north.

Birdie turned back to Cecil.

He told me he found Pop west of here. Cecil's a damn liar. But why lie about that?

Hair prickled on the back of neck. The tire tracks from the north led back toward Sandy Creek. Where the fire had started.

Her bare hand found the edge of the tailgate. Cold flowed up her arm until her elbow ached. In the truck box, an empty bottle of Bacardi rum rested against the wheel well, and just inches away a bright red Bic lighter nestled on the rusty metal.

Birdie cocked her head. Cecil had the sleeping bag under his arm and stood at the side of the truck a step away from her. His lips turned up in a grin, and phlegm bubbled in his nostrils.

Settle down. Cecil will lie just to lie. The whole county knows that.

She looked down at the phone in her hand.

Call failed.

Damn it.

She hit *send* again.

Over Cecil's shoulder she saw her Glock on the dashboard of the truck. Because . . .

Because when she drove the gun belt was too tight around her lardass. French fries and Hostess Fruit Pies were going to get her killed.

She glanced at her phone.

Nothing.

She put it to her ear and tried to keep Cecil in the corner of her eye.

"Can you hear me?" Birdie said into her phone. *Please?*

Cecil took a step toward her.

"Arlene, this is Birdie." She pushed confidence into her voice and spoke to the dead phone. "We found Pop."

Cecil's shoulder brushed her as he passed with the sleeping bag. He opened the passenger door to his truck.

"I'm with Cecil." She said his name loud as she dared. And said it again. "Yeah, Cecil. From Town Pump in Brandon. Listen, we're out on County Road Seventeen, 'bout ten miles south of Sandy Creek. Send an ambulance."

Cecil glanced over the top of his truck. The grin was gone.

Freezing wind cut through her jacket and shirt. Pinpricks of cold stung every pore on her skin. The wind chased its first wave of icy pellets across the prairie and scoured the dusty road.

"Pop got hit in the head. Might have a concussion. Tell 'em to hurry, Arlene." *Oh, please, someone hurry.*

Then Birdie was alone with Cecil. No phantom help on the other end of the phone. White mist rose from the tight line between his lips. He stood for a moment, then shook out the sleeping bag and draped it over Pop Weber.

"Cecil." She tried to swallow the lump of fear in the back of her throat, but it refused to move. "Shut that door. I don't want Pop to catch a chill."

Cecil didn't move.

"Get over here." Keep him busy thinking help is coming. She walked to her pickup's door. "I want you to show me exactly where you found him." Her lungs ached with the strain, and her pulse pounded in her head. "The sheriff will want to know. I'll get out my map."

She kept the map in the glove box. Just above her pistol on the car seat. Cecil sniffled up the slick wetness in his nose and held her stare.

"Damn it, Cecil. Let's get the spot marked while it's still fresh in your head."

Cecil shrugged his shoulders, took a step to the front of his pickup, and pulled out the shovel handle that held his hood open.

Birdie jerked with the crash of the hood.

Cecil looked down the road at the tire tracks his truck had left in the dirt. He lifted his head as if to follow the tracks to where they turned north, not west as he had told her. He swatted the shovel handle into the open palm of his free hand.

God help me.

With her toughest voice, she barked at him. "C'mon, I'm freezin' my ass off. Get over her. I'm not gonna bite ya." She pulled open her truck's door.

Cecil stepped closer. The handle smacked his palm again.

Birdie hit the button on the glove box. She felt his eyes on the back of her neck and the whoosh of air as the handle slapped his hand again.

She added the seconds it would take to grab the pistol, pull it from the holster, turn, and face him.

He's too close.

She plucked the map from the glove box, shoved by him to the hood of her truck and spread the map.

Wind shuffled the paper under her fingers, and icy snowflakes peppered the back of her hand.

Then she heard it. From over the only hill on the otherwise flat prairie came the sound of a car engine. A car crested the top. Not just any car, but a Sheriff's Department car.

Cecil tossed the shovel handle in the back of his truck and looked down, and a trickle from his nose splattered on the map. "Show me where we are now, and I'll figure out where I found Pop." A grin flashed across his face.

Gravel crunched under the tires of the car from the sheriff's department. Paco was behind the wheel. Birdie's shoulders sagged with relief.

CHAPTER TWENTY-THREE

Marty tried to think of how many times he had seen the coroner's van in the last year. Whatever that number was, it hadn't prepared him for three times in less than two days. He parked at the side of the road behind two pickups with volunteer fireman stickers in the back windows. The coroner's van had pulled in close to the yellow tape another deputy had strung along the charred fence post above the creek bottom. That deputy's four-by-four sat next to the van from the state crime lab. He'd seen that van three times, too.

The wind chased the first snow squall of the coming storm across the prairie and bleached the sky as pale as the two corpses he and the coroner had already seen.

As many times as he tried to push it way, still Marty wondered if the body of the girl would be pale or burned black by the fire. He told himself to keep thinking *girl* until he was positive it was Dolly.

Before he opened his car door he rehearsed one more way to tell Chase his half-sister was dead. Maybe there was a chance the body wasn't Dolly's, he lied to himself again.

He climbed out and turned his coat collar up against the chill. Soft voices floated up from the creek bottom. Marty followed the tracks along the blackened fence to the place where the first loop of yellow tape was tied. He swung his leg over the top strand of wire and lied to himself one more time.

It's not Dolly.

Marty slid down the steep bank to the creek. Craning his neck to shield his face from the cold, he followed trampled footprints through the scorched weeds toward the voices. The charred dirt stuck to his boots, and melting snowflakes turned inky black on the leather. Above him the branches of the burned cottonwoods hung like gallows' arms against the washed sky.

Lonnie Colby, a deputy from the other side of the county, nodded when Marty walked up.

"Where is it?" Marty couldn't say *the body* out loud.

Lonnie blinked the snowflakes off his eyelashes and jerked his head toward a spot where the creek twisted closer to the road above. "Over there. Coroner's with her and the two techs from the state."

"Is it—"

"They won't say for sure. You know how they are, Marty," Lonnie answered. "But it's her. She had on the Riley kid's letter jacket, and when they rolled her over there was a pay stub from Saylor's Café in her back pocket. Her body laid on top of it, kept it from gettin' burned in the fire. Coroner said the check was made out to Dolly."

Marty's chin dropped to his chest.

"Coroner won't say for sure. He called for dental records so he can make a positive ID when he gets her to the morgue. But it's her, Marty." Lonnie dug under his coat for a cigarette. He pulled one from the pack with his lips and lit it. "Chase know?" he asked in a puff of smoke.

"He knows." Marty shook his head. "He's just waitin' for me to tell him for sure."

"Listen, Marty. Chase'll want to hear this. Wasn't the fire that killed her. I heard the coroner talkin'. She was dead first. Somebody dumped her here."

It surprised Birdie that the head paramedic could bend over. The buttons of his blue uniform shirt gaped open, showing a paunch bigger than hers.

He struggled up from where he knelt beside Pop's stretcher in the back of the ambulance and climbed out to where Birdie stood. The pulse from the red strobe lights on the cab of the truck painted the shadows and falling snowflakes crimson. "You, Alice?" he asked Birdie.

"Nah." She shook her head.

"Didn't think so."

"Alice was his wife." Snowflakes teased her face.

"She dead?"

This time Birdie nodded. "For more than twenty years. Why?"

"He said 'Alice hit me.' At least that's what I thought he said. I asked him again, and he just started mumbling." The paramedic looked back at the ambulance, and the cold turned his breath to steam. "Poor old fart."

"How is he?"

"No way of telling how bad that bump on his head is until they run some tests at the hospital." He flipped open a metal clipboard and scribbled some notes. "Mostly he's just a wore-out old man. Let's hope all he needs is rest and a couple of nights in a warm bed."

"You take good care of him." Birdie's throat knotted. Pop had been on his own as long as she could remember. Drove the same truck and lived all alone in an old house too far from town for anybody to really look in on him. Just an old man who most people in the county felt sorry for. If Birdie didn't find someone who cared for her she'd end up just like him. The wind sent a shiver down her back. And Birdie didn't have an Alice to remember.

The paramedic climbed into the back of the ambulance and pulled the doors shut.

Birdie touched the closed door and breathed in the gassy fumes from the exhaust. *God, take care of Pop.* She'd never been any good at praying. She wasn't sure if God even heard prayers if you didn't use words like *thee* and *thou*. She looked up into the gray sky and she added one more thought. *If Thee got an extra minute, could Thee watch over me?*

The breeze sculpted the falling snow into mushroom caps on the tops of the fence posts. A couple inches of the white stuff covered the dirt road like the downy feathers hunters plucked off geese. It swirled around the tires as the ambulance, with Pop in the back, lumbered away.

The marks on the road that showed Cecil's truck had come from the north—not from the west like he had told her—were covered now. Would anybody believe her if she tried to tell them what she suspected? Would it matter?

"Officer Hawkins." It was the sheriff.

Kendall had shown up after Paco called in. Two State Patrol vehicles followed the sheriff, and the van from the TV station in Colorado Springs was right behind. After Paco wrote down everything Cecil could remember about finding Pop, the little TV blonde stepped up with a big smile and the zipper tugged down on her parka. Cecil was more than willing to talk with her.

"Hawkins, get over here." Kendall again.

Birdie moved close enough to the circle of cops beside Kendall's truck that the steam from her breath mingled with theirs.

"Listen up," Kendall started. "This storm could be a bad one." Powdery snowflakes sluiced from the brim of his cowboy hat as he moved his head. "We just got word that they closed the interstate from Fort Morgan to the state line. They're reporting a dozen semis have slid in the ditch. It turned icy fast, and they're guessin' it'll be all over us in a couple hours."

In the sky above Birdie, the sun showed through the gray clouds like a blurred white disc, and the snow turned from fluffy to hard and wet. Cold slipped up her jacket to the bare skin where her shirttail had pulled loose from her pants.

"Paco, I want you," Kendall continued, "to check out the place Cecil said he found Pop. It'll be dark in another hour, and snow will have covered most of the signs, but I want a set of eyes on it, pronto. Don't know about you, but I'm havin' a tough time swallowin' what Cecil's tryin' to tell us. If he lied about that, there might be somethin' else he's keepin' from us."

Birdie perked up. Maybe she should say something about the tracks. Kendall looked her in the eye.

"Hawkins, some of the volunteer firemen say they think they spotted Ray-Ray about an hour ago. He was on foot and headed back toward his farmhouse. You know him better than anybody, so get on over there and invite him to come to town and talk with us." A stream of mist flowed from the sheriff's nostrils. "I'm gonna send one of those state troopers with you in case he needs some persuasion."

"I don't need any help."

"My call. The trooper's goin' with you."

A hot rush replaced the storm's chill. Birdie gritted her teeth.

Kendall held her eyes for an instant more and then looked away. "We'll leave Cecil's truck here. He says he needs to get back to his job at Town Pump. One of the troopers will give him a lift into town. If this storm is as bad as they say, he won't be goin' anywhere anytime soon." The sheriff nodded at the TV truck. "I'll follow them into Brandon. All we need is someone else lost on these roads tonight." He wiped a drop of melting snow from his earlobe. "You know what you got to do. Now let's get with it before we all freeze our asses off."

The men moved away. Birdie caught Paco's arm and held tight until they were alone.

"I didn't say nothin', but Cecil was actin' real strange when I found him and Pop." She double-checked to be sure Kendall couldn't hear her. "Even strange for Cecil."

"What are you tryin' to tell me, Birdie?"

"He said he came up on Pop west of here. I'm tellin' you, the tracks his truck made came from up north." Birdie squeezed Paco's arm harder. "Where the fire started."

"Cecil will lie to you just to stay in practice, you know that. Why would he start a fire?"

"I can feel this one in my gut. Maybe Kendall's right."

Paco looked at Cecil still talking with the TV woman. "Where does Pop fit into all this?"

"I haven't figured that out yet. You know somethin' else?" Birdie reached under her jacket and tucked her shirttail into her pants. "The paramedic said Pop was mumblin' about his wife Alice and then blurted somethin' about her hittin' him. What you make of that?"

"Just the stress talkin', I'll bet. Pop isn't sure which day it is most of the time." Paco squeezed her shoulder. "Okay, if the snow doesn't shut me down, I'll see if I can find anythin'. Birdie, you be careful. Ray-Ray can turn mean if he thinks you're nosin' around what's his."

"I can handle Ray-Ray." She doubted Ray-Ray was still in the county, but she didn't dare say so to Kendall. She mopped the snow off her side window with her forearm and opened the door. Birdie snatched her pistol from the dashboard, sucked in a breath, and fastened the gun belt around her soft waist.

"Where's Marty?"

"You didn't hear? Fireman found a third body. Girl. Might be Dolly Benavidez." The old deputy turned for his car. "Marty's out helpin' at the scene."

God, Chase, I'm so sorry.

Paco's car headed down the snowy road. Cecil kicked the snow off his feet and slid into the front seat of one of the State Patrol cars.

Birdie climbed behind the steering wheel of her truck. The Glock stabbed her hipbone, and the belt pinched a roll of fat on her belly, but there was no way she'd take it off again.

Sheriff Kendall opened the passenger door of his truck and held the arm of the little blond TV girl as she climbed in.

The son of a bitch.

CHAPTER TWENTY-FOUR

Cecil tapped his thigh to the rhythm of the wipers swiping snow from the windshield. "They wanted me to be a state patrolman." He rubbed his nose with the one hand, never losing beat with the other. "That was back in Missouri. Not here."

"That so?" The trooper leaned forward, grasped the steering wheel in both hands, and squinted into the storm.

"Yeah. Yeah, it was. I'd'a been a good one, too." Except Cecil had never lived in Missouri or even been there. He hadn't finished high school, and he had a criminal record for possession, and petty theft, and he'd been nicked a few times for bad checks. "They was real interested in me, 'cause they knew I'd be good in high-speed chases. They saw me drivin' stock cars." He'd never done that, either. "That's when they asked me to join up. They were lookin' for a specialist to do that high-speed shit."

Sometimes he just couldn't shut up. Especially when he was pee-your-pants nervous.

The trooper driving the car had to be twenty-three or twenty-four years old. He had one of those buzz haircuts and hadn't said more than two words hooked together since they had left the place where Cecil's truck had died. Cecil thought this trooper had been specially trained in interrogation, and that's why the sheriff had made Cecil ride with him. They were looking for information, but Cecil knew how to keep his mouth shut.

The State Patrol car's back end fishtailed on the snow-slick pavement when they made the turn from the county road onto the highway west of Brandon. The trooper corrected, and they drove on.

Torrents of snowflakes slapped the windshield. The driver turned up the speed of the wipers.

Cecil's hand kept up with the new tempo. "Let me ask you somethin'."

"What's that?" Two words again.

"Supposin' a fella just left his vehicle by the side of the road. Kinda like we left mine back there. You know, with nobody around now, and a police guy like you wanted to look inside it. Could he just do it, or would he need one of those . . . whatcha call it?"

"Warrant?"

"Yeah, warrant."

"It depends on a variety of circumstances."

Cecil got the trooper to say more than two words. He was proud of himself.

He don't know I'm playin' him.

The trooper continued. "If a vehicle was just sitting there, we could look in the windows, but anything more would require a warrant before we could search it. In most cases."

"That's what I thought." Cecil let out a breath. He was safe for now. "Sheriff said you'd drop me off at Town Pump. You know they'll need my help, what with this blizzard and all." Cecil had drunk all the liquor in his trailer, but he always kept a pint of Bacardi in his locker. And there was one more thing he needed to take care of at the store.

The snow had come by the time Chase saw the town of Brandon in the distance. Wet flakes clumped in the tops of the tumbleweeds, and slop thrown by the tires drooled off the Dodge's windshield. Far out on the prairie, the tips of the sagebrush blended into the gray sky.

Where a culvert let some unnamed branch of Sandy Creek pass under the highway, Chase turned from the blacktop onto the dirt road that led to the house where Dolly had lived.

Something inside made him need to stop.

The house sat just at the edge of town, with goat pens, a chicken coop, and a corral in the back for a pair of horses.

Coach had said Dolly's stepfather, Victor, was a good man. In Brandon a good man worked hard. Many times, at two or three jobs. A good man did what he had to, to care for his family. A good man didn't drink up his paycheck.

When stringing fence, driving trucks, and swinging a shovel in the oil patch wore out his body, Victor washed dishes at Saylor's. He came in early and stayed late. He mopped floors, learned to cook, and after he'd been there five years, Mercy's mother made him night manager. Folks in town said after her stroke, he ran the place until Mercy came back to Brandon.

The weeds along both sides of his house were mowed short. The barbed wire didn't sag. One fender on the pickup in the front yard was a different color then the other three, but the tags on the license plate were current.

Chase nosed his truck into the drive closest to the goat pens. The house sat dark. The horses stood with their rumps to the storm, and snow streaked the wooly hair on their backs.

He checked his cell phone one more time to see if he'd missed a call from Marty. He hadn't, and down deep he knew Dolly was dead.

All the things he could have done to save Dolly stacked up in his mind. He could have brought her, her mother, and Victor to California with him. Or bought them a house far away from the little town where people still shook their heads and whispered about his father.

Instead, because it was easy, he'd stayed away from Brandon, from the people he had disappointed, from his home, and from Dolly, and he never did one thing to help.

Chase stepped out into the cold afternoon. Goats fidgeted in their pen.

Chase's mind drew the picture of the girl's body lying on the scorched ground. Dark hair burned away. Wrinkled, charred skin on arms wrapped tight around her chest. He wanted her to be sleeping, and he wanted to kneel down and touch her shoulder and have her wake up. And when the girl in his imagination lifted her head, Chase shut his eyes. It did no good; the girl looked so much like him.

Cold air filled his lungs and chilled every part of him until he thought the tears would freeze in his eyes. When he looked down again, she was gone.

"I'm sorry, Dolly." Not because she was dead now. Because he'd never known her.

A siren moaned in the distance. Chase could make out the roof of Mercy's house on the far side of town. He could see the goalposts behind the high school. Snowflakes sparkled from lights on the sign over at Saylor's, and the pastor brushed snow from his windshield in the parking lot at the church. Nothing in Brandon was ever hidden. But the town kept its secrets well.

Bright specks of snow clung to the roadside and dusted the ruts in the dirt parking lot as if some giant in the sky had emptied a great bag of powdered sugar into the wind. Mercy stepped to the café's front window and shivered. In the flat light of the afternoon, a stray paper bag did lazy somersaults over the asphalt in front of Saylor's.

"I hear something," she said to the smell of spice and sweetness that hung in the air of the empty restaurant.

The wail of a siren pierced the silence over Brandon before the pulse of lights painted the wet pavement red. An over-the-road rig's brakes moaned, and its driver eased to the side of the road so the ambulance could pass.

"What is it?" Hector called from the kitchen.

"Ambulance from Comanche Springs." She wiped her hands on her apron. "What more could happen today?"

When the ambulance passed, the semi pulled back onto the highway and headed toward Denver. From that west direction, Chase's Dodge drove by the café.

Mercy held her breath, hoping in spite of the madness that had seized the little town that Chase's truck would stop.

And that he'd come into the café. He'd reach out and gently touch her shoulder as he took a seat at the counter. She'd bring him coffee, and they could talk again. She'd watch the snowflakes caught in his long hair turn to droplets. He'd smile at her, and the two of them would be seventeen again. Before the murders. Before their marriages failed. Before they left for the world so far from Brandon.

Instead she watched his truck roll by.

"Hector, get the food ready for the sheriff."

"Already, *señora*? It's only four o'clock."

Mercy remembered when the workers called her mother *señora*, and she was the *señorita*.

She drew a deep breath to stop the memory. "You heard me. Box it up when it's ready and put it on the backseat of my car."

"It's getting cold out, *señora*. I can take it to the school."

"No. I'll take it." She leaned close to the window and watched Chase's truck turn into the parking lot at the high school. "When you're finished with the food, go ahead and clean up. We'll close early tonight. The weather's getting worse."

"*Si, Señora* Mercy."

"Lock up, Hector. I won't be back tonight."

Mercy stepped into her office. She took her comb from her purse, turned to the mirror, and ran the comb through her hair. She cursed the tiny lines that crowded the corners of her eyes and trembled at what she'd become.

Chase pulled into a spot between two county vehicles and killed the engine. Returning to the high school should have been a homecoming. He had spent what might have been the very best years of his life in the halls, classrooms, and gym of the school. There had been a time he thought he practically owned the old building.

The heat faded in the cab, and snowflakes turned to wet blobs on the windshield. Around him, Brandon's streets were empty. In the fading afternoon, falling snow angled through lights over the gas pumps at Town Pump, and a woman with a shovel scraped snow off the sidewalks in front of the store. Farther down, the lot at Saylor's sat empty, but the lights glittered behind the café's windows.

As Chase stepped from his truck, an over-the-road rig downshifted as it made the curve into Brandon. Windows rattled on the second floor of the school building.

When Chase was in school, kids would look up from their work or pause in their reading at the sound even though it happened dozens of times each day. He and Marty played a game with each other, betting on how long it took from the rattle of the windows for a teacher to say, *Never mind that,* or *Just go on,* or any of their pet ways of telling their students to ignore the commotion. The record was a minute and thirty-two seconds. Old Miss Anders had been asleep at her desk for that one.

The semi never slowed, and it sloshed through the wet snow on its way through town. Chase turned up his collar and went inside.

The state-championship trophy still sat in the center of the trophy case outside the gym, and there was a four-foot-wide picture of Chase's team over the door. Chase stood in the center of the row of players. He faced the camera straight on. The others around him turned their shoulders toward him. Chase hated the picture. Not the people in it. The way it made him look like the center of everything.

Inside the gym beneath the shaggy stuffed head of a buffalo was another picture. It was bigger than the one of the team, but this one was just him.

The photographer had captured an instant in that very gym. Chase hung in midair, his head and shoulders a foot above everyone else on the court. The ball had just left his fingertips, and in the background the scoreboard showed two seconds left and Brandon behind by a point. It was as if everyone in the county was waiting for him to win the game and save the day. That day the shot had gone in, but in the end he had disappointed everyone.

Usually Chase expected the sound of a bouncing ball on the wood floor, but a computer's printer ticked off pages, and folding tables with monitors and phones were set on his basketball court.

Cables and cords stretched over the circle at center court and the out of bounds lines.

What had been his was so different, and that was good.

Upstairs, windows rattled and another semi rushed by.

A man in brown pants and a blue shirt buttoned all the way to his chin looked up. He took a sip from a can of Diet Coke, excused himself from a table with two women perched behind computer screens, and crossed the gym floor to Chase.

"Mr. Ford?" He moved the Coke to his left hand and reached out to shake Chase's. "I'm Jim Doyle, Colorado Bureau of Investigation. I'm lead agent on the murders. Thank you for coming in."

"Before anything else, I need to know." Chase searched the detective's face for any sign of hope. "Any word on the body they found? Is it my sister?"

The corners of Doyle's mouth turned down. "There's no easy way to say this, but I've been led to believe so. We're waiting for the coroner to provide proper identification. I'm so sorry."

Chase's bit of hope fled. He thought he should cry. But he couldn't for a girl he didn't know.

"I should have come in sooner. I want to do all I can to help with this." Chase scanned the tables. Everyone in the gym looked back at him. "Can we go someplace and talk?"

"I made one of the classrooms into an office. Come with me."

Chase followed Doyle. "I didn't see the sheriff's truck outside. I thought he'd want to be part of this. The questions, I mean." It was Kendall who wanted him to be here, not this detective from Denver.

"I understand the sheriff is on his way in now."

"Should we wait until he gets here?"

"It might be best if we don't." Doyle paused just inside the gym door. "I understand there is a bit of bad blood between the two of you."

"That's why we should wait. Both of us have been puttin' things off for too long."

Doyle took his hand from the door.

Chase answered the question Doyle didn't ask. "Kendall was a year ahead of me in school. His family had money and connections, and he was used to gettin' things his way. He went to school in Comanche Springs. I was here at Brandon. I always figured he saw me as a threat. When I started gettin' noticed, it took the spotlight off him. He didn't like that. He was a good ballplayer, all right, but . . ."

"But what, Mr. Ford?"

Chase pointed at the picture on the wall. "I scored that basket over Kendall and drove his girlfriend home that night. But you didn't want to hear any of that."

"Not at all. Sometimes the smallest thing tells the most."

Chase had been in the offices of some very powerful men. Team owners who could buy and sell Brandon several times over. Media executives whose quick decisions impacted hundreds of lives. His agent had once told him that when in the presence of such men, he should remember that he had been invited there for a reason. And that reason gave him power.

The classroom Jim Doyle had taken over was not on the top floor of some mirrored-glass office building. Doyle's laptop sat on a folding table, not a cherrywood desk. The chair the detective settled onto wasn't Italian leather. It was plastic.

Doyle waved a hand over the stacks of neatly arranged paper on the table. "I've had my people interview teachers and students here at the school to see what we might discover about the murder victims. We talked to their parents, friends, businesspeople in town, the parents' friends—in a town this size it means we've talked to almost everyone." The detective took a sip from his can of Diet Coke. He paused and opened his lips, and Chase could hear the soda sizzle on the back of the man's tongue.

Chase looked at the empty chair and shook his head. "Where's Dolly's stepfather? Mind me askin'? I'd like to say, ah—you know."

Doyle tapped at his laptop. "Victor, that his name, right? He's with his sister in Fort Morgan. I guess he visits her on his day off from the restaurant. We notified him. He didn't take it well, as you'd imagine. He wants to be here. I suggested they wait until the weather improves."

"Good." Chase paced to the window and looked out at the snow.

"I do have some questions for you," Doyle said.

"I don't know what I can add. This is the first time I've been back to Brandon in almost sixteen years."

Doyle adjusted his eyeglasses. "And there are three dead bodies on the weekend you decided to come home."

"I know." In the instant after he spoke, anger flashed. "You thinkin' I had somethin' to do with it?"

"Not at all. Remember what I said to you in the gym?" He took another swig of the cola. "Sometimes the smallest thing tells the most." Doyle waved for Chase to take a seat. "Please? I understand you saw Jimmy Riley with a girl the night before his body was found. What did you see? Be specific."

Chase pulled down the zipper on his coat, took a chair, and told Doyle what he could remember about that night. Except for sips of diet pop, Doyle never moved, never took a note or so much as nodded his head.

When Chase had finished, Doyle asked, "We know Jimmy was dating Dolly Benavidez. Is that who you saw in the truck with him?"

"I can't be sure."

"But Dolly is your sister, isn't she?"

"Half-sister"—the image of a burned and blackened body filled his mind—"and I've never actually met her."

Doyle shuffled through some papers on the desk and lifted a single sheet with handwriting scrawled across it. "But on Saturday morning you went to the bank here in Brandon and set up a college account for her. And quite a sizeable amount, if I understand correctly."

"That's none of your business, and if my banker told you that, I'll have words with her."

"It came up in our conversation. She also told me that even though you haven't been back for sixteen years, you've been quite involved in the community here. Donations to the schools. Churches. You've paid property taxes each year for some who can't." He gestured with the pop can. "I take it that there are other things."

The hair on the back of Chase's neck bristled. "I am going to talk with my banker."

"Don't be too hard on her. The woman was nervous. She misunderstood me when I mentioned the word *subpoena*."

Chase took a breath. "Yes, I did set up a fund for Dolly's college. I'll give my banker permission to show you the records of the other kids from Brandon I've helped out. No need for a subpoena. And none of this is helpin' you find out anything about Dolly or Jimmy or Coach."

"I suppose it's not." Doyle slid a copy of the Brandon High School yearbook across the table to Chase. "I thought you might want to look at this. Dolly's picture is on page seventy-five. She was a lovely girl. I see a family resemblance."

Chase left the book flat on the table. He opened the cover. Sticky notes marked the corners of three pages.

"Those are so you can find the pages for Jimmy Riley and the coach." Doyle stood up. "I'll be back in a few minutes."

"No, you won't." Chase shut the cover of the book. "You'll tell me right now why I'm here." Ball games had trained Chase to harness his emotions, but this was not the same as being on the basketball court.

Doyle sat back in his chair. He slipped his eyeglasses from his face, pivoted, and held them to the light. The corners of his mouth turned down, and he took a plaid handkerchief from his back pocket. He lifted the glasses to his mouth, breathed out, and began to polish each lens. "You're free to go anytime. As much as the sheriff wants you to be involved, in my estimation there is absolutely no reason to believe you are. We checked out your story. You were in Cheyenne Wells when you said you were. We even found a hunter who saw your truck in the field just after dawn. All that will be in my report." He held his glasses to the light one more time and then put them on.

"So Kendall thought I had somethin' to do with all this?"

"More that he wanted you to be involved." Doyle tapped his pop can on the tabletop. "Was the girl you took home after the ball game all those years ago Ms. Saylor from the café?"

"Yeah."

"I gathered as much." Doyle folded his hands and looked across the table. "Mr. Ford, a significant portion of my job involves helping law enforcement in smaller communities. The state can offer resources and experience that they don't have or cannot afford. Most individuals I deal with are sincere and want justice done. A few times over the years I've encountered individuals who see someone else's tragedy as an opportunity to further their own personal ambitions."

"You're talking about Kendall?"

"Let's just say I raised a hypothetical." Doyle held Chase's stare for a moment and then looked at the screen of his laptop.

The corners of the windows fogged with gray haze, and in the parking lot outside snow twirled in the wind. "Everybody knows he's a prick," Chase said.

"Others wouldn't be so kind, Mr. Ford." Doyle stood up. "Off the record, the sheriff believes his bowel movements have no odor."

Chase grinned. "I think I had the wrong idea about you."

"I didn't about you." Doyle looked at the screen of his laptop. "Kendall should be here anytime. It might be best if you weren't here when he arrives."

"No." Chase shook his head. "Let's get whatever he thinks about me out in the open so we can figure out if whoever killed Jimmy and Coach murdered my sister."

Doyle didn't correct him. Maybe the detective hadn't heard him. But Chase doubted that Doyle ever missed anything.

"I'm needed in the gym." Doyle's fingers slid the yearbook closer to Chase. "Are you certain you want to stay?"

Chase nodded. "I have to."

He waited until the door shut behind Doyle before he opened the book. He flipped it open to the first of the pages Doyle had marked. Coach Porter stood in the center of the ball court, one arm over the shoulder of a player, the other pointing to be sure the boy understood some part of the game they were practicing. Gray showed in the coach's hair, but it was the same man Chase remembered. Teaching and caring. The two things Coach did best.

A few pages farther on, the next sticky note marked the Brandon Buffalos varsity basketball team. The players had been posed in the same way as in the state-championship picture outside of the gym. Jimmy Riley stood in Chase's center spot, and teammates on either side turned toward him. Jimmy held a basketball in both hands, waist high, and with a smile on his face the boy seemed to dare the whole world to stay out of his way.

The last image was the one Chase needed to see most. It was the smallest of the three. On a page with rows of other pictures, someone had used a ballpoint pen to circle one girl. Her hair was dark; his was blond. But her eyes, cheeks, and chin were so much like his father's. So much like his own. Where Jimmy's smile was daring, this smile showed innocence. Dolly Benavidez was a beautiful girl with so much to live for.

Chase let the book cover fall closed.

But his half-sister was dead.

CHAPTER TWENTY-FIVE

Sheriff Kendall bounced the county's new GMC pickup over the curb into the parking lot at the Sundowner Motel. The TV van followed him in and rolled to a stop in front of a door marked with the number three. No other cars were in the lot. Most of the deer hunters had headed home, and the old man who owned the motel had turned off the *no* on the *no vacancy* sign.

The gorilla who ran the camera and did all the technical stuff jumped out of his van, flipped up the hood of his parka, and dug into his pants pocket for the key to the door.

Kendall looked over at Jody. "Which one's your room?"

"On the far end." A gust of wind sent a wave of snow off the flat roof on the one-story stucco building. Jody put a purr in her voice and tilted her head the way he liked. "Looks cold. Wanna come in for a few minutes?"

God, did he. And not for just a few minutes. He wanted to spend all night getting into that little thing. But—"I saw Chase Ford's truck at the school when we drove by. I need to get over there and hear what he has to say."

"I could come along."

"Not now. I'll send someone to get you when Mercy brings supper over. I'll fill you in on what we find out then." He licked his lips. "And I'll give you a ride back here when we're done."

Jody touched his hand on the steering wheel. "Whatever you say, Sheriff." Her cell phone was at her ear before her feet touched the pavement.

He cut through the parking lot at Town Pump and turned left onto the four-lane road. When he got to the high school, he parked next to Chase's truck.

Birdie was sure that Ray-Ray had nothing to do with the murders. He was guilty as sin of hollering too loud when Puckett's buffalo knocked down his fence and got into his alfalfa. Guiltier still of being an odd duck. Even if he was guilty of hunting without a license, Ray-Ray wouldn't stop to answer any questions until Ray-Ray wanted to. Besides her, she couldn't guess at how many deputies and troopers had spent a day and a half proving that.

But Cecil. Just his name made her skin crawl. The way the slimeball had acted while they waited for the ambulance to take Pop to the hospital still turned her stomach. She knew he'd lied about where he'd found the old man. If Cecil had something to do with the fire, then maybe he had something to do with the murders. But what?

She mapped the fire in her head. Paco said that they'd found the body they thought was Dolly's about where the fire had started. West of where she'd found Cecil and Pop. West, not north.

Was Cecil trying to hide something? Was he that smart?

Scuffs in the snow alongside the dirt road showed the deer were on the move. Spooked out of the creek bottom by the fire, no doubt they were looking for shelter to ride out the storm. A set left by a coyote probably meant he was on the lookout for an easy dinner before the rabbits and other tasty critters hunkered down in their burrows to hide from the coming cold.

The next marks in the snow were different. She tapped her brakes and felt the back of her truck slip on the snowy road.

The tracks that crossed the dirt road at the Butt Notch hadn't been laid down by any animal she had been entrusted to protect.

She eased her pickup to the side of the road and checked the side mirror to see if the state trooper would do the same. He pulled in behind her and they met at the back of her truck.

The footprints came across a stubble field, ducked under the fence, crossed the barrow ditch and snowy road, and padded off across the bent prairie grass on the other side. From the length of the stride, Birdie could tell the man was in a hurry.

"Think these belong to him?" the trooper asked.

"Ain't nobody but Ray-Ray who'd be out in this weather on foot." She zipped up her Carhartt and adjusted the pistol on her hip. "His farmhouse is a couple miles from here, but that ain't where he's headed." She shook her head. "He's up to somethin'."

The trooper squinted and looked out to where the tracks disappeared in a tangle of weeds and red tamaracks. "What's out there?"

"Just two square miles of the roughest damn country God put in this county. And Ray-Ray's spent all his forty years huntin' and hikin' in it. He knows every wrinkle out there." Birdie lifted her foot to the running board on the side of her truck, pulled up her pant leg, and retied her boot laces. "You get on your radio and tell 'em what we found and say that we're gonna follow those tracks for a ways."

While the trooper did what she told him, Birdie dialed Marty's number on her cell phone.

No answer.

She found a stocking cap and a pair of gloves behind her pickup's seat. Snowflakes settled in her short hair. If there was one thing she hated more than walking, it was walking in the cold.

The trooper pulled on mittens. "Should I bring my shotgun?"

"Hell, if Ray-Ray's as mad as I'm bettin' he is he won't let us get close enough for a scattergun to do any good." She shut the door to her truck. "Do you got a machine gun with you?"

The trooper's jaw dropped open. "There's an M16 in the trunk."

"Better bring it and all the bullets you can carry." Birdie wiped her nose on the back of her glove.

"So you think he might shoot at us?"

"Not us." Birdie slipped her pistol from its holster, checked to be sure there was a cartridge in the chamber, and snapped the gun back in place. "Ray-Ray's been after me to come to dinner for years. If he shoots at anybody, it's gonna be you." She clomped out across the snowy ground. "You might want to walk behind me. Ray-Ray's an awful good shot."

Nowhere on the strands of DNA that made Chase who he was had the Creator thought to add patience. Waiting was something Chase didn't do well.

He paced across Doyle's classroom office again and stopped at the window. No sign of Kendall's truck in the snowy parking lot outside. Chase pivoted on the heel of his boot and walked the eight steps to the far wall then turned and walked back.

He hated waiting.

That was why basketball suited him so well. The game moved. The back-and-forth on the court, the jumping and running, and the challenge of the opponent satisfied his senses. The hardest year of his life came during his freshman year of college when he was relegated to watching from the bench while older teammates played his game.

It had been almost as difficult during his rookie season with the Lakers, but an injury to a veteran player provided an opportunity that Chase wouldn't give back. By the tenth game of that season he was being introduced to the crowded arenas as part of the starting lineup.

When the torn knee took basketball away, he spiraled inward, first waiting for the surgery, then waiting to heal, and finally waiting through long days for the rehab to give back his strength. The pills made waiting easier.

He took the last two steps to the window, paused, and looked again. Doyle had said Kendall was on his way. Chase glanced at the clock over the door. Eight minutes had gone by since Doyle had left him in the room alone and two since he'd last checked the time.

The footprints on the fresh snow were easy enough to follow. Maybe too easy.

What was Ray-Ray up to?

Cold air found its way up the back of Birdie's coat and teased the bare swatch of skin where her shirttail had again worked loose from her pants. When Birdie paused to hitch up her britches, the state trooper bumped into her.

"Watch it," she said.

"You said to stay close."

"Not that close." She glared at the trooper. "Gimme some room, Junior. Ray-Ray might miss you and hit me."

"I thought you said he was a good shot."

"Everybody misses once in a while."

The trooper hung his head and stepped back.

Birdie clomped on. The more she thought about it, the more it didn't make sense. If Ray-Ray didn't want to be found, he was just too good to leave tracks like the ones they were following. He had to know they were after him. She pushed aside a tree branch, stepped through, and gave the branch an extra tug before she let it go.

Junior yelped as the branch smacked the top of his head.

"Damn it," Birdie hissed. "I told you not to be watchin' your feet. Ray-Ray's out there somewhere." She pointed through the brush. "You keep your eyes on where you're goin', not where you're steppin'." Her words turned to gray mist in the fading light. "If you get shot, don't expect me to drag you outta here."

She ducked under the next spray of branches and sent the last springing back toward Junior.

No yelp.

He's learning.

But she'd rather have Marty with her than the still-green trooper. She fished her cell phone from her coat, thumbed Marty's number up, and hit Send.

Call failed showed on the little screen.

Crap.

Ray-Ray's tracks never so much as showed a stumble. Never

showed any signs he was tired and always stayed where they were easy to see. Almost as if he wanted to be found.

Double crap.

Birdie shook her head.

What's he up to?

Hair stood on the back of her neck, and cold goose bumps popped up between the hairs. She knew each step put her and Junior farther from the road and closer to wherever it was Ray-Ray was leading them. Her arm brushed a thick tamarack, and powdery snow cascaded over her face.

Triple crap. And put a cherry on top of it.

Birdie dabbed at her eyes and blew through her lips. When she drew the next breath, she stopped stock-still.

"Junior. Smell that?"

He made a slippery sucking sound with his nose. Then sniffed again. "Yeah," he whispered. "I smell something. What is it?"

"Wood smoke." She sank to her knees and pulled the trooper down beside her. "Like from a campfire."

In two more trips back and forth across the room, Chase ate up a minute and thirty-five seconds by the clock over the door. He traced a circle with the tip of his tongue onto the inside of his cheek and started the next trip. Outside the window, snowflakes the size of quarters replaced the smaller flakes from earlier. A gust of wind spun the snow into swirling funnels between the vehicles parked in the lot.

Chase stopped at the window and painted a steamy circle on the cold glass with his breath. Outside a semi rushed by, spraying slop and shaking the windows in the old building. Near the lights at Town Pump, a pickup turned onto the highway and headed toward the school. Between swipes of the truck's windshield wipers, Chase recognized the black hat on Kendall's head.

About time, Sheriff.

Chase waited to be sure that Kendall would stop, and when the sheriff stepped out of his truck, Chase went to meet him in the hallway.

A puff of cold followed Kendall in from outside. He slipped out of his jacket as he walked, brushed the snow from his hat, and placed the Resistol, crown down, on top of the trophy case outside the gym.

Doyle must have been watching for the sheriff to arrive. The detective came through the gym doors and met Kendall before Chase could get to him. Doyle had a clipboard of papers under his arm and a can of Diet Coke in his hand. He held out the clipboard for the sheriff.

Kendall glanced down the hall at Chase, hesitated for an instant, and then took the papers from Doyle. His head nodded and the muscles along his jawline tensed.

Even in the shadowy hallway Chase could see the shiny scar at the tip of Kendall's left eyebrow. In a tight basketball game in that very building almost twenty years before—when Chase was a sophomore and Kendall was a junior—Chase had poked the ball loose from a Comanche Springs guard. The ball had rolled toward the sideline in front of the visitor student section, just at half court.

Mercy Saylor sat in the front row, determined to let everyone from Brandon know she was dating the captain of the Comanche Springs team. In a flash of muscle and sinew fueled by jealousy and teenage bravado, both Chase and Kendall dove for the loose ball.

The skin on four knees sang out as they scraped across the hardwood floor. Elbows gouged for ribs. Kendall's head smacked the bleachers at Mercy's feet, making a cut that took ten stitches to close, and Chase came up with ball.

Standing in the hall all those years later, Chase remembered his satisfaction when he saw Kendall's blood on the floor that night.

Just like then, Kendall wouldn't look at Chase. When he patted his snow-damp hair, his fingers lingered an extra second on the shiny pink place near his eye.

Chase walked up to Kendall and Doyle. "Sheriff."

"Not now, Ford, can't you see I'm busy?" His eyes stayed on the papers.

"Sheriff."

"I said not—"

Chase grabbed Kendall's shoulder and turned the sheriff to face him. The clipboard clattered to the floor, and papers scattered among the wet footprints. "Listen to me, Kendall. Whatever happened when we were in high school is long over. I'm here to do what I can to help find who killed Coach and my sister."

Kendall's hand hovered over his holstered forty-five. The pink scar on his face turned as red as the blood that flowed in the veins behind it. He took a half step closer to Chase.

Everything around Birdie was as quiet as the falling snow except for the chatter of the trooper's teeth. "Quiet," she hissed through her lips.

"I'm—I'm—I'm freezin'."

"Hush yourself," she said in a hoarse whisper, and then added, "Man up. I haven't had any feeling in my butt for half an hour."

Snowflakes drifted through the tamaracks where they hid. Birdie's knees cramped, and tiny icicles formed where her stocking cap touched her eyebrows. She squinted into the last light of the day, trying to find some faint glow from the fire that sent the smoke wisps teasing her nose.

"Can you see anything?" she asked the trooper.

"No," he moaned.

"Are you trying?"

"No."

"You're as worthless as tits on a boar hog." She shifted her seat on the snowy ground. Leaves crackled, and a branch snapped under her. "Listen, Ray-Ray's gotta be sittin' out there by a fire toastin' his behind, while we're freezin' ours. It's gonna be pitch dark in a few minutes. Maybe I can spot the fire then." Cold stabbed the two inches of naked skin where her shirttail had worked loose. "When I tell you, you're gonna crawl outta here. When you're good and gone, get up and run back to your car. Radio in and tell 'em to send all the help they can spare." She caught a nose drip on the back of her glove. "I'm gonna sit here and keep watch. When the others get here, you bring 'em to this spot. And tell 'em to keep quiet."

"You'll freeze to death."

"No, I won't."

One advantage of being a fat girl was the extra layer of insulation around her middle.

Junior struggled onto his knees. He looked at Birdie. "I'll bring a thermos of hot chocolate back with me."

"Hell, no. You better bring me a pint of whiskey." She winked at him. "Be sure to keep your butt down. Now get, and do it now."

The trooper scrambled on all fours until he'd cleared the canopy of brush where they'd hidden. He looked back over his shoulder at Birdie and lunged to his feet.

Out of the twilight, the boom of a rifle shot shattered the stillness.

"Junior," Birdie screamed.

Mercy watched the sheriff's truck pull into the parking lot at the high school. Like Chase, he hadn't stopped at the café.

She locked the front door to the café, flipped off the lights in the dining room, and hit the switch to kill the neon *open* sign. The light sputtered, and its pink shades faded from the steamy window. She took her wool coat from a hook behind the office door, slipped it on, and draped a scarf around her neck.

"Is the food for the sheriff ready, Hector?" she called to the man in the kitchen.

"Yes, *señora*. There's a couple boxes. I'll take them to your car."

"Just put it on the backseat."

"Might not be room. The trunk might be better."

"No." She stomped to the kitchen doorway and bristled. "If you can't get it all in the back, put a box on the front seat. Is that too hard for you to understand?"

"No, *Señora* Mercy." Hector bobbed his head. "I'll do what you tell me."

Mercy felt her shoulders drop. "Hector, I'm so sorry. I shouldn't have spoken to you that way." She touched the dampness that filled her eyes. "I'm just upset. Dolly and her boyfriend. The Coach. Pop. The fire. Now this storm. What more can happen?"

"I understand, *señora.*"

"I'm so sorry, Hector." She hung her head.

In the office she put on her gloves, found her purse and the bank deposit bag, and tucked them under her arm. She held the door for Hector and watched him slide the boxes onto the backseat of her mother's Lincoln.

While he brushed the snow off the car's windows with an old broom, Mercy climbed in and started the engine.

"Don't stay too much longer," she said through the top two inches of the window. "It's getting bad." And before she rolled the window up, she added, "Hector, please forgive me for the way I spoke to you."

"De nada, señora."

She waited for him to go inside and then turned on the car's dome light. She tilted down the rearview mirror, checked her makeup, and dabbed fresh lipstick on her lips.

Chase stared into Kendall's eyes.

Neither man blinked.

Sweat dampened Chase's palms like in those seconds before the tip-off of a big game. The sight of the burned-over prairie where Dolly had been left, the smell of bloody carpet in Coach's house, the touch of the prairie breeze while Jimmy lay with the dead buffalo filled his senses. Each pump of his heart echoed off the hallway walls and floor.

They stared at each other for hours or seconds, years or only an instant, until from somewhere far away, a voice broke the spell.

"Sheriff." It was Doyle, and the man wasn't far away. He was standing next to them.

"Sheriff."

With just the bat of an eyelid, Kendall shifted a glance to the state detective. "What is it?"

"Mr. Ford and I have already talked. He was most cooperative. We have witnesses to corroborate his statements. I told him he could go, but he wanted to talk to you."

Kendall touched the side of his face. The tip of a finger lingered at the scar near his eye. "What is it you want, Ford? Say it, and then you can get out of here."

"It's simple. I want to do anything I can to find who killed my sister and my friend."

Kendall's face twisted into a cruel grin. "This ain't a ball game. Even if it was, your best is way behind you."

Chase swallowed hard. He looked at Doyle. Doyle shook his head and began to gather the spilled clipboard and papers from the floor.

"No matter what Doyle says, I think you know somethin'. Why else would all this happen the first time you show up in Brandon in sixteen years?" He took the clipboard and papers from Doyle. "When I figure it out, I'll come for you. Just know that." He looked down at the papers and tipped the top of his head. "Now get out."

"You're wrong, Kendall." Chase fought to keep from screaming. "And I will find out who killed my sister."

Chase barreled down the hallway, struggling into his jacket, and was reaching for the handle when the door opened. Snow swirled in and Mercy, with a box balanced on her hip, swung the door wide open.

"Now be careful," she said to two troopers on the concrete steps. Steam rose from the boxes both held in their arms. "It's beginning to get icy." Mercy stepped back, propping the door open with her hip. "I don't know what I would have done without your help. Go on. I'll hold the door."

The troopers nodded as they passed Chase, trailing the spicy aroma of beans, chili, and tortillas from the boxes they carried.

"Take those to the gym." Mercy stepped inside and let the door shut behind her. "Oh, Chase. I didn't see you." A smile washed over her face, and snowflakes sparkled in her hair. "C'mon, eat with us. There's more than enough for everyone."

She held her box for Chase to take. "You always liked my mother's burritos."

Chase didn't raise his arms. "No, Mercy. Not now." He glanced back down the hallway to the spot where he'd almost lost it with Kendall. "I gotta go."

The smile left Mercy's face. "There's trouble, isn't there? You and Kendall?"

Chase nodded. "It's just best I leave."

Mercy raised a knee to ease her grip on the box in her hands. "I get it." She stepped closer to him. "When I'm done here, I'm going back to the café. Come over. I'll make us both something to eat. It'll be like old times."

"I don't know, Mercy."

"Please." Her lip trembled. "Too much has happened today. I don't want to be alone. Not tonight." She bit her lip. "Just you and me?"

The chill from outside raced up his spine, and Chase bit down on his lip.

Mercy's eyes pleaded.

Chase thought he saw a warmth he needed. "Yeah. Okay, I'll be there."

"Good, I'll park out front. When you see Mom's car, you'll know I'm back." She pushed by him, and the clack of her cowboy boots echoed from the tile floor.

Through the front windows of Town Pump, Cecil watched the State Patrol car pull out onto the snowy highway. After he waved goodbye to the trooper who had dropped him off, Cecil went to the coolers at the back of the store. He took a twelve-pack of Bud from the bottom of the shelf, tore open the cardboard, and pulled out a can.

"Hey, you gonna pay for that?" Diana called from the counter.

Cecil popped the tab and guzzled half the can. "Bite me." And he finished the rest.

"Asshole," she said, and gave him the finger.

He dropped the empty can between the potato chip bags on the top shelf of one of the gondolas, plucked another can from the box, and pushed through the door to the back room. Cecil went to his locker and spun the combination on the lock. He upended the can and tossed the empty on the floor.

Under a stack of dog-eared *Hustler* magazines on the bottom shelf of his locker, Cecil found what he was looking for. He tucked the bundle into the front of his jeans, pulled his sweatshirt down over it, and started his third can of Bud as he went out the back door.

Kendall sat down at a table with Mercy.

"I saved this for you." She pushed a plate loaded with tamales, frijoles, and tortillas across the table. "Your deputies and the troopers ate up all the burritos. I hid some pie, though. Lemon still your favorite?"

Kendall nodded.

Mercy smiled. "You're worn out, aren't you?"

"Long day. Now this storm. I'm gonna send folks home, and we'll start over in the morning." Kendall lifted a forkful of tamales to his mouth. "Umm, good, Mercy. Tastes just like your mama's."

"What about—what's his name—Doyle?"

"He says he's gonna stay and work through the night. I don't know what else he thinks he can do."

"Has he found anything?"

"You know I can't say anything specific, Mercy." He stuffed another forkful in his mouth. "He's a worker, that one. He pours over the interview manuscripts and the coroner reports. Then studies the pictures they took where Birdie found the hay bales used to lure in the buffalo. He's sees something he wants to remember and types it into some computer program he's got. Then studies some more."

"So, it must be useful?"

"Oh, yeah. He's good at what he does. No doubt about that. When he figures it out, I'm gonna swoop in and arrest the killer." He smiled and reached for a napkin to wipe his chin. "That's why I asked for Doyle. He's a strange one, but he's good."

He swiped a tortilla through the remains on his plate and stuffed it in his mouth. "Now, how about that pie?"

Mercy came back with the slice. "Will you drive home to Comanche Springs tonight?"

"Naw, I rented a room at the motel. I told that reporter girl I'll give her a statement for the ten o'clock news, and then I'll turn in." Kendall thought of Jody Rose and hoped he'd read the invitation correctly in the way she'd talked to him in his truck.

Mercy reached across the table and laid her hand on top of his. It was warm and soft. He shifted on the hard plastic chair.

"Lincoln, I don't want to be alone tonight. I'm going to take the dishes back to the café." She trailed the tips of her fingernails over his arm. "I'll leave the back door unlocked. I keep a bottle of scotch in my desk. It'll be like old times."

Two offers in one night? Two pretty women. Who was he to say no?

Paco Martinez burst into the room. "Sheriff?"

"What is it?"

"We just got a call from that trooper you sent with Birdie. Somebody took a shot at 'em."

The night sky above the high school churned with snowflakes captured in the yellow glow of the second-floor windows. The glimmer from the signs at Town Pump added color, and some flakes seemed to sparkle with reds and blues and oranges. Chase hustled around Mercy's car and across the parking lot to his truck. Falling snow filled the tracks Mercy's cowboy boots had left just minutes before.

Chase climbed in, slammed the door shut, and cranked the engine. Cold air funneled up from the vents and bit through his coat until great shivers shook his shoulders and stung his core. He banged both fists on the steering wheel.

He hated that Kendall was right.

What could he really do to help find who killed Dolly?

Wisps of warmth teased at the cold truck cab. Chase leaned forward until his forehead rested on the steering wheel.

Just one pill.

Behind his closed eyes he imagined the warmth from a pill chasing the ragged pain from his knee and numbing his thoughts. The pills made it easy not to care.

Not to care about Billee. Or even himself.

Chase lifted his head and flipped the switch for the wipers. They hesitated an instant, broke free from the ice, and swept across the windshield.

Damn Kendall. Damn him, and damn this stupid town. Why did I come back?

Light spilled from the back door of Town Pump, and a bent figure hurried out into the snow. In the headlights of an oncoming semi, the man pulled up the hood on his sweatshirt and clutched a box close to his side. With his free arm he waved for the truck, and its driver pulled over.

The man in the sweatshirt waded through the slush on the roadside and pulled open the passenger door. The man's head bobbed as he talked to the driver, and then he climbed inside and the truck pulled away.

Whoever it was, he was leaving Brandon.

And Chase should, too.

Chase slipped the truck into gear and rolled onto the highway. The lights of the semi ahead of him touched the place where Dolly had lived.

In a town as small as Brandon, no part was too far from any other.

Once, nothing could make him back down. The challenges on the court fueled him. He vowed to show the people who said he wasn't good enough how wrong they were. But when his knee crumbled under him, giving up became easy.

Kendall's mockery thundered in his head and blended with his own doubts.

When the knee wouldn't let him come back. When Billee was away so long. When the pills took away more than the pain . . .

Chase made a sharp turn at the next street. He wouldn't give up this time.

Maybe there was something at Coach's house the police had missed.

He left his pickup at the end of the block and walked down the alley like he had all those years before—when Coach's house was a refuge from Big Paul's rage.

On the south side of the house, where a foot-tall ridge of drifting snow sheltered a bare swatch of earth, Chase spotted the faint impression of a boot track in the dirt. Not a man's. Maybe a boy's? He flipped over a flat rock with his foot and picked up the hidden aspirin bottle. When he shook the plastic container, a key rattled inside. He smiled. Coach still left the key for his players now the same way he had sixteen years before, for Chase and Marty.

Chase groped inside his coat for his cell phone, scrolled for Marty's number, and pressed Send. At his feet, snow began to fill the lines and marks from the boot track.

Call failed showed on the small screen.

Chase pushed away the police seal on the back door, pressed the key into the lock, and turned the knob.

Marty knew the only place in the county with worse cell reception than the spot along Sandy Creek where Dolly had been found was at the Butt Notch. His phone told him he'd missed a call. He dropped it on the car seat beside him and twisted a knob on the police radio.

No matter. If the department needed him, they'd use the radio.

He tried Chase again. But no luck. Birdie's phone: the same.

The wind had changed. The storm had blown in from the north. Now it had moved more from the west. Big, wet flakes that froze when they touched the ground replaced the smaller ones. Even with a coat on inside the patrol car, he shivered.

Kendall had told him to head home after he checked with the coroner. Officially, he was off the clock. It didn't feel like it. How much longer would this day go on? The worst part was still coming.

Telling Chase the body belonged to Dolly.

But they'd found Pop. That was good. The fire was out, though Marty knew that sometime tomorrow, or the next day, Kendall would chew his butt about Connie Mason and the car. He glanced down at the phone and thought he should call Deb to let her know he was okay. If she'd heard about his stunt with the tractor at the Masons' place, she'd leave bigger teeth marks on his hind end than

Kendall could do on his best day. He shook his head. Kendall could fire him, but Deb was stuck with him.

It was probably best the phone had no service. Still, when it was time, he'd take whatever Deb dished out and tell her how sorry he was and that he'd never do something so stupid again, just for the chance to snuggle up with her in their bed.

Especially on a night as cold as this one.

Even with their baby growing inside her, Deb was a beautiful woman, and he didn't tell her that near enough. One thing was for sure: he loved her and their boys more than he ever thought he'd love anything.

He made the turn on Sandy Creek Road, clicked down the high beams to cut the glare from the oncoming snowflakes, and let the patrol car creep ahead.

The night and snow turned everything to shades of black and white. Even so, the marks the wildfire had left were plain to see. It was almost as if someone had drawn a line just where Sandy Creek curved up close to the county road. Snow draped the trees and brush in the creek bottom on the west side of the line like a wintertime picture from a calendar hung on a café wall. But the blackened branches of the charred trees on the other side fought the new white snow, like fingers twisting just before death.

He was glad that the coroner had had Dolly's body in a bag by the time he'd climbed up to where they found her. But the picture his imagination had drawn crept in every time he shut his eyes.

It had to be worse for Chase.

The back end of Marty's car drifted as he followed the curve in the road. Tires spun, and the back slid toward the ditch. He fought the wheel and gunned the engine, but the car continued to slide. With a thump a back wheel dropped off the shoulder of the gravel road.

He hit the gas, and the spinning sound made him sick. As he climbed out of the car, one hand shot to his Stetson and clamped it tight to the top of his head.

Shitfire.

When Marty did something, he did it good. Now he was stuck.

Good and stuck.

His car's radio squawked. "Marty?"

He slid back into the car, out of the wind and snow, and grabbed the microphone. "This is Marty. What is it, Arlene?"

"Where are you?"

"Down on Sandy Creek Road. About twelve miles west of town. On my way home." He didn't want to tell her he was in the ditch. "Why?"

"Oh, Marty. We got more trouble. Somebody took a shot at Birdie."

"When?"

"Maybe twenty minutes ago. You might be her closest help."

Ray-Ray peered out into the night through the notch he'd carved in the log walls that made his stronghold. Nothing moved except the snowflakes and a puff of steam from Birdie Hawkins's nose.

His rifle shot had sure put the hurry-up in that lanky kid from the State Patrol who was with her.

Ray-Ray took another drag on his hand-rolled smoke and grinned.

That kid should try out for the Olympics. He flat hauled ass out of there.

But Ray-Ray wasn't sure just what Birdie was up to. After she was sure the kid wasn't hurt she'd just hunkered into that spot in the tamaracks and sat there watching. Smart girl, that Birdie. She picked a place out of the wind. He was sure a big girl like Birdie wouldn't chill too soon. One of them skinny little girls would be shivering and thinking hard about getting back to where it was warm, he'd bet. Not Birdie. She was one tough woman.

Ray-Ray used the barrel of his rifle to open the door to his wood stove. The steel box teetered back and forth. He should have leveled it better, but it threw good heat. He banked the coals with a foot-long piece of split cottonwood and tossed the log on top of the small fire.

Keep the fire small and sit close. Those who didn't know better built big fires and had to sit far back. Used their wood up quick, too. Not him. A small fire would keep the stronghold plenty warm.

He'd planned things that way. Wood, water, food, guns, and bullets, all hidden in a place not much bigger than the bed of a pickup. He'd built it all himself and tucked it just below the crest of the highest point in the Butt Notch. No one knew it was there but him.

Even Birdie had almost parked her truck right on top of it on opening day when she came to the Notch to try to catch him poaching. She hadn't seen a thing.

Ray-Ray speared the bail of a cook pot with the barrel of his rifle and lifted the pot from the top of his stove.

The deer stew smelled good.

A drop of melting water fell from the tin flashing around the stovepipe and sizzled when it hit the iron stovetop.

Ray-Ray stuffed a spoonful of stew into his mouth. Tasted good, too. Maybe Birdie would like some. He chuckled and looked out at her.

Boy, that friend of hers sure was comical running and sliding in the snow. He musta thought I was tryin' to hit him.

Birdie needed his help.

Marty slammed the patrol car in reverse and hit the gas. The car rocked backward a few inches before the tires started to spin. He left off, moved the gearshift to drive, and gunned the car again. Three inches forward, then the tires slipped and spun.

Again. Reverse. The car moved backward. Spin.

Slam into drive, hit the gas, lurch forward. Spin.

Reverse.

Spin.

Drive.

Once, years before on a Friday night, Marty and Chase had been hurrying to get two girls from Comanche Springs home before their curfew time struck. A shortcut to the highway across Sandy Creek seemed smart. But Marty buried his old man's pickup halfway to the axles in the muddy clay along the creek. One girl started bawling about how much trouble she was going to be in.

So Marty started rocking the truck back forth. Reverse then

forward. Reverse then forward. Again and again. Sand and water flew in the air. Tires whined. The girl cried. Chase screamed *Eastwood* and laughed until Marty thought he'd bust.

Inch by inch and little by little, that old truck pulled itself out of the muck. They bounced up from Sandy Creek, across the pasture, busted through a barbed-wire gate, hit the highway, and made to Comanche Springs with ten minutes to spare. Laughing the whole way.

Marty wasn't laughing now. He slammed the patrol car from reverse into drive and jammed his foot into the gas pedal. One back tire found the edge of the road, and the car heaved ahead. He turned the steering wheel, and the spinning tire grabbed the ridge of gravel along the shoulder and with a bounce the car freed itself of the ditch.

I'm comin', Birdie.

And he never let up. He took chances he shouldn't have and drove faster than he would have ever dared before.

Deb'll kill me if I break my neck.

But Marty gripped the wheel tighter and willed himself through the blizzard to Birdie, trying to chase away all the thoughts that tumbled around in his head.

Out across the prairie, the pulsing flash of the red and blue lights on the State Patrol car from a mile away let him know he was close. It didn't slow him down. If anything, he drove faster.

Down the next hill and then up. Tires sliding.

Around the hard corner at the next junction.

He used the brakes for the first time when he slid to a stop in the middle of the road next to the State Patrol car. The young trooper had an assault rifle slung over his shoulder and was at his door before Marty could jerk it open.

"Tell me what we got." Marty scrambled from the car and jerked a thumb for the kid to follow.

Marty had to give one to the trooper—he was precise with his report. The kid and Birdie had followed tracks, Birdie had smelled a campfire, and they'd hid in some brush trying to spot where the smoke came from. The kid told Marty it was cold—real cold. He'd said that to Birdie half a dozen times. Finally, when he was ready to give up, Birdie had sent him to radio for help, and when he got to his feet, there'd been a rifle shot.

"Just one shot?" Marty asked.

"Yes, sir."

Marty shook his head. "How long ago, do you think?"

The kid trooper looked down at his watch. "An hour and twenty-three minutes."

"You sure Birdie didn't get hurt?"

"Yes, sir. She hollered for me to get out of there."

"Anything else? More shots?"

"No, sir."

"Okay, you're doin' good." Marty opened the passenger door and unhooked a short-barreled shotgun from its bracket on the dashboard. "One more thing, kid." Marty eased open the gun's action and checked to be sure there was a load of double-aught buckshot in the chamber. "What did that rifle shot sound like?"

"Sir?" The kid took a step back. "It sounded like a . . ." His face screwed up like his was thinking. "Like a rifle shot, sir."

"Anything you can remember might help. Think hard now," Marty said. "Was it a sharp crack like from that gun of yours? Or . . . ?"

The kid looked to one side, then the other. Snowflakes blew by his face. "No, it was a deeper sound. More a boom then a sharp crack."

"Good."

"Why you askin'—"

"Ray-Ray hunts with an old forty-five-seventy. Buffalo gun. When it goes off it bellows real mean. Not a polite bang like a modern gun."

"That means it's him, doesn't it?"

"It does, and I don't know if that's good or bad."

"Why do you say that?"

"Ray-Ray usually hits what he's aimin' at, and you don't have any holes in you."

"So?"

"He must not have wanted to hit you. Probably just wanted to scare you off. Ray-Ray's a strange one, but I bet he just wants to be left alone." Marty pulled on his gloves. "One thing I am sure of. He won't miss next time."

The trooper wiped the melting snow from his face. "What are we goin' to do now?"

"You're gonna wait here." Marty tossed his Stetson into the car and rolled a ski mask over his face. "When help gets here, tell 'em what you know. Nobody will listen to me, but you tell 'em that I think it's best if everyone goes and finds a nice warm place for the rest of the night and that we leave Ray-Ray alone until morning." He shook his head. "But that's not what they'll do." Marty left the trooper and tromped through the snow out into the field.

"What are you gonna do?"

"Goin' Eastwood," Marty muttered.

"Whatya say?"

"I said, I'm gonna find Birdie." He didn't look back. "And do everythin' I can to keep your friends from gettin' killed."

CHAPTER TWENTY-SIX

Chase stood for a minute to let his eyes adjust to the darkness. The lights from the neighbor's house filtered through the frosty window glass and painted everything in gauzy grays. On the vinyl floor, shadows of falling snowflakes danced between his boots.

Like the negative of an old black-and-white snapshot, the shades seemed reversed. Walls were silver pale and open doorways as dark as deep water. Even in the confusion the house was just as he remembered.

So many times he had sat with Coach at the kitchen table for meals, and when they'd finished, a flipped coin decided who did dishes. The archway opened to the living room where Coach's big-screen TV was always set to ESPN when it wasn't being used to study tapes of the Brandon Buffalos. The silent TV in front of the couch where Chase had slept when he lived in the house proclaimed for certain that Coach was really gone. Chase's throat clamped closed, and he muffled a sad sound.

Dark streaks marred the carpet outside the bathroom where Marty had said they found Coach's body. Chase couldn't let himself look at the gore or go into the bedroom where Coach had slept.

He stepped into the short hallway, took a breath, and swung open the door to Coach's office. The curtains were drawn on the only window, and darkness wrapped the little room tightly. Blurred rectangular images hung on the walls, each a picture of a squad of boys in their basketball uniforms. The biggest, of Chase's state-championship team, hung over the desk, with two smaller beneath it—Chase's college team and a picture of Chase with the Lakers.

If Coach was anything, he was a man of details. Every minute at ball practice was planned. Notes were taken and filed. Each game was dissected for mistakes to eliminate and successes to build on. The file cabinet next to his desk bulged with those records.

Chase knew if there was any clue to be found it would be in Coach's other notes. Not the careful ones filed in the cabinet, but in the jots and scribbles he made on the sheets of his desk calendar.

A bottom drawer hung open on the old metal desk. Coach would prop his feet up there when he leaned back to talk on the phone. Chase wrapped his fingers over the screen of his cell phone and turned it on. Bright light slipped out between the tight gaps of his fingers and cast just enough light to see the desktop.

The phone sat on one corner, and stacks of papers to be graded, sports magazines, and newspaper clippings lined the edges, each slumping over until it blended with the next. In the center, three felt-tipped pens rested on the open calendar.

The calendar was open to November's page. Coach's way of coding things was printed in the blocks of the calendar. Appointments were written in blue, errands and shopping lists in black. Now, they were only trivial reminders of a man who had shaped Chase's life in so many ways.

Chase ran his fingers over the page, looking for anything in red. In Coach's system, notes in red were the spontaneous ideas, things to be remembered, and more important notes about his players. Chase's name in red had covered Coach's calendar sixteen years before.

Looking down at the page, two initials, printed in red, showed three times in the month. The first, *J-R*, was circled three times and the name *Slater* was scribbled next to it. J-R had to be Jimmy

Riley, and Slater was head coach at the University of Denver. Slater had called Coach or Coach had planned to call him. Scholarship offer for the boy?

In the middle of the page, next to the score of Friday's game, a dash separated the *J-R* from a carefully printed *27 pts*—Jimmy's total for that game. But when his fingertips stopped near the red ink on the top of the page, Chase's breath stopped in his chest. Away from the numbered blocks, on a corner of the paper, in small, tightly printed red letters, a name Chase knew too well was written. The name was circled in blue—Coach's code for an appointment—and *11 P.M.* with a question mark twice the size of the letters was drawn below it.

Chase reread the name.

No. No. Could it be?

He let his cell phone go dark so he couldn't see the name again, and sickness burbled up from his stomach.

Outside, sirens wailed.

Every State Patrol and Sheriff's Department vehicle had emptied out of the high school parking lot. Lights and sirens filled the snowy night over Brandon. Sheriff Kendall's truck was the last in line. Mercy set a box filled with dirty silverware and empty serving plates on the backseat of her mother's Lincoln. Twenty years before, it had been the nicest car in Brandon.

While the car idled, she brushed snow from the windshield. The oldies radio station from Lamar played a song she hadn't thought of in years. She'd slow danced to that melody with Lincoln Kendall at the Comanche Springs junior prom in 1993. She moved as if she were dancing to the other side of her car, and she could still feel his fingers edging down her rear end while they swayed with the music.

Maybe later tonight he'd want to dance with her again.

The song on the radio confirmed that everything Mercy had planned was what the universe intended. Instead of turning onto the highway, Mercy followed the town streets home. It was only six blocks. Six blocks was about as far apart as anything was in Brandon.

If the two best boys in the county were coming to call, Mercy had to get herself ready. She'd been planning every part of it all day.

She ran her fingers through her hair and tossed her head back. Her giggles flowed out and surprised her, because she hadn't giggled in years.

CHAPTER TWENTY-SEVEN

"Birdie?"

"Hush." Then, "Over here."

Her whispered answer pointed Marty to a snow-bent stand of tamaracks near where the cottonwood branches drew patterns against an almost black sky. The kid trooper's directions had been right on, but the wind and falling snow made following the kid's tracks as close to reading Braille as Marty ever wanted to get.

He ducked low and wrestled through the heavy branches. Clumps of snow fell free and tumbled around him. Birdie's muffled curse made him sure that she was only a few feet away.

He stopped and stared into the tangle. Only the flash of teeth as she mouthed the next string of profanity betrayed Birdie's hiding place. When Marty dropped to his knees, a thorn bit through his jeans and long johns and found the soft patch of skin between his shinbone and kneecap. He winced but never let out a sound, and then propped himself with the stock of the shotgun while he dug the sticker from his leg. He was sure the knee was bleeding, but he bit down on his lip and crawled the last couple yards to where she sat.

"What took you so long?"

"That all you can say?" Marty knew Birdie was happiest when she was unhappy.

"I'm freezin' my ass off waitin' for you. And take that stupid mask off."

She was having a good old time. "Next time pick a place closer to the road to get shot at." Marty peeled the ski mask from his face.

"Yeah, yeah." She brushed the snow from her nose. "Got anything to eat?"

Marty tugged a mitten off with his teeth and dug into his coat pocket. "Brought you this." He handed Birdie a crushed and twisted Slim Jim.

Birdie tore the wrapper away with her teeth. "My nose is so damn cold I can't smell anything. Is it teriyaki or smoke flavor?"

"What difference does it make?"

"Don't be so pissy. It's me that's been sittin' in the middle of a blizzard for two hours waitin' on you." Birdie bit the end of the meat stick. "Ugh, this thing's as old as I am."

"Shut up and tell me what's goin' on. Ray-Ray out there somewhere?"

She stuffed the rest of the sausage in her mouth. "No shit, Sherlock, and he knows we're here, too. I just can't figure out what he's up to." She sniffed in a dribble of snot. "But I know one thing. There's a reason we're not both shot dead."

He shook his head in rhythm with hers. "Lord, it's cold, Birdie."

"That it is. Got another Slim Jim?"

Chase sprawled in the pickup's seat and mashed his eyes shut. The heater blew full force, and from under the edge of his Lakers cap, strands of his hair danced in the warm flow of air.

He'd killed the truck's lights and parked at the edge of Brandon's little cemetery. He wanted a place where the quiet would let him sort out all he'd found. The more he searched for an answer, the more he knew he could never climb from what trapped him.

Could the name on Coach's calendar have something to do with Jimmy's murder? And Dolly's? What did Coach find out?

Chase turned down the fan and pulled the zipper on his jacket halfway down his chest. His knee throbbed, and when he tried to untangle his long legs from under the steering wheel, the pain cramped the muscles in his thigh.

A pill.

Just one.

At the bottom of his shaving kit, back at his trailer, he'd hidden a plastic prescription bottle. There were two pills left in the bottle. One would be enough. It would soften the pain in his leg and chase the confusion away. That one pill would let him sleep.

In the morning, the worst of the storm would be past. He'd call his agent. Tell him to accept the broadcasting job in San Diego. And drive away from the homeplace forever.

Even if the red ink had nothing at all to do with the killings, the name would be his secret.

The first gaps showed in the storm clouds. The snow came slower, and it fell straight to the ground, not carried on the wind like before. Marty could see farther out onto the prairie, and the dark, charcoal-colored shadows turned gray. Far out, away from the trees and brush, the untracked snow sparkled as if some giant had let a thousand dirty diamonds trickle from his fingers.

"Why would Ray-Ray kill those people?" Marty whispered to Birdie.

"What makes you think he did?"

"Why else has he been hidin' out?" Marty's teeth chattered. "Why shoot at the trooper?"

Birdie shook her head. "He's probably got another one of his wild hairs up his—" She stopped. Drops of melted snow hung on the very tips of her eyelashes, and when she blinked they rolled down her cheeks like tears. "You really think he did it?"

"He's always talking about wantin' to be left alone. How nobody can tell him what to do. He hates you and me up one side and down the other just 'cause we work for the government. Most around here thinks he's a little crazy, but harmless." Marty strained to see something, anything that would show where Ray-Ray was hiding.

"Maybe he's been out there, big-time crazy all along, and somethin' finally set him off. Maybe he ran into Jimmy and Dolly after they left the Ford place. Saw what they was up to and thought it was up to him to punish them. You know how he thumps the Bible."

"I don't think so." Birdie hung her head. "But . . ."

"But what?"

"We gotta do somethin'." She touched his arm for the first time since he'd found her. "We gotta do somethin' now."

"Maybe we can." Marty's eyes strained into darkness. "Look. Out there, do you see it?"

Snow high enough to cover the bottom strand of fence wire covered the fields along the highway. Drifts, knife-edge sharp, hid mailboxes and snaked up the sides of pickups and tractors parked beside farmhouses. Here and there moonlight found the cracks in the stacks of gray clouds and reflected off the new snow in an eerie brightness.

Kendall stared through the windshield of his truck, not sure if the storm had blown past or was preparing for its next punch. The digital thermometer on his dashboard showed 0°.

He gripped the steering wheel tighter as a burst of wind-whipped flakes skated across the icy road in lights from his pickup, like angry ghosts seeking souls to haunt.

He fumbled for the cell phone on the console, scrolled to Jody Rose's number, and pushed Send.

Jody sat in the passenger seat of the TV van, two car lengths ahead of him. The cameraman hovered over the steering wheel. She picked up on the first ring. "We heard on our scanner that something's happening and decided to follow. What's going on?"

"Ray-Ray took a shot at a state trooper and that woman game warden. We're sending every trooper and anybody I can spare to help out. Do what I say. You follow 'em, but if they hightail it after Ray-Ray, stay back. I mean it. There's liable to be shootin', but you'll have your story."

"Thanks, Sheriff. I owe you."

Lights on the police radio flashed.

"You can settle up later. Maybe even later tonight." Kendall licked his lips. "I got a call comin' in."

He hit a button on the radio, and Arlene's voice filled the cab. "Sheriff, a semi laid over in the ditch about twenty miles west of Brandon. I guess it's real bad. Ambulance's on the way. The trooper at the scene says he found somethin' you need to see."

"Send someone else. You know what we got goin' on here."

"The trooper said the truck was runnin' under forged DOT papers. . . ."

"That's their business, not ours."

"I tried to tell him that, but he said he's sure it's one of the truckers they've been after. Said you need to see what he found. He said that twice."

Kendall tipped his hat back. The line of troopers' cars and department vehicles ahead of him turned off the highway onto the county road that led to the Butt Notch. The TV van with Jody Rose followed.

He tapped his brakes. "Damn it all." He flipped on his flashing lights. "Arlene, tell 'em I'm on my way, and tell 'em that this better be good." Kendall gave his truck all the gas he dared and headed west on the highway.

With every second the night sky grew brighter, and with every second the temperature dropped colder.

"Birdie." Marty hoped the word didn't freeze solid, drop to the ground, and shatter into a thousand pieces. "Birdie, look out there, maybe fifty yards, side of the hill, where that big tree toppled over. See it? Maybe two-thirds of the way up. Just to the south of where those dead branches kinda fan out."

"Yeah?"

"See that dark spot settin' down in kind of a bowl in the snow?"

"Uh-huh. Just a rock."

"You see any other rocks around it?"

"No." He heard her teeth chatter. "No, they're covered with snow, shit for brains."

"Why ain't that one?"

"Huh?"

"Watch it close." His belly clenched with the cold. "When the light is right, I think I see a puff of smoke every now and then."

Icy air threatened the moisture in his eyes. The next seconds turned into a minute. Then two. He dared not blink.

A minute more.

Then he saw it again: grayish smoke, just a wisp, hung for an instant in the grayer moonlight above the dark spot on the white snow.

"See it?" he whispered.

"Think so." Birdie shifted, and snow crunched around her. "That dirty pecker's dug him a cave under that dead tree, and he's sittin' by a fire while I got icicles growin' off every part of me. Damn him."

"He didn't just dig a cave tonight."

"Like you said, Ray-Ray's always rantin' on how the big, bad government's gonna take over and do away with anyone that can think for themselves." White vapor streamed from her wet nostrils. "I got tired of hearin' it. But he believes it for sure, and I betcha he's built himself a hideout." Birdie muffled a cough. "Hell, he could have tunnels dug all over this hillside, he's that crazy."

Silence froze in the air around them until Birdie spoke again. "Marty, if those troopers come out after him . . ."

"Yeah, as riled up as he is, Ray-Ray could think everythin' he's been sayin' is comin' true." Marty struggled up to his feet. The bloody spot on his jeans tore away from his skin.

"Where ya think you're goin'?"

"I gotta do somethin' before they get here."

Birdie tried to stand. "I'm comin' with you."

"No." Marty pushed her back down on the snow. "I'll do this one by myself."

CHAPTER TWENTY-EIGHT

The dress on the bed wasn't exactly like the one Mercy had worn to the prom. Sixteen years before, other girls had tried to hide their envy, but the sideways glances let Mercy know just how jealous they really were that night.

And the boys looked, too.

That dress had been blue satin. A jade green one lay across Mama's bed. She'd picked it because it went so well with her eyes.

The clothes she'd worn all day with their smells of stale coffee, bacon grease, and chili from the café had been kicked into a pile in the corner of her mother's room. Mercy finished the last brush-stroke of makeup along her cheekbones. She turned slightly and mugged for the mirror, liking what she saw. Just as in high school, every bit of makeup and each detail of how she would dress had filled her mind since the minute Chase had walked into the café again. She tangled her fingers in her hair and lifted it from her bare shoulders.

No, Chase liked her to wear it down.

Mercy ran a brush through her hair, checking to be sure last night's touch-up had covered the gray roots. Lacy white under-things would send the wrong message, and black would be too predictable. She'd chosen a color the catalog called dusty rose. The bra had a single clasp, not four like the ones her ex-husband had ridiculed.

Mercy lifted the dress over her head, careful to keep it from smudging her new makeup. She ran the zipper up the side, following the curve of her hips, breathing in as the fabric pulled tight across her stomach, and with a last tug the zipper closed just below her arm.

No need to hurry.

Chase would be early. He always was. With all the trouble in the county, there was no way of knowing when Lincoln Kendall would arrive. But they'd both be there, she had no doubt.

Mercy picked up a pair of shoes that matched her dress, but she slipped into her Tony Lama boots because of the snow and cold outside. She'd change into the green ones at the café. She put on her coat and checked her hair and makeup one more time.

With the candles and perfume in her purse, Mercy added one more thing from the dresser in front of the mirror.

A box of cartridges for her father's deer rifle.

Snow crunched under the truck's tires. The noise stirred a soreness hidden in Chase's brain. Each crackling sound stung like the tremors that had chased the pain through his body the night his knee failed him. Chase slammed the Dodge into four-wheel drive and powered through the drifting snow that had covered his tire tracks on the lane to the cemetery.

The truck bounced onto the pavement. Barely touching the gas, he crept along the streets through Brandon's small neighborhoods, past the houses where friends had lived, now dark reminders of the many who had fled the small town. He pushed away the thoughts of what he'd seen at Coach's house. And as much as he tried, the pills in the trailer still teased him.

Maybe he shouldn't sleep at the trailer.

Pack up and leave.

That would be best.

Be far away from Brandon by the time the sun comes up.

Chase turned toward the highway. Mercy's house was four blocks away. Coach's home was near the school. Everything held too much badness. He stopped for the sign at the four-lane highway. The snow had slowed to twirling bands of wind-driven flakes. Hints of moonlight threaded through the clouds.

A semi downshifted at the curve into town, and the windows on the second floor of the school vibrated with a moan. Down the street the lights were off at Saylor's and on at Town Pump. He waited as the big truck whined past, sending waves of slop up from its tires. An old sedan followed the truck. The car's blinker came on, showing its driver wanted to turn left toward the silos, railroad tracks, and trailer houses south of the highway in the old part of town.

While he waited, Chase fiddled with the radio until he found the oldies station from Lamar. He tapped his thumbs on the steering wheel to the rhythm he hadn't heard in years and tried to remember the song's name.

He wished for the simple times of long before. When his knee was sound and basketball was fun, and before three bodies haunted Brandon.

The car on the highway started its turn and splashed through dirty slush in the middle of the roadway. The back tires lost purchase on the icy pack and began to spin. The driver corrected, but too late. Almost in slow motion, the car slid sideways across the road, bumped a utility pole at the corner, and dropped both back wheels into the ditch in front of a boarded-up building.

The driver gunned the engine, but the wheels just spun.

Maybe I should help?

He answered his own question.

It's what people do.

Chase checked both ways and eased across the road to the stranded car.

Birdie waited until night and the curve of the hill swallowed up Marty. Why was he so cocksure? Going after Ray-Ray all by himself?

Birdie felt an uneasy twinge in the bottom of her gut.

It was Marty's job to go after Ray-Ray. She'd done her part chasing the wild man across the biggest part of Comanche County. Now, it was up to Marty to do the rest. Birdie knew damn well that he was good at what he did. If any man had to go up against Ray-Ray, Marty was the best bet.

But if Birdie was sure of anything, it was that no matter how good a cop he was, Marty was one dumbass. He took chances he shouldn't and just didn't think things through. He'd proved that when he pulled that stunt with the tractor during the fire. Back in high school, Coach even said right in front of the whole team that Marty would lead with his face in a fistfight.

More than anything else, he never thought of how what he did might affect his wife.

Birdie shook her head.

There was no scare in Ray-Ray, and he could be mean enough to make a pit bull nervous. If Marty and Ray-Ray met nose to nose, neither was apt to back down.

Dumbasses. Both of 'em. They deserve each other.

Birdie lifted herself from the crater her butt had melted in the snow. Marty had a wife, two little boys, and a baby on the way. Somebody had to be sure Ray-Ray didn't shoot Marty's ass off.

She tugged her jacket up over her hip, slipped her pistol from its holster, and blew the snow off the rear sight. The knee-deep snow made for tough going. As much as she tried to step from one of Marty's footprints to the next, she couldn't. His stride was too long for her stubby legs, so she kicked her own path to follow him.

Damn Marty for makin' me walk in the cold.

Hunting Ray-Ray was way different from taking a twenty-two and putting the sneak on a plump rabbit in a weed patch behind an old farmhouse. Or taking his bow and stalking whitetails along the creek bottom. Rabbits and deer didn't carry forty-five-seventies.

Marty's toes had passed cold and now burned numb. He pulled the ski mask up over his ear and cocked his head into the breeze.

Maybe? Just maybe.

He thought he'd heard something far out across the prairie, back toward the road where he'd left the kid trooper. He tucked the mask back over his face and checked his watch.

Ten thirty.

Reinforcements should be there by now. Sheriff Kendall would be leading the cavalry out to do battle. Kendall would lead from the rear. That was his style. The sheriff wouldn't take a chance at getting shot at, and he'd stay close to the back. Directing things, he'd tell everyone. He'd really want to be the first to tell the story to the newspaper or that little TV gal from the Springs. That's how the man got re-elected.

All that mattered was who got to Ray-Ray first. If it was Kendall and the troopers, there'd be red blood on the new snow.

Marty dropped off the hill and into the brush along the creek. If he was right, Ray-Ray had dug his cave into the east side. If Marty could get far enough west and come over the hilltop, chances were best that Ray-Ray wouldn't hear him. If he had to, Marty could belly crawl the last bit.

So many ifs.

He planned on kicking snow onto the dark spot where he'd seen the smoke coming from. It had to be a chimney of some kind. Stop up the smokestack and wait for Ray-Ray to come out. Sounded easy in his head, but Marty knew nothing was ever as easy as it seemed.

He and Chase had found wild bees in an old hollow tree along Sandy Creek. It was the summer before they started junior high. He told Chase he'd read in a farm magazine how they could light some rags on fire and stuff them into the hole. The smoke would chase the bees away, and they'd have all the honey they wanted. The plan went just like it was supposed to, except that not all the bees had read the same magazine as Marty. A few illiterate ones hung around, and when Marty stuck his hand in, they let him know they were still there. His fingers swelled up to twice their size and what honey hadn't melted in the fire was full of ashes.

Marty sucked in a breath of cold air and replayed his plan in his head. Everything seemed right, except Ray-Ray's stinger fired bullets as big around as a man's thumb.

Marty left the creek to make his way up the hill. With every fourth or fifth step he stopped and clawed away the icy clumps that packed the soles of his boots. He didn't dare stomp his feet. The thorn tear on his knee throbbed. His breath came in hard gasps, and frost from the icy air settled deep in his lungs.

Shadows cast by the moonlight tangled in the different world the night painted on the snow. From the top of the hill his own shadow stretched out and touched the dark spot above Ray-Ray. Smoke drifted back to him.

The shotgun hung like a club from his frozen fingers. Before he did another thing, Marty said a prayer for his boys and Deb and asked God to be sure that she knew how much he loved her.

Far off, out east on the prairie, he spotted specks of light from the State Patrol cars.

In his next prayer he pleaded for just enough time to do what he needed to do. Before he said amen, Marty asked for forgiveness.

He dropped onto his knees, pushed aside the snow-covered tree branches, and crawled through the cold snow down the hill.

Following Marty wasn't hard. He'd tromped a path plain enough for a blind man to find. Keeping up was something else. Soft snow covered the brushy creek bottom. Each tree branch Birdie touched sent a cascade of white, cold powder down her coat collar.

The snow turned icy at the base of the hill. Where it was deep enough to only cover Marty's boot tops, Birdie sank to her knees. Sweat poured off her face and mingled with the melted snow on her neck. She used her hands and knees and some cuss words she hadn't said in years to help her climb the hill.

That dumbass was bound to do something stupid, and she needed to be close by to bail out his sorry butt.

CHAPTER TWENTY-NINE

Chase opened the door to his truck. "Looks like you might need some help." He hung a smile on his face. Maybe the first one since he'd laughed with Marty beside the tractor in Mason's field.

Snowflakes swarmed in the headlights from his truck, and freezing air slapped his face.

The man beside the stranded car flipped his sweatshirt's hood off his head and looked over his shoulder at Chase. Like a box turtle trying to hide in its shell, the man pulled his neck into the folds of his shirt and hunched his shoulders in the cold.

"Thanks for stopping. We drove over a hundred miles in this storm." He nodded to a woman in the passenger seat. "And got stuck two blocks from home."

"Roads are bad, huh?" Chase joined the man at the back of the car.

"Sure are. Thought I'd hafta use a crowbar to pry my fingers off the steerin' wheel."

"Get back in, and I'll give it a push. If that doesn't work I've got a chain in my truck."

"Thanks." The man raised an arm to shield his eyes from the

glare of the headlights and looked up. "Hey. You're Chase Ford, aren't you?"

Chase nodded.

"You probably don't remember me. I was in sixth grade when you guys took State. Biggest thing that ever happened around here." He stuck out his hand. "Eddie Payton's my name. Doris is my oldest sister. She was a junior that year."

Chase shook his hand. "I think I remember you, Eddie." He didn't really, and a fuzzy reminder of a high school girl with braces named Doris flashed across his mind. "What's your sister up to these days?"

"Livin' outside Oklahoma City. I can't wait to tell her that I saw you right here in Brandon."

Chase fought off a shiver. "Let's see if we can get this car unstuck."

"Wait." Eddie walked to the side of his car. "Come here, I want you to meet someone."

He opened the door, and the dome light came on. A woman with red curls poking out from under a green Carhartt stocking cap was stretched over the console checking a chubby redheaded boy strapped into car seat in the back.

"Karen," Eddie said. "You're never gonna believe who stopped to help us. It's Chase Ford. You know, I talk about him all the time."

Karen slipped a pacifier into the little boy's mouth. Vestiges of old acne pocked her cheeks, but her smile was pure. "He does talk about you a lot. See this?" She pointed at the purple sweatshirt with the Lakers logo her little boy wore.

"Yes, sir." Eddie beamed. "I want you to meet Chase Ford Payton, future Brandon Buffalos basketball star. We named him after you."

Chase's knee threatened to fold. His breath caught in his lungs. "Wow" managed to seep from his lips.

"Shoot, there's four other little boys named Chase that I know of in this end of the county."

"I, uh, I . . ." Chase's insides went watery. "I don't know what to say." When he looked up, moonlight reflected off the town's water tower, and a single beam seemed to rest on the painted letters celebrating that state championship so long before. "I hope he grows up to be a better man than I am."

The little boy's father shook his head. "Nobody's better than Chase Ford."

Mercy tucked the bundle under her arm and slammed the trunk of her mother's Lincoln closed. The blanket-wrapped package was the last thing she needed to bring in. And the last jigsaw piece to her plan.

A semi truck hauling a flatbed of pipe lumbered down the highway, flinging blobs of dirty slush to the edge of the café's parking lot. Snowflakes, pink from the neon sign, danced in the air, like she had danced with Chase when the whole world ended in the crepe-paper-draped basketball court at the high school.

Everyone. Everyone had watched the star player and the girl he had chosen that night.

The whine of spinning tires seared the air. Uptown, in front of the boarded-up hardware store, two men pushed the back of a car that had slid into the ditch.

Mercy shut the café's front door behind her. She had already pushed all the tables to the side except for a two-top with a pair of chairs at the center of the room. She kicked off her boots and crossed the cold floor in her stocking feet. She hung her heavy coat on the hook inside the office door, smoothed the front of her satin dress, and fumbled in her purse for her reading glasses.

If it had been the start of her morning at the café, Mercy would have looped the cord that held her glasses around her neck. She'd need them close to work the cash register, tally receipts, and perform all the other little tasks that required younger eyes.

She perched the glasses on the end of her nose and adjusted the thermostat up two degrees higher than she ever had. She wanted the chill off the room. It would have been nice to have a fire in a fireplace. But that was something the old café didn't have.

Six candles sat evenly spaced along the length of the breakfast counter and one sat on the table in the middle of the room. She lit each candle and hid her glasses under the counter.

Tonight she needed to be young again.

Nobody's better than Chase Ford?

Didn't Eddie Payton know?

Chase turned and took a step away from the car. Bile swam in the back of his throat and threatened to gag him.

He named his son after me?

Every sin and shortcoming of the last years tumbled through Chase's mind. All the broken promises and all the people he had let down bubbled to the surface. In the center of it all he saw who he had hurt the most.

When Chase turned back, Karen stood by her husband. He'd slipped his arm around her hips. Both smiled back at him.

"I told Karen all about you," Eddie said, and he hugged her tighter. "Not just the Lakers stuff. Everybody guessed you sent money back here to Brandon. You know, for the new computers at school. Scholarships so those kids could go to college. There was even a rumor that you paid the taxes for a couple of the farmers who stood to lose their farms. People around here owe you a lot."

Chase needed to ask. What about my divorce? And the stories in the magazines? And on TV? And the pills? But the words wouldn't form in his mouth.

Because everything since his knee failed him had been wrong.

He'd proved that when he told himself that he'd come back to be sure that Dolly would have money for college. Things would be different at the homeplace. He craved its peace again. He could have made arrangements with the banker over the phone, but he wanted to see Brandon once more. On that one weekend in sixteen years, three people had died. As if the evil and everything he regretted had followed him to the prairie.

"Chase?"

Eddie's voice coaxed Chase away from his thoughts. He took the invitation.

"We heard on the radio about you out at the fire. Must have been somethin'," Eddie said.

"It was really Marty Storm that—" *Don't make me the hero. I didn't do anything.* Chase pointed to the car. "Hey, have Karen get behind the wheel, and we'll give this a shove and see if we can get you and that little boy home to where it's warm." Chase motioned for Eddie to follow.

"Yeah, you're right."

Karen's cowboy boots crunched in the snow. The door shut behind her.

Chase and Eddie put their backs to the car, caught the edge of the bumper with their fingertips, and braced themselves.

"Go," Eddie shouted.

Karen hit the gas, and the car lurched forward.

Just as the tire began to spin, the two men heaved, and with a jolt, Eddie's car pulled itself from the icy shoulder and slid onto the snow-packed road.

Karen came to thank him. Chase shook his head and flexed his cold fingers. "You two get on home." While Eddie took her place in the driver's seat, Chase opened the passenger door for Karen.

"Take care of that little boy," he said softly.

Little Chase's eyes were shut as he sucked the pacifier back and forth in his mouth.

"And when he's ready to play ball, find me and I'll come coach him some." Chase reached in and squeezed the baby's shoulder.

A puff of exhaust from the car swirled the snowflakes around his ankles. Chase stood and watched them drive away.

Maybe the one he'd hurt the most was himself. The best punishment would be to leave the place where a few people still thought he was good.

Chase started his truck. The wipers chased feathery crystals of snow from the windshield. Down the highway, Mercy's mother's car sat in front of the café. Tiny lights flickered in the dark dining room. Chase pulled in next to the Lincoln.

Before I leave I need to know if her name on Coach's calendar means anything.

He took the slippery stairs two at a time and pulled open the door. A pair of wet boots sat just inside.

"Mercy?"

CHAPTER THIRTY

Clouds covered the moon, and darkness gulped up everything around Marty until his whole world became the next few inches he could crawl down the hill. He pushed the thoughts of Deb and the boys to a small secret place in the back of his mind. Cold stole all the feeling from his hands. If what he feared came true, he doubted he could curl a stiff finger around the shotgun's trigger. He grabbed the next snowy handful and pulled himself forward.

Above the edge of the depression his body made in the snow, hard kernels of wind-whipped ice brushed over the covered ground and found the tender places around his eyes and lips not covered by the ski mask.

Far out on the prairie, perhaps a mile from the hillside, dots of white from headlights told him how precious the next minutes would be.

Could he save the troopers? Could he save himself?

A swirl of wind brought a wisp of smoke. Marty squinted though the harsh sting, and his tears froze at the slits in the fabric around his eyes. Then the warmth brushed across his face, teasing with false comfort for only an instant.

His goal on that lonely hill—the stovepipe—was only an arm's length away.

He eased forward, daring the snow not to crunch under his knees and hands, paused, and strained for any sound from below him. As carefully as he'd ever done anything in his life, Marty peeled off his ski mask, packed it full of snow, and smashed the wet bundle over the chimney.

The snow evaporated around his fingers. Hot steam teased his nose and water hissed. The first warmth in hours lured him to hold his hands close for a second more, but he rolled back away from the stovepipe and kicked more snow into the opening.

Will I have to kill him?

Marty pulled the shotgun close to his chest.

At the sound above him, Ray-Ray turned from the slit in his fortress's log walls and stared in the darkness above his head. Dust drifted down onto his face.

Somebody's up there.

He pointed the muzzle of his rifle at the ceiling and thumbed back the hammer.

One more noise, you son of a bitch.

Seconds stretched. The blackness thickened around him until a splash of water showered down the stovepipe. Droplets danced across the hot metal. Steam merged with smoke and filled the chamber.

Ray-Ray's eyes clamped shut. He buried his face in the dirty canvas at the crook of his elbow and gagged for breath.

Blindly he waved the rifle at the roughhewn boards that made the ceiling and jerked the trigger. A white flame rocketed from the barrel, and the sound fused with the smoke and steam around him, and all at once, Ray-Ray went blind and deaf.

Birdie caught hold of the tips of sagebrush that poked through the snow and held tight. For every three steps she climbed up the hill she'd slid back one. Marty had disappeared over the top, and the breeze stole away the sounds of his hands and knees on the snow.

A gust of wind cut through her coat, shirt, and long underwear. A dozen goose bumps rose on every square inch of her skin. Birdie was sure that hell had frozen over and at any minute the devil himself would hand her a pair of ice skates and invite her to follow him through his icy inferno.

She cussed Ray-Ray for what he had done. Said a few choice words to Marty for telling her not to follow him and saved the vilest for herself. For not listening to him. Birdie sucked in a breath of the frigid air, braced herself to start to climb again, and whispered out a string of the foulest words she'd ever said all at once.

A blast rocked the night.

Rifle shot. Ray-Ray.

That was all it could be.

Her lips quivered as she took in everything around her.

Marty?

Birdie moved faster than she knew she could. Up the hillside. Feet sliding, fingers grabbing for anything she could hang on to. Knees and palms in the snow. Clawing for the Glock on her hip.

Not because of the sound of the rifle.

Because she'd heard a man moan.

Ray-Ray struggled up from his knees. A foot slipped on the wet floor. He lurched toward the hot stove. His arm went out to stop his fall.

Hot steel bit into his hand. The stove rocked off the stones he'd set it on, and a stew of wet, smoldering wood spilled onto his boots. Acrid smoke funneled into his nose and stung his eyes. He tried to fill his lungs, but the air around him was thick and gritty, and his throat closed and lungs rebelled.

Instinct worked the lever of his rifle and racked another shell into its chamber.

Leave me alone.

He wanted to scream it and kill each of the devils that drove him to this.

Everything in his stomach filled his mouth. Ray-Ray doubled over and spewed the contents on the floor. Air wouldn't come. He threw himself against the crude door on the side of his fortress.

Hinges squeaked. Lag bolts groaned against timber.

He fumbled for the cross bolt and tumbled outside into the snow. Frozen tree limbs snapped under him. He sucked in the cool air. The snow quenched the burn on his hand.

But Ray-Ray ran. Away from the place that was supposed to keep him safe. Down the hill through the snow to the tangles of trees and brush in the bottom of the Butt Notch. To where he knew best.

Leave me alone.

Leave me alone.

Or you'll make me kill every one of you.

Marty's ears rang from the gunshot. He waited for the pain to take over his body, and deep inside he knew what had happened.

He did it. He shot me.

Emptiness filled his chest.

Stay calm. Think. Think.

They'd taught him what to do at the academy. One morning an old lawman peeled back the front of his shirt and rubbed a shiny purple scar just below his shoulder. Every green kid wannabe in the room had sat stock-still. The old man looked at each face one at a time and said, "If you can think, you're alive. Find the hole and start first aid. If you're lucky, your partner's already radioed for backup and the EMTs. If you're all by yourself"—he was looking at Marty–"you're the only sumbitch that can save ya."

Marty knew the stories about gunshot wounds.

You don't feel pain at first. The impact shuts down your nervous system.

He lay still. Wishing he'd waited for the troopers.

The shotgun stayed glued to his hands. He let it drop to the side. Still on his back, Marty flexed both hands.

Fingers and arms work.

He pulled off his gloves and ran his hands over his stomach, expecting warm blood to bubble up from a gut shot.

Nothing.

He found his belt buckle and inched his fingertips lower.

Please, no. Not there.

But the fellas were okay.

Thank you, God.

He raised himself onto his elbows. The clouds above stirred, and brushstrokes of gray moonlight parted the shadows over his legs and feet. He bent his right knee, set that foot flat on the ground, and leaned forward to examine the dark blotch on his pants above where his left ankle stung so.

He imagined his foot hanging from fibers of skin, and muscle, and shattered bone.

What would he be if his leg was gone?

He made up his mind right then that if it was bad he'd lay down and let the blood run out of him until he was dead.

Deb didn't deserve a one-legged gimp.

He didn't want to touch his leg, but he had to. He held his breath and moved his fingers closer to the dark spot above his ankle.

Find the blood.

But there was none. Black dirt covered the cuff of his pants. One of his fingers found a ragged hole the bullet had torn through the denim. When he probed further, he found a wooden splinter, no bigger than a matchstick, had stabbed through his sock and into the flesh on his lower leg.

He missed me. I'm not shot.

He pulled the sliver out and the cold air on the raw flesh felt good.

Thousands of *thank yous* filled his mind and he said prayers to the God that had watched out for him.

He climbed to his feet. Both feet.

Dark smoke billowed from an open doorway below. Fresh tracks led away from the door, and Marty spotted Ray-Ray running down the hill.

Birdie made the top of the hill on her hands and knees. Faint fingers of smoke filtered up against the dark sky. She found Marty's ski mask wadded over the top of the metal pipe and could see from marks in the snow where he had lain on his back. His tracks led down the hill.

She gritted her teeth and followed.

Ray-Ray slapped branches away from his face, lowered a shoulder, and bulled his way through the tamaracks along the creek. The moon peeked through the clouds, turning the night a silvery hue. Ice splintered under his boots and freezing water soaked his pant legs and socks.

Some government man was following him. He could hear him fight his way through the brush.

In the shadows just ahead, a fallen cottonwood trunk leaned into the tangle of willows. He splashed through the frozen, swampy ground to the tree, ducked under, and turned back the way he came. He fed another cartridge into the magazine and pointed the big rifle at where his tracks crossed a clear spot in the brush patch.

Come and get me, you bastards.

Marty stopped where the tamaracks thinned and opened into a clearing. The wind had chased the clouds away, and the night was nearly as bright as day. He held the shotgun tighter to his chest and flipped the safety on and off with his thumb. Something didn't feel right. Hair all along the back of his neck prickled.

He lowered the shotgun and swept the muzzle from side to side over the trail in front of him.

This had gone too far. Whatever happened if the troopers found him, Ray-Ray had it coming to him. And Marty cussed himself for thinking he could do anything about it.

Deb'll kill me again if I get shot out here.

He lowered the shotgun and backed away.

"That's far enough." A voice boomed from the shadows.

Marty's insides went watery. "That you, Ray-Ray?" he croaked. "It's me, Marty. I come to help you."

"With a shotgun?"

"Look, the state troopers are on their way. It'd be better if you came with me." Marty squinted, trying to find where the man was hiding.

"Better for who?"

Marty knew the Winchester was aimed at his belly.

"Drop that gun," Ray-Ray called out.

In all his training Marty had been told never to give up a gun. Ray-Ray had already fired at him. No matter how quick he could be with the shotgun, Ray-Ray's gun was already aimed. If Marty didn't do what Ray-Ray wanted, all Ray-Ray had to do was pull the trigger.

Marty let the shotgun slide from his hands.

"Now the pistol. I can see it under your coat."

Marty's only chance was to keep the man talking. "Listen, Ray-Ray, the shotgun belongs to the county. I don't care if it gets scratched up, but the pistol's mine, and I'm still payin' off the credit card bill. How about I just lay it down?" Marty raised his jacket with his right hand, reached across with his left, and lifted his forty-five out the holster with his thumb and little finger. He held it up so he was sure that Ray-Ray could see he meant no harm. "I'm gonna put it down here so it doesn't get snow on it." He bent his knees and lowered himself. He put the pistol on top of a clump of weeds.

"You all alone, Marty?"

"Yeah. I swear it."

"I got no reason not to trust you, right now. Don't give me one."

The brush rattled, and not ten yards away the ghostly outline of the man materialized near a fallen tree.

"That's a big gun you got, Ray-Ray."

"Big enough to beat a man to death, not worth shootin'." Ray-Ray pulled back his shoulders and drew up to every bit of his height. A moonbeam rested on his face.

"Am I worth shootin', Ray-Ray?"

"That's gonna be up to you."

The crashing in the brush stopped. Muffled voices drifted back in the night. Birdie strained to hear what they were saying. But it was just faint garbles.

She pulled her pistol out from under her coat, double-checked to be sure there was a cartridge in the chamber, and tiptoed into the brushy jumble.

Despite the cold all around him, sweat trickled down Marty's forehead as if it were as sunny as a Fourth of July afternoon.

"Leave me alone." Ray-Ray's voice was just a harsh whisper. "Your kinda law don't mean nothin' to me."

Marty had been right. The rifle was pointed at his belt buckle. His mouth went dry, and his tongue scraped the roof of his mouth. "You need to put down your gun and come with me. Sheriff needs to ask you a few questions."

Slowly, Ray-Ray lowered the muzzle of his rifle a few inches until it trained on Marty's knees. "Sheriff send papers?" The clouds stirred, and a shadow hid the man's face.

"Papers?"

"A warrant, damn it. I know my rights." Moonlight flashed on his teeth and Marty was certain Ray-Ray had a smile on his face. "You ever read the Constitution, Marty?"

"What are you talkin' about?"

"The Constitution, fool. The laws you swore to uphold."

"This has nothin'—"

"It has everythin' to do with right here and now. I asked you a question. You read the Constitution of these United States?"

Marty wasn't sure he ever had. He knew about the Fifth Amendment. He had a little speech printed on a card he was supposed to read if he had to question someone after an arrest. It meant the perp could decide not to talk and he had to have a lawyer if he wanted one. He knew the second was about the right to own a gun, and he thought the first had something to do with free speech. Somewhere in there was something about how no one could tell you what church to go to or if you had to go at all. The rest was just little bitty print.

"This doesn't have anythin' to do with the Constitution," Marty said.

The muzzle of Ray-Ray's gun bobbed up and down, and the smile in the shadows disappeared. With each word his voice grew louder until he shrieked, "This has everythin' to do with it."

He tried to recall all the training he'd had on how to talk to suspects under stress, but it blurred in his mind. He struggled to make the next words out of his mouth sound calm and even. "Listen, Ray-Ray, we can work this out."

Ray-Ray waved his rifle in a wide circle. In the dark, Marty couldn't be sure where the muzzle came to a stop, but he guessed it now pointed at his face. Marty took a half-step backward.

Birdie stalked as close as she dared. She braced her Glock on the trunk of a twisted Russian olive tree and studied the two men. Ray-Ray's voice grew louder, and he raised his rifle. Birdie took a deep breath and put the pistol sights square on the man's chest. But when Marty stepped back, he blocked any shot she'd have to save him.

Shit. Shit. Shit.

She ducked under the tree's branches and stalked closer.

"Calm down, Ray-Ray." Marty knew it was a stupid thing to say as soon as the words left his mouth.

"No." Ray-Ray raged.

Marty tried again. "We can work things out. Listen—"

"You're gonna listen to me." Ray-Ray's voice boomed, and he cocked the rifle. "Then we'll do what has to be done here."

Marty knew his only chance was to keep Ray-Ray talking until he could think of something. "What you got to say?"

"They don't want people like me."

"Who—"

"Listen to me." The voice went as still as the night around them. "The government of this country don't want people like me that think and do for themselves. They want everybody the same. Earn the same money. Nobody works harder than anybody else. Just do what they want you to do." The gun jerked in the old man's hands. "I can't be that way."

A shiny spot at the muzzle of Ray-Ray's Winchester flashed in the moonlight, the forest faded away, and all Marty could see was the muzzle of the gun. He bit the inside of his cheek until he tasted blood.

Then Ray-Ray's voice changed. The demands became a plea. No. A prayer.

"Somewhere, we got things all screwed up." Ray-Ray fought for his next words. "The Constitution says what the people allow the government to do for them. It's not about the government makin' people do things. You gotta read it, Marty."

Ray-Ray stepped into the moonlight. The muzzle of the Winchester was ten feet from Marty's face. In a voice made raspy by four decades of Marlboros, Ray-Ray whispered, "One side gives you more rules and regulations and promises to take care of you from your first cry until they pound nails in your coffin. The other makes up just as many new laws and calls it the Patriot Act." He spit on the ground and his voice rose again. "I don't want no help. I'll make my choices and take my chances. If I fail it's on me. I won't come cryin' for someone to clean up any mess I got myself into." He jabbed the rifle at Marty's face.

"Think what happened here the past few days. The power of the county, state, and army helicopters chasin' after one man 'cause they think I didn't buy a state license to hunt deer on my own land. How much tax money got spent up? Leave me alone, Marty. And tell all of them to leave me alone." Ray-Ray's proud shoulders slumped, and he lowered the gun.

Marty took a deep breath. "Ray-Ray? This ain't about any huntin' license. Boy named Jimmy Riley was killed, and some of Andy Puckett's buffalo were shot. Coach and a girl from town got killed, too. Sheriff thinks you know somethin' about it?"

"Huh?" Cloudy mist flowed out of his nostrils.

"Three people killed? Know anything?"

"I ain't been to town in months. I don't know nothin' about a dead boy or buffalo."

A gust of wind drove the cold deep in his chest. A cloud of snowflakes stirred from the trees. Marty looked into the darkness on one side and then the other. "It's my job to take you in, Ray-Ray."

"I'm not goin' with you." Ray-Ray tightened his bare fingers around his gun.

"I believe you didn't have anythin' to with those folks gettin' killed. But, Ray-Ray—"

"I seen the dead girl."

"What?"

"Girl's body. Along Sandy Creek. Where the fire started. That her?"

Marty nodded. "It was Dolly Benavidez. Firemen found her."

"Somebody dumped her there."

"How you know that?"

"There was tire tracks on the road. Drag marks where they took her from the car. Boot prints all over the side of the road." Ray-Ray's breathing blended with the sounds of the breeze. "New Tony Lama's. Woman's size, I'd guess. You tell that to the sheriff."

It made sense. Ray-Ray could have seen the tracks the traffic from the fire trucks and snow had covered. "Come with me. Tell him yourself."

"Bold talk for a man whose guns are layin' on the ground." Ray-Ray winked. "I'm leavin' now. Follow me and I'll have to kill you." He backed into the brush, and in a moment there were only the sounds of his movements through the brush along the creek.

Marty's knees failed him, and he dropped into the snow. More cold than he'd ever known stabbed up at him.

"Son of a bitch." He cursed at himself.

Birdie stepped out of the darkness. Her pistol hung in her hand. "Let him go, Marty. He didn't have anythin' to do with those people gettin' killed." She held out her hand and pulled Marty up from the snow. "None of the boys from the state'll ever catch up to him on a night like this. He'll show up back here in a couple of weeks after everythin' blows over."

All went quiet except the wind. Clouds boiled and covered the moon. Night and cold wrapped tight around them.

Marty looked up at Birdie. "What are we gonna tell Kendall?"

"We got a long walk out of here. It'll give us time to think of a good lie. C'mon." She turned and walked away. "Don't forget your guns, dumbass."

CHAPTER THIRTY-ONE

Sputtering signal flares, stabbed into the snow banks, dotted both sides of the road. The snow had mostly stopped, and when Kendall checked his watch it was coming up on midnight.

The ambulance's flashing lights disappeared on the dark road headed west toward Hugo. Both state troopers climbed in the front seat of one of the cruisers. They tugged off their parka hoods and slouched back into the car seats, no doubt as tired as he was. Steam, painted pink by the glow from the taillights of their idling car, rose from the coffee cups in their hands.

Nothing for anyone to do but wait until the wrecker from Limon got there. Then there'd be a shitload of standing around in the cold while the crew lugged the big rig up onto its wheels and pulled the whole mess out of the ditch. Kendall wouldn't admit it, but a good part of a sheriff's day was spent standing, pointing, and nodding, and Kendall had done enough of that for the rest of month.

He turned the fan on the truck's heater down a notch and unzipped his coat for the first time since he pulled up at the scene. When he was sure the troopers weren't looking his way, he snuck a pint of Old Yellowstone out from under the passenger seat and poured two inches in the Styrofoam cup he had bummed off the ambulance driver. The twelve-hour-old coffee was cold, and sipping cold coffee was part of his job.

Old Yellowstone gave it some life. He drained half the cup with his first gulp and let the liquor's warmth flow down to his feet and toes.

Kendall flipped on the radio and waited for Arlene to answer.

"I'm fixin' on headin' back to Brandon," he told her. "Nothing more for me here. The driver's banged up pretty bad. They'll get him to Hugo and decide if they need to send him on to Denver."

"True it was Cecil with him, boss?"

"Yep, and how the little turd didn't get all busted up in the accident is beyond me. The trooper told me that when he found the meth right there in the cab with 'em, suddenly old Cecil started havin' chest pains and couldn't remember anything about what had happened except that the crystal wasn't his. Dumb shit." He took a sip of the whiskey. "I got to read 'em both their rights and handcuffed Cecil to the gurney myself. One of the few joys I get from bein' sheriff." Kendall rubbed the bridge of his nose between his thumb and finger.

"Long day, Sheriff?"

He nodded. Arlene knew the answer. "So Colorado's finest couldn't catch up with Ray-Ray, huh?"

"That's what they tell me."

"I thought with Storm and Hawkins out there we stood half a chance." He drained the cup and slipped his pickup into gear. "I'll spend the night in Brandon, and we'll start all over tomorrow."

"Get some rest, Sheriff."

"Yeah." *Not if what I got planned for the TV reporter comes true.*

He checked both ways on the highway and then cranked a hard U-turn. The lawman nodded to the troopers as he drove by, and when he was down the road far enough, he took another sip of Old Yellowstone. Right from the bottle.

Birdie turned off the blacktop and followed the faint ruts in the snow down the lane to Marty's double-wide. In the corral just past the trailer, the truck's lights flashed off the eyes of Marty's horses. Snow covered their shaggy backs and steam trickled up from their nostrils.

"Thanks for gettin' me home, Birdie." It was the first time either of them had spoken since they left the troopers on the prairie.

"Think they bought our story?"

"Who knows? Maybe everyone was just cold and tired and wanted to get back to where it was warm." He slouched back in the seat and stared ahead. "If I can convince Kendall tomorrow morning that Ray-Ray gave us the slip, I did the right thing. If not? Well . . ."

"Something botherin' you?"

"Just tired I guess. But"—Marty shook his head—"Ray-Ray didn't kill those people, and they didn't kill themselves. Who did? Used to think this county was a safe place and I helped keep it that way. Stuff like this happened somewhere else. Not here."

Birdie leaned over the steering wheel. Her breath fogged the windshield. A light came on in Marty's trailer house.

"Is that Deb?"

"I reckon. She's got a way of sensing when I get home."

The light in another room flipped on.

Marty reached for the door handle. "She's in the kitchen now. She'll make some hot chocolate and want to hear about what happened. Wanna come in?"

"Naw. I gotta get home."

Marty popped the door latch open. "Cross your fingers about tomorrow."

"Wait."

Marty turned to look at her.

"Somethin's been eatin' at me. 'Member, I told you I found boot prints out where we think Jimmy Riley got the hay bales he used to lure in the buffalo?"

"I remember."

"Before Ray-Ray walked off, what did he say about boot prints where he saw Dolly's body?"

"What the hell, Birdie?" Marty slammed the door shut and looked at her.

Birdie told him what she had seen each piece at a time. "Last thing, the paramedic told me Pop said 'Alice hit me.' He wasn't sure he heard it right, and when he asked again, Pop just started gibberin' about somethin' else." Birdie pounded a fist on the steering wheel. "You know who Pop confuses for Alice almost every morning?"

"We gotta find Chase."

CHAPTER THIRTY-TWO

A speeding truck sent beads of slop splattering across the back of Chase's truck. The glare from the eighteen-wheeler's headlights erased the candlelight and painted a flash of twisted shadows around the single table in the center of the dining room. Chase stepped over the wet cowboy boots in front of the door. "Mercy?" he called out again. "Power go out?"

Over his shoulder, lights shone from the houses near the school. The lights at Town Pump reflected off the icy parking lot and colored beer and cigarette signs sparkled in the windows. Down the highway, stray snowflakes danced in the streetlights.

Something twisted in the pit of his stomach.

"Mercy?" He called louder.

Yellow candle flames turned the edges of the room ghostly. Shades and shadows tickled the walls. Chase looked at where Mercy had kicked her boots off. The feeling in his stomach tightened.

Something about the boots?

He nudged at one with the toe of his own boot. It toppled over. Grit ground into the sole sparkled in the candlelight. The edges of the heel were sharp, not yet rounded from wear. It seemed about half the size of his own boot. About the size of—

The shoe print on the bare ground at Coach's.

That image became clear in his mind. The corner of the house had shielded a patch of sandy ground from the drifting snow. Flakes had dusted the boot print like grains of sugar sprinkled over cereal. It was just where someone would stand and reach down to get the key Coach kept under the rock.

Chase had been sure the track was left by one of the boys from the team, stopping by like he'd done all those years ago.

He could remember Coach's invitation. "Let yourselves in. You know you're welcome anytime."

But what if it wasn't a boy's track in the dirt?

The footprint was about the size a woman's boots would make.

A door somewhere behind the counter creaked, and a sliver of light stabbed the dining room. "Chase?" It was Mercy's voice.

He couldn't take his eyes off the boot. It was Mercy's name scribbled in bloodred ink on the edge of Coach's calendar.

"I'm so glad you came," she called from kitchen. "I have something very special planned."

Birdie gunned her pickup onto the highway.

Marty pulled his phone away from his ear. "He's not answering."

"He's asleep in his trailer, or he's in town somewhere. That's the only places he could be." She was guessing. "Where do we go?" She tapped the brakes and felt the rear wheels begin to slip on the icy road. She let up, and the truck slid through a stop sign.

"You choose, Birdie."

"God, I hope I'm right." She swung the wheel and tromped down on the gas. "Keep callin' him, Marty. Keep callin'."

"Mercy?" Chase nudged her boot again.

Half the women in Brandon wear boots like that one. It doesn't mean anything. He cleared his throat and called louder. "There's something I need to ask you."

All was dark except for the candles. Behind the counter, a bright sliver of light outlined the café's office door.

"You hear me, Mercy?"

The door swung open wider. The bright light painted Mercy's shadowy silhouette across the café floor.

The woman in the shadow fiddled with her hair. Her head tilted, mouth puckered, and she dabbed on new lipstick.

"Chase, I made your favorite. Remember how much you liked Mama's meatloaf? I used her recipe. Mashed potatoes with brown gravy. Corn, too." The shadow smoothed the front of her dress. "I brought a bottle of wine."

She didn't hear me? "Stop it, Mercy. We need to talk."

Her shadow turned, and the curves of her figure filled the doorway.

"Oh, Chase, have dinner with me. Let's pretend we're in high school again. We'll talk about all our dreams. How we're going to leave Brandon and never come back."

"Are you drunk?"

"Oh, no, Chase." The silhouette rested a shoulder on the door frame. "You don't understand, do you, Chase?"

"Understand what?" When he stepped back, his foot came to rest on her fallen boot. "I'm not sure I know what you're talking about."

"You and me, Chase. We both made mistakes, but we're back together now. A second chance, just for us."

The tiny hairs along the back of his neck stood on end, and spiders' feet danced over the end of each strand. "Mercy, tell me what you know about Jimmy Riley and Coach."

"No." Her voice was different, almost faraway. "I invited both you and Lincoln to come to the café. He liked Mama's meatloaf, too. I wanted the two of you to choose. But he's not here. You came, Chase. It was meant to be this way. We both made mistakes, and all that's over now. We can leave Brandon. Together this time. Like we should have all those years ago."

Her words came too fast for his mind to sort out. "Mercy, answer me."

"No, Chase." When she stepped out of the doorway, light wrapped around her and candlelight glimmered off her shiny green satin dress. She took two steps to the end of the counter. "You always liked this color. That's why I chose this dress."

But Chase couldn't look at the dress. All he saw was the rifle.

Sheriff Kendall turned off the highway and nosed his truck into the curb in front of the office at the Sundowner Motel. The *vacancy* light was lit, and the office sat dark. Big letters on a laminated card hung over the doorbell said: *Ring for after-hours service and give me time to find my robe.*

The sheriff's truck was the only vehicle in the parking lot except for an idling eighteen-wheeler near the street.

No sign of a TV van or Jody Rose.

He dug his personal cell phone out of his shirt pocket, scrolled down to her number, and hit Send. She answered on the first ring.

"It's me. The sheriff." He tried to put a little bit of country charm in his voice. "Where are you, Miss Rose? I thought we had plans."

"Yeah. Hey, listen." She spoke softly, as if she was trying to be sure no one else would hear. "We got called back to the Springs. I guess this storm is really something, and the station manager wants the whole team ready to cover the school closures and road conditions for Monday morning. I think it's a bullshit thing to do to my story. But it's not my call." She sighed. "When the troopers couldn't find Ray-Ray, I lost any bargaining power I had. I promise I'll be back as soon as they let me. I still want that interview with Chase Ford. He hasn't left Brandon, has he?"

That motel bed was going to be awful lonely. Cold, too.

Kendall slumped back in the car seat and turned his head. "I'm not sure about Ford. We cut him loose. No reason to ask him to stick around." From where Kendall was parked, he could see the back door to Saylor's Café. He remembered Mercy's invitation and sat up. "Okay, Jody, let me know when you get back to my county. You know you can count on me to help out."

He ended the call, unscrewed the cap on the bottle of Old Yellowstone, and thought over what Mercy had said earlier that evening.

He sipped his whiskey. The night was shaping up to be a little bit warmer.

Every fiber of muscle in Chase's body drew taut. Nerves stood on end and adrenalin pumped.

Dancing candle flames reflected along the rifle's blue-black barrel. A star-shaped spot of light glimmered from the center of the scope mounted on the rifle. The glow from the candles showed one finger curled over the trigger. She held the rifle's muzzle level with the middle of his stomach.

Run.

Wrestle it away from her.

Talk to her.

Like a man standing belly deep in a rushing stream, everything swept around him. Thoughts jumbled, emotions twisted, and fear ran cold. Confusion focused into one thought, and it spilled out of Chase's mouth.

"It was you, Mercy. You killed them."

Her head nodded. "I had to."

Kendall parked behind Saylor's. He tapped a breath mint out of a tin box and popped it into his mouth to quell the smell of Old Yellowstone.

Smart woman, that Mercy. Tellin' me to use the back door. This time of night no one's apt to see the truck and start talkin'.

He finished his whiskey and went to the door. The knob turned in his hand, and before he could call out, he heard her voice.

Shadows hid Mercy's face, but Chase could hear tears in her voice.

"Don't you understand? She was about to make a big mistake."

"Who, Mercy?"

"Dolly. I tried to tell her. Tell her that Jimmy Riley would leave her like you left me. Dolly could make something of herself. Leave Brandon like I tried to and never come back. That boy was no good. I had proof, I did. But Dolly wouldn't listen."

"What proof?" Chase asked the question to keep Mercy talking while he stalled for a plan.

"Jimmy would look at me. You know the way boys do when they want something." Her teeth flashed in the darkness. "He'd come by the café late at night after he dropped Dolly at home. At first we'd just talk. After a while, we'd share a sip of wine. Then he came to my house. It went on for three months."

"What else, Mercy?" he edged a half step closer.

"I went to tell Dolly. I waited until Jimmy dropped her off after the game on Friday. Victor was here at the café closing up for the night. She was surprised to see me. I told her I had her paycheck. It was such a nice night I pretended I wanted to see her animals, and she took me out by the corrals. When I told her Jimmy was with me, she cried and ran away. I tried to stop her, but she slipped and hit her head." Sorrow left her voice and a coolness took its place. "I put her in that big old trunk in Mama's Lincoln."

Her words punched Chase in the gut. "My sister? Dolly was my sister, Mercy." He felt tears on his face.

"You didn't care about her."

Chase climbed out of his numbness. He tried to move closer, but she raised the barrel of the rifle so it pointed at the center of his chest. "They found her out on Sandy Creek," he said. He closed his eyes for an instant and saw the crumpled body of his sister in the ashes of the fire.

"I had to do something with her. I took her out there before I opened the café on Sunday morning." She took her left hand from the rifle and dabbed at her eyes.

"And Coach?"

"He was suspicious about me and Jimmy. I asked if I could

come over after the game. I told him I'd be there after I closed things up at the café. Maybe eleven. I wanted time to be with Jimmy first. Coach was waiting for me. I tried to explain it was over. He said it was too late. He'd already decided to tell the sheriff what he knew." She rested her head on her shoulder and then like a child said, "He turned his back on me and walked away. The knife was there on the counter, and . . ."

She'll kill me like she killed him.

His muscles trembled, but he had to know the rest. "Jimmy? Did you kill Jimmy?"

"It was me, Chase." She stepped forward, and for the first time he could see her face. Her lips were pulled so tight across her teeth that the lipstick looked thick and waxy. Shadows played over her face, and her eyes turned to hollow sockets. "It was me in his truck. You saw us. Down in the trees at the homeplace—where we used to go."

The muzzle of the rifle dipped in her hands. Chase tensed. Mercy gripped the rifle tighter.

"We drove away laughing at you, and we saw those stupid buffalo in the field. Just like the Brandon Buffalos." She spit the words out of her mouth as if they were something vile. "Like the high school team that everyone in this county is so proud of." The muzzle of the gun rose until it pointed at his face. "Jimmy said he knew how to get them to come closer to the fence, and we went and got the hay. I took the gun and shot them when they came in. He laughed at me and I made him go out in the field with those precious Brandon Buffalos and I killed him there because that was all he was ever going to be. A basketball player for Brandon High School. And I hated him for it."

Lord Almighty.

Kendall couldn't believe what he was hearing.

Bright slivers of light framed the half-open door to the restaurant's side office. Mercy's voice came from just past the arch-shaped opening between the café's kitchen and dining room. The door shielded him from seeing all but Mercy's left hip and shoulder. She was talking to someone.

Who's out there with her?

Her voice was soft and the words garbled, but he'd heard enough. Mercy Saylor was admitting to three murders.

Keep talking, Mercy.

He took his cell phone out of his shirt pocket and cupped it in his palm. He found the record app and turned it on. He knew he was smiling.

He wanted every bit of what was happening recorded on some little microchip in the phone. He'd solved the crime. Mercy would stand trial. He'd be called to testify.

Re-election for sheriff was a sure bet. State legislator would come next. And why stop there?

He held the phone out with one hand and drew his father's forty-five from its holster with the other.

Congressman Lincoln Kendall. It had a certain ring to it.

Mercy must have lit candles in the other room. Orange shadows painted the walls. She took a step toward whoever was in front of her and when she turned, Kendall saw the rifle barrel.

"That's your father's deer rifle isn't it, Mercy? Three hundred Weatherby Magnum. He bought it at the same time Big Paul bought his." Like on the basketball court, find your chance and take it. No one would come to rescue him. "It's a powerful gun." He rocked forward onto the balls of his feet. She'd be watching his face and eyes. That's what his opponents did on the ball court. He coiled the muscles in his legs to be ready for the one instant when she looked away. "But you know that. That rifle dropped each one of those buffalo with one shot." He slid one foot forward an inch. "I didn't see the body, but they said one shot from that rifle took off the whole back of Jimmy's head. Think what it's going to do to me, Mercy."

She raised the rifle to her shoulder. "Don't make me do it, Chase."

Chase Ford?

Kendall almost licked his chops.

It would be so simple. As soon as Mercy shot Chase, he'd shoot her. He'd tell everyone he had pieced the evidence together and found Mercy at Saylor's. Chase blundered in. Mercy had the rifle. He tried to save Chase but couldn't and had to kill her. Everything would be recorded on his phone. He could fill in any missing parts about the murders. They could trace the bullets in the buffalo to the rifle. Everything was falling in place.

Mercy was on edge. He could hear it in her voice. She would kill Chase. What else could she do?

He moved to the side. To have a clear shot past the door.

C'mon, Chase. Make a move. Force her.

Do something stupid.

His hip brushed the stove top. When his hand shot out to steady a teetering pan, his heel caught and he stumbled.

Somewhere behind Mercy, a pot clattered onto floor.

Mercy whirled toward the sound.

The door to the office swung wide open, flooding the room with light.

Over Mercy's shoulder, Chase saw Kendall. The man's eyes peeled wide and his mouth hung open. The seconds stretched into slow motion. The sheriff's pistol dangled in the air a few inches from his outstretched hand as he tumbled forward.

Chase lunged. His shoulder smashed into Mercy's back. He grabbed the rifle's barrel with both hands and pushed it toward the ceiling just as the blast rocked the room. Splinters, chunks of plaster, and a cloud of dust cascaded from the ceiling.

Then Chase was on the floor with the rifle under him and its scope biting into his sternum. Breath wouldn't come. The sound of the gunshot rang in his ears. He caught the edge of the counter with one hand and pulled himself onto his knees. Kendall crawled across the kitchen pawing at the shadows for his gun.

High-heeled shoes clattered across the floor.

The café's front door slammed shut behind Mercy.

Spray from the semi truck splattered Birdie's windshield. She swung her pickup into the left lane and pressed the accelerator to pass. Oncoming headlights filled the cab.

"Shit," she screamed. She let off the gas and pulled back in behind the semi. The oncoming big rig rumbled by.

"Easy, Birdie." Marty jammed both hands onto the dashboard. "We're almost to town. Don't kill us before we get there."

Birdie tapped the brakes and let the truck and trailer in front pull away. She pried one hand from the steering wheel and wiped it across her forehead. "We're gonna be too late."

"You don't know that," Marty said.

"God, let you be right."

She caught up to the semi as the road made the downhill curve into Brandon. Lights from the high school flashed by on her left. Town Pump was a blur. She knew she was driving too fast.

"Watch it, Birdie."

Brake lights from the semi glowed red. The big truck veered into the oncoming lane and then jerked right. The pickup's headlights danced along the side of the aluminum trailer. Brakes squealed. Her pickup went sidewise. The back end of the trailer swung toward them. Then it was broadside.

Jackknife.

"Watch out." Marty's arms shot to his face.

Birdie spun the steering wheel.

"Mercy," Chase called as he stumbled through the front door.

She stood in the middle of the highway. Headlights glared off the icy roadway and shimmered from the folds of her green dress. Mercy turned and looked at him. In that second he saw the girl she'd been in high school, not the woman in the café. She mouthed the words, "I'm sorry."

The eighteen-wheeler slid. Its horn blared.

Chase screamed her name.

Marty wrapped his arm around Chase's shoulders and pulled him up from his knees. "There's nothing anyone can do now." And he turned Chase from the gore on the road.

At the front of Saylor's Café, Kendall doubled over and emptied everything in his stomach onto the tops of his boots.

When Chase shut his eyes, he saw Mercy and the truck. Again, and again.

CHAPTER THIRTY-THREE

It was still two hours until dawn when Marty followed his head-lights into Brandon. The gas pumps at Town Pump were lit. Porch lights dotted the neighborhood near the high school.

Dirty snow filled the gouges in the roadside where the big truck had lost control. At the spot where Birdie's pickup had taken out the telephone pole, a shiny new pole stood in the line of weath-ered brown ones.

All that was left of the yellow tape hung from shredded tufts tacked on the power poles and street signs in front of Saylor's Café. At the makeshift memorial on the edge of the highway, a lone red rose lay atop a pile of dried flowers.

Chase left one each morning. He hadn't missed a day.

Farm trucks and cars filled all but a few spaces in the parking lot at Saylor's. Marty pulled in behind one of the fire trucks on the street and went into the café.

The scent of warm pancake syrup, frying bacon, and fresh cof-fee filled the dining room. Winter coats hung on chair backs and men in work clothes nursed steaming mugs. Nearly every table was full.

"Got yourself up before breakfast, huh, Marty?" Earl Collins motioned to an empty chair at a long table surrounded by volunteer firefighters. "C'mon and join us. We were wondering who the sheriff would send." Earl slopped a flour tortilla through the green chili sauce on the half-empty plate in front of him. "We thought you'd draw the short straw for this one. Still in his doghouse?" He stuffed the tortilla in his mouth.

Marty turned the chair around and straddled the seat. He tipped his Stetson back and rested both elbows on the chair back. "He's still got me runnin' overnights on the back end of nowhere, but I wouldn't miss this shindig for anything."

The men around nodded their agreement in between forkfuls of eggs and pancakes. A waitress set a cup of coffee in front of Marty.

Earl came up for air. "We was just talkin' how the ball team has won five straight, since"—he dabbed his lips with a napkin and stared at his plate—"you know, what happened."

"Sure is good to see Chase on the bench with the team," a man added from the end of the table. "That's got to be a big thing for those boys."

"Birdie, too," Earl said. "You know, at the game last night, she looked almost like a woman in that dress." Heads nodded. "Principal did a smart thing naming her head coach." He pointed in the air with his next tortilla. "You know somethin' else? I'll bet all ya a hundred bucks she gets tossed out of a game before the season over. I like the way she cusses the refs."

Marty smiled. "I wouldn't bet against you."

"Speaking of Chase." Another of the firemen spoke up. "I'm sure I saw his truck out at Pop Weber's place."

"You probably did," Marty said. "Chase promised Pop he'd watch his farm. I think he had to, to get that old man to agree to stay in the nursing home."

"I hear Chase is paying for that."

Marty shook his head. "I can't say for sure."

"Somebody said Jimmy Riley's father is buildin' a fence for Chase."

Marty shrugged his shoulders.

Earl studied Marty's face. "My wife's sister works at the old folks' home where Mercy's mother lives. She said she heard that Chase fronted Victor the money to make the down payment on the café."

"Don't' know about that, either." Marty hated lying to his friends. He finished his coffee and set the mug on the table. "It's 'bout time to be headin' that way. Chase'll be waitin'."

Men pushed away from the table and stood. Some wrestled into their heavy coats. Dollar bills were tucked under the edges of plates and saucers.

"Marty, can I ask you one other thing?" Earl put his white fire helmet on his head. "Cecil's back over at Town Pump. I thought when that truck wrecked, they found drugs on him."

"Didn't have enough on him to press charges. Somebody screwed up."

"Kendall?"

"I can't say that for sure."

The fireman set his white helmet on his head. "Kendall musta had his mind on his campaign for state representative."

"Don't know about that, either."

"For a smart guy, you don't know much. You know that, Marty?"

Chase turned off the flashlight.

Alone in the dark, he walked the last steps to the foot of the staircase in the old farmhouse. He shut his eyes to seal in the darkness.

Memories, like ghosts, crowded around him. His mother came to him first. Smells of her cooking teased his nose, and the hair on his arms prickled as she passed near him. In the next room, the mattress springs of her hospital bed groaned with her weight.

From faraway, his father called him to help with the chores. The voice turned to anger and then slurred as Jim Beam stole him away. Big Paul climbed the stairs behind him and met his lover in the bedroom he had shared with Chase's mother.

Then suddenly Chase was all alone.

"You still sure you want to do this, Chase?" Marty stood next to Earl Collins and the other volunteer firemen. The first spikes of dawn nudged the horizon.

Chase nodded.

"And you got everything out of the house you want?" Earl asked.

"There wasn't anything."

"Okay, then?" Earl shot a glance at Marty.

"Tell him how you got it planned, Earl," Marty said.

"We cleaned out as much brush and dried weeds as we could yesterday. I stationed a truck with hoses and a team of men on each side of the house. Sent three more out to watch the barn and corrals. Not much wind this early. That's good." Earl looked over his shoulder and raised a hand to shade his eyes from the glare of the headlights behind him. "Old places like this tend to go up fast. When it's fully involved, we'll push the walls in and let her burn. Mostly, we'll just be sure it doesn't get away from us." He whistled through his teeth. "This is gonna be somethin'. Anybody bring marshmallows?"

"I did." Birdie walked up from around one of the fire trucks and stood by Marty. She held a plastic bag from Town Pump. "Brought graham crackers and Hershey's, too. Ya need that stuff for a bonfire, don't ya?" She jerked a thumb toward the road. "The whole damn town came."

Pickups and cars lined the gravel road. A school bus pulled up, and high school kids in letter jackets and winter coats piled out.

Birdie hitched up her pants and grinned. "Hope they brought their own. I ain't sharin'."

Marty tucked his hands in his coat pockets. "That's their way of tellin' you that they're glad you're here, Chase."

Chase smiled for the first time. "Let's give them something to watch, Earl."

Two of the firemen jostled up the front steps with five-gallon jerry cans in each hand. From the lights on the men's helmets Chase saw them slosh the liquid onto the floors and walls of the farmhouse. When they came out the door, one raised a hand and looked at Earl.

"Let's do it," the Brandon volunteer fire chief called. "This is gonna be fun."

The fireman flicked a lighter and lit a bundle of newspapers and tossed the fiery torch into the house. Flames crawled across the floor. Window curtains curled in the blaze. Fire climbed the steps one at a time. Dancing yellow light spilled from the windows. Old shingles caught, and fire rose fifty feet high against the night sky. People along the road hooted their approval. Birdie munched a marshmallow and refused to share.

As waves of heat touched their faces, Marty nudged Chase. "Give any more thought to where you'll build the new house?"

"I just decided." He turned to his friends. "I'll build the new one right here." Over the sounds of dawn he said, "I'd almost forgotten, it's my homeplace."

Chase turned his back to the fire. A ribbon of red showed far out to the east. The sky sizzled as the warmth of the sun touched what was left of the cool darkness. Night tore away along the horizon, and day took its place.

And Chase Ford heard each sound.

ACKNOWLEDGMENTS

When this author determined to put one of the stories that occupied his mind on paper, he assumed that writing would be a lonely, solitary endeavor. He was wrong.

The Homeplace would not have come to be without the help of so very many. First, the Southwest Critique Group. Mary Ann, Leisa, ZJ, Mindy, Val, Ed, Laurence, Michael, Sue, Nikki, Janet, and Lizzy who endured and encouraged. Thank you so much. Next, Rocky Mountain Fiction Writers hosts one of the best writers' conferences in the nation. Mark, Shannon, Susie, Angie, Pam, and so many others. You guys are the best. Barbara and Theresa from Crested Butte Writers. There wasn't a better place to learn the craft.

To my agent, Gina Panettieri with Talcott Notch Literary, who took a chance on this writer and always reminded him that writers write. To Peter Joseph and his assistant, Melanie Fried, from St. Martin's Press, who guided this project through the world of publishing. To Anne Hillerman and Jean Schaumberg for establishing a contest to honor a great author and providing an opportunity for new ones. Please know that each of you has my most sincere appreciation.

To my wife, Nancy, who reminds me each moment of how much she loves me. Thank you.

Finally, here's a bit of the story that readers should know.

In the summer of 1909, my great-grandfather, Starling Harry Gray, came to the prairies of eastern Colorado to stake claim on a homestead. After searching, he decided to purchase a 160-acre tree claim. The following spring, Starling brought his wife, Essie, and their two children to Colorado.

They built a two-story house on the property he had purchased, four miles south of the town of Kit Carson. In an era of dugouts, soddies and lean-tos, others in the county called their home the Tall House. The house had one door and four windows. The main floor was divided into a kitchen and bedroom and the sleeping area upstairs was a single room. The Tall House swayed in the prairie winds and, though long abandoned, still stands.

Starling deeded the land to his youngest son, giving the property the unique quality of being owned by only two persons.